GWEN BRISTOW & BRUCE MANNING
THE MARDI GRAS MURDERS

Gwen Bristow was born in Marion, South Carolina in 1903, and Bruce Manning in Jersey City, New Jersey in 1902. In 1924, following Bristow's graduation from Judson College, her parents moved to New Orleans. In the late 1920s, Gwen Bristow and Bruce Manning, both Louisiana journalists at that point, met and married.

Their first joint novel, *The Invisible Host*, was a success, and enjoyed stage and film adaptations. Three further mysteries by the writing duo were to follow.

The couple moved to Hollywood in the early thirties, and there Bristow established herself as a prolific and bestselling writer of historical fiction, while Manning became a respected screenwriter, producer and director.

They continued to live in California until their respective deaths: Manning's in 1965, Bristow's in 1980.

GWEN BRISTOW
AND
BRUCE MANNING

THE MARDI GRAS MURDERS

With an introduction by
Curtis Evans

DEAN STREET PRESS

Published by Dean Street Press 2021

Copyright © 1932 by Gwen Bristow and Bruce Manning. Renewed 1960. By arrangement with the Proprietor. All rights reserved.

Introduction © 2021 Curtis Evans

All Rights Reserved

The right of Gwen Bristow and Bruce Manning to be identified as the Authors of the Work has been asserted by their estate in accordance with the Copyright, Designs and Patents Act 1988.

First published in 1932 by The Mystery League

Cover by DSP

ISBN 978 1 915014 56 6

www.deanstreetpress.co.uk

INTRODUCTION

OVER several years in the early 1930s the spousal writing team of Gwen Bristow (1903-1980) and Bruce Manning (1900-1965) published four crime novels: *The Invisible Host,* (which possibly inspired Agatha Christie's classic mystery *And Then There Were None*), *The Gutenberg Murders, Two and Two Make Twenty-Two* and *The Mardi Gras Murders.* The couple later went on to enjoy highly successful careers in entertainment, she writing historical fiction, including her bestselling Plantation Trilogy, he writing screenplays in Hollywood, including most of the scripts for the hugely popular films of youthful star Deanna Durbin. Before turning to writing crime fiction and these other rewarding pursuits, however, Bristow and Manning had experienced at first hand, during their time as Roaring Twenties newspaper reporters working the mean moonlight and magnolia streets of New Orleans, Louisiana, more than their share of real life crime, including a great deal of bloody murder. Bristow, a diminutive but daring brunette originally from South Carolina, particularly distinguished herself as what George W. Healy, Jr., a colleague of hers at the *New Orleans Times-Picayune*, the Bayou State's leading newspaper, termed "our star sob sister." Although "sob sister" was a somewhat condescending term for women journalists covering human interest stories (the most interesting of which invariably concerned murder), another of Bristow's colleague's recalled of her, with what he no doubt meant as the highest of praise: "She was the kind of woman reporter you'd send to do the type of story you'd send a man on. She was perfectly capable of doing it."

Bristow proved just how capable she was of doing nasty jobs in 1927, a banner year for bizarre and grisly killings in Louisiana, even by the old French colony's own impressive Baroque Gothic standard. First there came in July the murder of Morgan City utility company engineer James LeBoeuf. Murder in this case was only outed when the engineer's bloated body, which had been submerged with three hundred pounds of railroad irons in the depths of Lake Palourde, was exposed by receding water in the aftermath of the Great Mississippi River Flood. James's unfaithful wife Ada, the mother of the couple's four young children, was arrested and brought to trial for his shocking murder, along with an older, socially distinguished local doctor named Thomas Dreher, with whom Ada had been having an affair. The trial, which dragged on for two years, became an immediate sensation in the state and even made national newspaper headlines, with Ada LeBouef finally becoming the first white woman in the state's history to be judicially executed. The state hanged Dr. Dreher as well, on the same day as Ada.

Along with her colleague, drama critic Kenneth Thomas Knoblock (who later authored three crime novels himself, including one which drew directly on the infamous Moity murders; see below), Bristow handled coverage of the LeBoeuf-Dreher trial for the *Times-Picayune*. She "manfully" detailed every aspect of the affair for her readers, despite admitting in an anguished letter to her mother, written after the guilty verdicts had been handed down, that her job exacted an enormous emotional toll on her. The two year LeBoeuf-Dreher trial was "the most horrible experience I ever had," she confided. "When I rushed into the Western Union office behind the courtroom to flash my story, my hand was shaking so I could hardly write. I slept only three hours that night...."

Bristow proved considerably more hard-boiled when, about four months after the James LeBoeuf murder, she and her colleague George Healy found themselves on the scene of a ghastly double trunk slaying in the French Quarter. Early on the morning of October 27, black "scrub woman" Nettie Compass, who lived in the back of the small stucco French creole style two and a half story building at 715 Ursulines Street with her husband Rocky and daughter Beatrice, trudged upstairs to clean at the second-story apartment of housepainter Henry Moity and his wife Theresa, a couple who lived unharmoniously in cramped and dingy quarters with their three small children and Theresa's sister Leonide, who recently had left her own husband, Henry's brother Joseph, and two children. Discovering a pool of blood seeping out from under the door to the Moity's apartment and down the stairs, Nettie promptly fled for her life, screaming for help in classic crime novel fashion.

Nettie's cries attracted two insurance salesmen who ran a business next door. After a brief inspection of the premises one of the men, Frank Silva, doubtlessly did what any other true blue American would have done. He alerted the press, which soon arrived on the scene in the form of the *Times-Picayune*'s intrepid George Healy. Silva, Healy and several local neighbors effected entry into the Moity apartment, where they found more blood on the floor and a large, partially open trunk in the couple's bedroom. Upon lifting the lid of the trunk, Healy discovered a dismembered woman's body, its severed limbs and head piled over the torso. Healy then doubtlessly did what any other true blue American reporter would have done. He alerted his city desk, asking for a lady reporter to be sent to the scene as soon as possible to help chronicle this blockbuster story. He also suggested that the city desk might want to get in touch with the police and the parish coroner.

Star sob sister Gwen Bristow arrived on the scene at the same time as the coroner, George F. Rowling, but she was in no way intimidated or inhibited by this man's official presence, bounding into the apartment at his side and immediately sighting several repellent objects on the bed in the Moitys' bedroom. "Look," she ghoulishly announced as she held these loathsome items up for the others in the room to descry, "ladyfingers." Four human fingers they were, severed from a woman's hand. Placing the "ladyfingers" back on the bed, Bristow then charged into the second bedroom, where Leonine had slept, and thereupon discovered a second trunk with another woman's body. The disjointed bodies being identified as those of the Moity wives, New Orleans Police Superintendent Thomas Healy, a "ruddy, pot-bellied Irishman" (who was no relation to George, though the two men had an amicable relationship), sent out an all-station bulletin calling for the arrest of the dead women's husbands.

Joseph Moity soon turned himself in the authorities, opining all the while that his brother Henry, driven to madness by Theresa's wanton ways with other men and resenting Leonide's influence over her sister, had committed the murder and fled; this indeed proved to be the case. There followed another bulletin from Superintendent Healey to the seven ships which had sailed from New Orleans on the day of the murders, warning their crews to keep a lookout for a desperate man with "dark, bushy hair," "very dark brown eyes" and a tattoo mark on his arm, depicting a flower with a woman's face and a nude female body.

The telltale tattoo did the trick and Henry, who had been working under an assumed name as a deck hand on a fishing lugger on Bayou Lafourche, soon was identified and turned over to the police. Once confronted with the ghastly killings, Henry attempted to pin the blame on a big, red-haired, psychotic Norwegian sailor he had dreamed up, but soon he broke down and confessed to the awful crimes. He admitted that after hearing rumors his unhappy wife was planning to run off with Joseph Caruso, the Moitys' landlord and the owner of a store on the ground floor of the building, he became possessed with thoughts of killing her and her meddlesome sister. Catching sight of Nettie Compass on the evening before the murders, he had whispered to the cleaner not to be frightened if she and her family heard the Moity children crying in the early morning hours. A few hours later, Henry after a heavy bout of drinking stabbed Theresa and Leonide to death, then expertly disjointed their bodies and deposited the pieces in the trunks. (His former employment as a butcher proved most helpful in this regard.) After cleansing himself of his bloody work in the bathroom he gathered the children and deposited them at a relative's and made his futile attempt at escape.

At the conclusion of his trial the next year Henry was sentenced to life imprisonment for the murders. Deemed a model prisoner by authorities, he was eventually placed under minimal supervision and as a result casually strolled to freedom by catching a cab in 1944. Although he was recaptured two years later, Henry received a pardon from Louisiana's governor in 1948, on the ground that he had committed the murders during a fit of temporary insanity (i.e., that bout of heavy drinking). It is interesting, and perhaps instructive, to compare the difference in the punishments which the state meted out to Ada LeBeouf for peripheral involvement in the murder of her husband and to Henry Moity for the bestial slaying and dismemberment of his wife and her sister. Henry went on eight years later to shoot his then girlfriend in the state of California. For this attempted murder (his bullet had pierced the woman's lung, but she managed to survive), he was sentenced to a term in prison at Folsom State Prison, where he passed away the next year.

George Healy and Gwen Bristow covered the Moity murder trial from start to finish, Healy writing the straight news report and Bristow the imaginative "color" (i.e., the sob sister stuff). However, near the end of the trial the two reporters, having gotten rather bored with the whole sordid mess, secretly switched bylines. George ruefully admitted that his color was not up to Bristow's impeccable standard and that it "was my last attempt to write like a woman." While he did not divulge how successfully Bristow had written "like a man" on this occasion, certainly she proved able to put her experiences covering murder trials to good use when she wrote four crime novels in collaboration with another male, her husband Bruce Manning, a fellow New Orleans newspaper reporter with black hair, dancing eyes and an infectious grin, whom she met and married while covering the LeBoeuf-Dreher trial.

* * * * * * *

Critics of Bristow and Manning's most successful crime novel, *The Invisible Host*, have carped over the wickedly baroque novel's artificial setting and general lack of realism, criticisms which to me seem entirely beside the point. The Golden Age of detective fiction for a time gloried in its very artificiality. However, the trio of Bristow and Manning crime novels which followed *The Invisible Host* are, if less outrageously inspired than *Host*, also more credible as well as quite enjoyable in their own right, demonstrating that the crime writing couple had not exhausted their murderous imaginations with a single book.

Although not published consecutively, *The Gutenberg Murders* (1931) and *The Mardi Gras Murders* (1932)—both of which novels, like *The Invisible Host*, are set in New Orleans—comprise a two book series and share a number of characters, both major and minor. The major series characters in the novel, all of whom are memorably presented, are Dan Farrell, district attorney of Orleans Parish ("not society but . . . nice people"), ace crime reporter Wade of the *Morning Creole* (decidedly homely but the possessor of a "sardonic grin that conveyed a perpetual assumption of the superiority behind the grin and the stupidity in front of it"), Captain Dennis Murphy of the New Orleans Homicide Squad ("broad, ruddy and Irish") and the *Creole*'s star photographer Wiggins (a "very small, very brown young man with a screwed-up face, hopping like a firecracker"). These colorful characters, along with assorted police and press men (sadly no sob sisters ever put in appearances) link and enliven the two novels, providing as well an air of big city verisimilitude to a genre that was then still dominated by the country house setting, both in the United Kingdom and the United States.

Although its milieu is more realistic than that of *The Invisible Host*, *The Gutenberg Murders* nevertheless offers readers an ingenious, highly classical puzzle, with D.A. Farrell, the police and the press all working together to discover the malefactor behind a rash of gruesome, fiery slayings of individuals associated with the Sheldon Memorial Library, which had already been reeling from the scandalous theft of its recent prized acquisition of nine leaves from the Gutenberg Bible. (Farrell improbably deputizes Wade, although in real life Bristow herself would seem to have had rather a cozy relationship with the police in the Big Easy.)

For murderous inspiration Bristow and Manning unexpectedly drew on the ancient Greek playwright Euripides. (Indeed the novel might have been called *The Euripides Murders*.) Another source of inspiration very likely came to the authors from England's recent Blazing Car Murder, a notorious killing which took place shortly after the passing of Guy Fawkes Night in the early morning of November 6, 1930. After a slain body was discovered in a burning automobile, another man, Alfred Rouse, was arrested and brought to trial for the crime on January 26 1931, and convicted and sentenced to death five days later. Upon the failure of his appeal, Rouse was executed on March 10. Bristow and Manning published *The Gutenberg Murders* four months later in July, likely after having been composed the novel during the winter of 1930-31, so assuredly would have been familiar with the case.

The second and final entry in what might be termed the Wade and Wiggins mystery series, *The Mardi Gras Murders*, was published in November 1932, about sixteen months after *The Gutenberg Murders* and eight months after the non-series *Two and Two Make Twenty-Two*. Farrell, Murphy, Wade and Wiggins all reappear, with Murphy's and Wiggins' roles enlarged from the first novel relative to Farrell's and Wade's. Indeed, Wiggins, whose first name we now learn is Tony, plays the leading role in solving the crime, as Wade had done in *Gutenberg*. The story concerns another rash of bizarre murders in New Orleans, this one taking place over Collop Monday, Shrove Tuesday and Ash Wednesday and plaguing members of the secretive and sinister Mardi Gras parade society Dis, dedicated to the Greek god of Inferno. Once again Bristow and Manning served up an intricately plotted mystery with fiendish murders (including a "locked room" killing on a parade float) and plenteous local color, although it must be admitted that *Mardi Gras Murders*, completed after the publication of Dashiell Hammett's hugely popular novels *The Maltese Falcon* and *The Glass Key*, has a more hard-boiled consistency to it than *Gutenberg*.

In particular Police Captain Murphy, with his repeated bellicose threats of inflicting the "third degree" upon persons of interest in the case and his bigoted treatment of Cynthia Fontenay's black butler Jasper (an important witness in the case), likely will be viewed far less indulgently by modern readers than he is by Farrell, Wade and Wiggins. Yet should we really fault authors like Bristow and Manning for portraying things as they were in those days? (And of course many would question just how much things have changed today.) As New Orleans crime reporters themselves, Bristow and Manning knew of what they wrote, unlike most crime writers of the day (Dashiell Hammett certainly excepted), although they often shared the cynicism of their profession, a quality which they portray in their depictions of Wade and Wiggins, who often get so caught up in the story they are covering that they forget about the finer human feelings. Bristow and Manning refer to "the newspaperman's paradoxical quality of combining a genuine sympathy for people who got into trouble with a naïve eagerness to put their troubles in the paper," which is perhaps a bit too indulgent a way of characterizing it.

Wade and Wiggins are similarly indulgent in their view of Murphy's practice of "stowing away recalcitrant suspects" in the "dripping, rat-ridden, unlighted depths" of the Ninth Precinct station house under the authority of Ordinance 1436, on the assumption that a night or two spent there would loosen stiff tongues. "[E]ven the toughest of gangsters had been known to confess with teary appeals for mercy after two days in sparse fare among the rats," write Bristow and Manning, without any obvious sense of disapproval. As the pair of former reporters would well have known, in real life Henry Moity had made his confession at the Ninth Precinct station house a few years earlier in 1927 and at his trial his legal team argued that he had confessed essentially, as George Healy out it, "to get away from the rats" in that "disintegrating, ill-kept, rodent-infested dungeon."

Two and Two Make Twenty-Two, the crime novel which appeared between *Gutenberg* and *Mardi Gras*, is more of a throwback to the pleasing artificiality of *The Invisible Host*, at least in terms of its enclosed setting on an island off the Mississippi Gulf Coast, which is obviously drawn from the time which Bristow and Manning themselves spent in the area in 1930-31. As a powerful storm bears down on the high-toned pleasure resort of Paradise Island, the small number of hotel personnel and guests remaining there has to cope not only with a squall but drug running and a most determined murderer. Regular police being absent from the scene, the case is solved by a sprightly and engaging elderly genteel lady sleuth, Daisy Dillingham, one of a series of well-drawn women characters who appear in the Bristow-Manning detective novels. At one point Daisy pronounces: "Men always see the obvious. You'll run around putting two and two together and making your own chesty fours out of them. Sometimes two and two make-twenty-two." And the novel's jaw-dropping conclusion proves that she is right. Gwen Bristow and Bruce Manning may have only moonlighted in mystery for but a short while, but vintage mystery fans are fortunate that they did.

Curtis Evans

COLLOP MONDAY

It was Carnival time in New Orleans.

It was Collop Monday, the night before Mardi Gras. Proteus, king of the sea, came in a pageant of miracles and led his parade through the sparkling city while thousands of merrymakers stood along his line of march and cheered. Then the parade dwindled out of sight and the last twinkle of tinsel died in the darkness; the crowds shouting in the streets untangled themselves from the swirls of confetti and went home, to go to bed early, that they might wake at dawn of the town's magic holiday; and Proteus came down from the royal float and led the court to his ball.

The ball of Proteus is Collop Monday's shining preface to Mardi Gras. Mardi Gras is Shrove Tuesday, the day before Ash Wednesday. Ash Wednesday brings the season of penance and fasting and prayer; but Shrove Tuesday is a splendid, glittering day, when the people wave goodby to pleasure for the holy season of Lent.

But there were other merrymakers in New Orleans who did not dance at the Proteus ball. They danced under the rule of Dis, god of the Greek Inferno, and in the court of Dis they all, men and women alike, came dressed and masked as devils. The revelers of Dis met in the French Quarter. Some of them did not go to the ball of Proteus because they had not been asked, others because they did not want to go. They had formed their own Carnival court and they held their own parade on the afternoon of Mardi Gras; for they existed to burlesque the traditions of Carnival. Nobody knew who attended the revels of Dis, though it was known that the ball of Dis on the night of Collop Monday was always held at the house of Cynthia Fontenay. It was said that they had chosen their patron god not only because Dis was the lord of the nether world, but because his name prefixes the words that stand for lost illusions—discontent, disappointment, disenchantment, dismay.

So while Proteus ruled his laughing tinsel court, downtown in Cynthia Fontenay's house the members of Dis danced a devil's dance, their faces hidden behind ugly slant-eyed masks.

A square away the hands of the clock in the gray old St. Louis Cathedral tower crept up toward midnight. When the clock struck twelve it would be Mardi Gras.

CHAPTER ONE

"Sure, Mrs. Fontenay knows I'm coming. Tell her Wiggins from *The Morning Creole* is here to make the pictures."

Mrs. Fontenay's impassive butler bowed. "Yes sir. Will you wait in the courtyard, please sir?"

"Okay. But make it fast."

"Yes sir. I'll tell her right away, sir."

Wiggins of the *Creole* placed his camera on the stone flags of the courtyard, sprawled his diminutive person in a canvas deck chair near the fountain, and squirmed around to screw up his countenance at the butler's departing back. As that functionary noiselessly ascended the iron staircase that led from the courtyard to the upper floor of the house, where the music of Mrs. Fontenay's Mardi Gras party tinkled through the window-hangings, Wiggins sat back and glumly reflected that Mardi Gras was a nuisance and a trial from Twelfth Night to Ash Wednesday morning.

Parades. Mobs of people packed together like cotton-bales. Pictures and more pictures. And then when a fellow was hot and tired, he had to be picked on to get out at midnight and make a lot more pictures of nitwits who had no better way to spend the time than stay up and have a party all night, when tomorrow was Mardi Gras.

Wiggins looked around indifferently. Mrs. Fontenay's courtyard was a swell place all right. But he viewed it with less admiring awe than those visitors from Up North who paused in their excursions through the French Quarter to peer through the high wrought-iron gate. The titter of the fountain at his back and the swish of the banana plants along the tall brick wall had no charm for Wiggins. He was tired and mad and sure that city editors had mighty few brains and practically no hearts at all. He sat lumpily, his blasé brown eyes lifted to the lights above the balcony, waiting to be told everything was ready.

"Mrs. Fontenay says serve you a drink, sir."

Wiggins started and sat up, and his weariness fell from him like a worn garment. He scrambled to his feet.

In the doorway stood a girl.

The light from within flooded out on her shoulders and surrounded her like a halo, and the shadows of the courtyard ended at her feet, as though she came followed by a train of brightness and the dark receded before her. Wiggins gazed and gulped.

For she was small and slim and gracile, and she wore a soft gray dress and an organdie cap and apron, like a luscious actress dressed up as a parlor-maid for the first act of a Cinderella play. Her hair was red, the exciting sort of red that changes sheen with every change of light; and though she did not know it, seldom had greater tribute been paid to her loveliness than that Wiggins of the *Creole* noted all these details before he saw the tall frosted glass on the silver tray she was carrying.

"You're a life-saver, babe," said Wiggins as he approached her. "This must be my big day." He grinned. "A little drink and a little girl, supplied by the management."

"All you're to get," said the vision tartly, "is the drink."

Wiggins put out a hand in a pleading gesture. "Now don't freeze up. I ain't never done you nothing, have I?"

"Do you want this drink," snapped the girl, "or don't you?"

"Sure I want it." Wiggins grinned again. For freeze or no freeze, Wiggins felt he had a way with girls. He took the glass. "What you so sore about, beautiful? Don't you read the papers? This is Carnival time. You oughta be having fun."

The girl flicked up a pair of impertinent eyebrows. Wiggins noticed that they were amazingly black, and so were the eyelashes that curled away from eyes which even in the dimness were blue as the water-hyacinths of the Louisiana bayous.

"Thanks," he said as he gazed at her across the rim of the glass, "but I sure do hate to drink alone, honey."

"Honey?" she countered. "You've got lots of nerve."

Wiggins gave an impudent shrug. "Still don't want to be playmates, eh? Well—" he lifted his glass—"here's to the big frost of '98. Compared to you it was a heat wave."

He watched her as he drank, and he was sure that in spite of her severity he had caught a glimpse of a mischievous crinkle at the corners of her eyes. Wiggins set the glass on the edge of the fountain and launched a plea that rarely failed.

"Say, gorgeous, while we're waiting let me take a coupla pictures of you standing here by the fountain. I got lots of flash lamps, and it won't cost you a cent."

The girl tilted a shoulder. "No thanks. I only work here."

"Oh, that's all right. I'm working here too." He smiled ingratiatingly. "What's your name? I'm Tony Wiggins and I make pictures for the *Creole*."

She hesitated. "My name's Lucy Lake."

"Lucy Lake." Wiggins whistled ecstatically. "Sounds like a summer resort. Gee, that's a pretty name."

Lucy laughed and sat down on the rim of the fountain. "You like it?"

"It's the nertz. It's got sex appeal and everything."

She regarded him unbelievingly. "I suppose you hand that same line to all the girls."

"Not me, babe," he protested. "I never look at a girl. I'm in love with my work, no fooling. To get a break from me girls have to be red-headed and blue-eyed and be named Lucy—see?"

"O yeah?" she retorted. "That's what they all say."

Wiggins sat down on the fountain-edge by her. "I bet they all say it to you, Lucy. Say, you oughta be in the movies. What makes you waste your life in a place like this?"

Lucy held her hand under the trickling water and watched the drops sparkle off her finger-tips. "Well, I was at a finishing school in Paris, and I had a grand duke in love with me, then papa lost his shirt in the market and the duke lost his head in a revolution and I had to get a job."

"That ain't a bad line either," Wiggins observed with appreciation. "Well, I ain't no duke but I got artistic talent and a big blue roadster, and I look like Maurice Chevalier when I'm wearing a straw hat. I guess it's a good thing I came along. Let's go to ride when I'm through here."

Lucy shook her head vigorously. "Umnha."

"Which means?"

"Ummnaumnha."

"No go?"

Lucy smiled sadly.

"What's the matter, afraid?"

She shook her head again. "I live in. I don't get a day off till Thursday."

Wiggins nodded. "Thursday's my day off too. I'll make your picture then, huh?"

"Maybe."

"That's good enough for me."

She gave him a look that was roguishly hardboiled. "But don't forget: All you make is the picture."

"Maybe?"

5 | THE MARDI GRAS MURDERS

"Not maybe. Positively."

"Okay, kid. The customer's always right."

Wiggins gave a shrug and a grin. His philosophy was based on the premise that you couldn't hate a guy for trying. Lucy picked up the tray. "Say," said Wiggins, looking toward the lighted upstairs windows, "what's holding up the parade here? Anything special tonight? I got to get to work."

Lucy replied with stoical calm. "I don't know. I guess some of them passed out."

"Huh. Some drunken brawl these Dis bums put on, ain't it?"

Lucy stood up. "Keep your mind on your work, boy, and pipe down about what's none of your business. Mrs. Fontenay wouldn't like it, see?"

"Wait a minute," he protested. "I ain't putting the zing in on your boss. I've taken her picture lots of times. But the others. I hear they're a bunch of lushies."

"Shh," Lucy cautioned. "Don't let them hear—"

Wiggins came close to her and dropped his voice. "Okay. I don't want to get you in a jam, honey. I'm just curious. I know Mrs. Fontenay. She's regular, even if she is always getting married or something. I shouldn't think she could remember her right name."

"Don't say that out loud," Lucy warned. "She's getting married again soon."

Wiggins' face puckered. "Again?" He held up three fingers. Lucy shook her head and held up four.

"Say," Wiggins whispered, "that's almost a new record for this town. Who's the new lamb?"

Lucy shrugged her slim shoulders. "How should I know?"

Wiggins smiled tantalizingly. "Well, come closer and *I'll* whisper it to *you*. It's Boss Hildreth. I see them at the racetrack a lot."

Lucy gave him a scornful blast from under her black eyelashes. "That's not true," she said.

"Pardon me." Wiggins backed away. "I don't want to marry her. It's okay with me, babe. She didn't even ask my blessing the other times, and she ain't gonta have to this time."

Lucy put a warning hand on his arm. "Don't be spreading that Hildreth stuff."

"But who's the guy?"

"I don't know," Lucy answered, with an emphasis that made it clear to Wiggins that she did know and wasn't telling. "She just said it was going to happen."

"How about Roger Parnell? I've made his picture. He's the good-looking one—the collar ad guy."

Lucy laughed. "Mr. Parnell's the best-looking man in town. All you other men are jealous of him."

Wiggins answered with scorn written from his wide eyes to the upturned palms of his hands. "Horse feathers. How about Arnold Ghent? He's a big hero. Wins cups at swimming meets and dives from high places."

"You know them all, don't you?" she said skeptically.

"Sure, I mug them all, and so I—"

Lucy sent out a warning "Sh!" as the butler crossed the upper balcony and looked down at them for a second. He went in by a side door.

"Maybe," Wiggins hinted, "he's gonta bring down some more drinks."

Lucy gave a cynical shake of her head. "All you newspapermen are just alike. Sponges." She turned.

Wiggins sprang forward to face her with a pained look. "Why, you been to the movies too much, babe. We members of the Fourth Estate work hard and behave like bishops."

"Yes, you do!" she contradicted assuredly. "Say, I used to be a manicurist in the *Daily Star* building. I *know*."

"Oh," he exclaimed. "That makes it all plain. That crowd on the *Star* is terrible. They're always drunk. But say, honey, I'm different. Don't you think you could learn to like just one newspaperman?"

"Well—" Lucy balanced the tray on one hand and considered. "I never thought I'd get to like olives." Before he could answer she was gone. Her spiky heels clicked on the flags and he caught a glimpse of the kitchen, where a fat cook was waddling about in lugubrious activity. The butler reappeared on the gallery and came hurriedly down the stairs.

"Mrs. Fontenay says everybody's ready, sir."

"All right." Wiggins picked up his camera and peered along the passage that led under the balcony. "You tote the box and the other dingus there."

The butler picked up the tripod and the box of flash lamps and started for the stairs. "Right this way," he directed. There was a clatter as the tripod slipped from his hands. Wiggins started.

"Save the pieces. Whatsamatter, your gloves get in your way?"

The butler muttered a series of apologetic noises. He picked up the tripod and again started up the stairs.

"I'll be along." Wiggins peered toward the kitchen.

As the butler made his dignified ascent Lucy reappeared in the passageway with another drink. Wiggins swallowed it gratefully, threw her a kiss and turned toward the path of duty that lay before him in the shape of a scroll-iron staircase, and went up. The butler was waiting for him. There was a scared look in the former's eyes. "Where's Mrs. Fontenay?" Wiggins asked airily.

"Everybody's in the front room, sir," the butler advised, and opened the door. Wiggins nodded jauntily and went inside.

But as the door closed he stood still an instant to gasp at his surroundings.

Wiggins was used to Carnival groups, and with the sulkiness of his trade he regarded most of them as infernal nuisances. It took a great deal to surprise Wiggins. But this was his first adventure with Dis, and he had a sudden strange sense of wickedness, almost of depravity, in Cynthia Fontenay's flaming inferno of a party.

The room was red and hideous and grotesque; an arrangement of shifting lights gave it the appearance of being lit by rapid fires. From behind the screen of palms an orchestra beat a demonic thrum. Some of the maskers were dancing, others were whispering in corners or sprawled across red divans; and several of them sat on the steps that led to a fiery throne at one side. They all wore long red cloaks and horned red and black head-dresses and ugly leering masks, and there was nothing in their costumes to indicate age or sex. To Wiggins the confusion appeared a tumble of red devils with horned heads and black hands, cavorting to abandoned music in a quivering fiery room. So this, he thought, was the Dis party he'd heard so much about.

He saw Mrs. Fontenay coming toward him.

She had taken off her mask, and even the lunatic lights could not destroy the charm of her finely-chiseled features, nor her hideous costume the grace of her famous figure. She was taller than Wiggins, and as he trotted over to meet her and stood looking up into her long-lashed hazel eyes he caught himself thinking what a pity it was that so beautiful a lady should be so completely haywire. She smiled down at him, and in spite of the hardness of her mouth her smile was invitingly gracious.

"Good evening." Her voice was low and husky. "I hope we haven't kept you waiting too long. We were having a meeting when you came."

"That's all right, ma'am," Wiggins gallantly assured her. "I got here early. If everybody's ready, I'll go to work."

"Fine." Cynthia smiled and turned to look toward her orchestra. As she did so the music stopped, and the revelers noticed Wiggins. They shouted and waved to him.

Wiggins waved back. He felt pleased. There was nothing high-hat about this crowd. He smiled as he fixed his flash-lamp and tightened the screws on his tripod. Then, straightening up, he took a long squint at the crazy pattern of the figures against their red background.

"Herd 'em over by the throne, please ma'am," he said. "I'll try to get 'em all on one plate."

Carefully he took a lens out of his pocket and adjusted it, marveling at the swift efficiency with which Cynthia marshaled the group into order, though some of them were obviously difficult to direct. Wiggins studied the figures as they came over to the throne, noticing that each one had a black number sewed on the back of his cloak. Cynthia came back to the camera.

"How many are there?" he asked, clamping his tripod.

"Forty-nine Dis members and one guest. She'll be here in a minute."

Wiggins grinned up at her. "This looks like a hell of a good party, Mrs. Fontenay."

She chuckled. Wiggins decided that he liked her. She had a way of making a fellow feel that he and she were good friends.

"They're all right," she answered. "A little bit noisy, that's all. Do you think you'll need any help?"

"I guess I can manage, ma'am." He looked through the finder. "Now if you little devils will just sit down in front—" he waved his hand—"that's it. And you fellows on the ends. Push in a little bit. Like that. Fine."

He looked into the finder again. "Good so far. Now you with the pitchfork—get back just a little." He glanced up at the hostess and back toward the throne, and suddenly he saw the girl in white. She had just come in.

Among this group of tipsy red devils she looked strangely young and innocent. She was not masked, and her childish features had a touch of uncertainty; her black hair was loose on her shoulders, and glinted in the light like a silken cascade. Wiggins drew a long breath and looked back at Mrs. Fontenay. "Who," he asked, "is the angel?"

Cynthia smiled. "That's Miss Morse—Esther Morse. She's the guest of honor tonight. Do you want her in front?"

"Right in the middle. I'll fix 'em."

Wiggins hurried forward to rearrange the group. He turned the front row into a crescent, and guided Esther Morse to a place in the curve. Cynthia mounted the throne. Wiggins returned to his camera and took one more look.

"Hold steady now." He picked up his flash-lamp switch. "There." A blinding light blinked on and off. "Hold it!" he shouted quickly. "Just one more in case it went blooey." He connected another lamp, and it flashed.

"Thanks everybody. That's all. See you in the paper."

The butler began gathering up the equipment. Mrs. Fontenay came back to Wiggins.

"Thank you for coming."

"No trouble, ma'am. I hope they turn out good."

"I'm sure they will. Good night." She smiled as she turned away. Wiggins hurried out and down into the courtyard.

The butler went with him to the gate.

"Put the stuff in my car," Wiggins ordered in an undertone. "I gotta wait here a minute."

The butler looked at him apprehensively, then dropped his eyes. "Yes sir."

Wiggins waited. The kitchen door was closed. He looked in at a window. Nobody was there but three servants.

The butler was coming back. Wiggins met him. "Everything in okay?"

"Yes sir." The man's dignity seemed gone entirely. "I'm glad I didn't bust up that dingus when I dropped it, sir."

"That's all right." Wiggins dropped a half-dollar into the butler's palm. "Just to show there's no hard feelings."

The butler thanked him and went upstairs. Wiggins wondered if such a small event as dropping the tripod had scared him, or if Mrs. Fontenay had been bawling him out about something.

He whistled softly for Lucy.

She did not come. He whistled again. Still no Lucy. Then, as if in a hurry, he walked toward the gate. No Lucy.

He fumbled with the latch. The gate swung open. Wiggins looked back. There was a soft "Sh" behind him. He looked around, but still he did not see her.

"Here I am," her voice said cautiously.

Wiggins looked around again. The top half of a blind in the corridor wall was open, and Lucy's head and shoulders were silhouetted against the light inside. Wiggins hurried toward her.

"Snapshots all made?" she whispered.

"Yeah. All washed up for the night."

"Were they very drunk?"

"Not bad."

Lucy rested her elbows on the closed lower half of the blind. "Was Mr. Ghent making a nuisance of himself?"

"They were all Ghents to me. I don't know which one was him."

"He was acting awfully funny awhile ago," said Lucy. "I guess he passed out."

Wiggins sniffed. "Let me know if he gets rough."

Lucy smiled. "He don't bother me," she said. "It's just if Mr. Hildreth—" she stopped. "Say, what am I gassing to you for? Go on home."

But Wiggins smiled the cynical smile of an innocent man wrongly accused. "Don't go screwy, kid. I don't care about any of those apes. They're just bum assignments to me."

"I guess you're right."

"Sure." Wiggins was more interested in the flecks of light on Lucy's red hair than in pursuing the hypothetical conduct of the Dis revelers. He rested an elbow on the sill beside hers.

"Say, you're really beautiful, honey."

A buzzer sounded inside the room. "Save it," she retorted. "I've got to be going. Good night."

She made as if to shut the blind. But Wiggins put his hand out.

"How about the pictures Thursday?"

"All right. I'll give you a ring. I've got to go. Good night." The blind closed softly.

Wiggins gazed rapturously at the shut blind for a moment and went out to his car. As the engine started he glanced back, hoping unreasonably for one more glimpse of Lucy. But he saw nobody.

The night was clear and cool, and the street-lanterns threw soft shadows over the time-stained walls of the Quarter. Wiggins' car hummed peacefully along, through the narrow streets of the old city and into the blazing white light of Canal Street. There was something about that girl.

Canal Street and St. Charles Avenue were singularly quiet as the car ambled along. There was no hurry. The picture of the Dis ball was for Sunday. Everything looked fine. He'd drop these plates in the darkroom, hop home and get some sleep. Maybe he'd see Lucy again when he photographed the parades tomorrow. And then there was Thursday.

Wiggins drove in peaceful contemplation to the building that housed *The Morning Creole*. He nodded abstractedly to the lone man behind the classified counter and walked to the elevator.

"Mr. Koppel wants you," the elevator operator informed him. "Said go right into the city room." Crash went the amber glory of Wiggins' dream. "Hell," he groaned. "Another assignment. And me out on my feet."

He left his equipment in the elevator and banged his way through the door that led to the city room. He could see that something had happened. Koppel, the city editor, was yelling into the telephone; three reporters were leaning over his desk, all nodding at his parenthetic instructions; and Wade, the lanky star of the *Creole*, was sliding into his coat. Wiggins' Graflex and flash lamps were waiting for him on the city desk. As the door banged Wade looked up and dashed forward to grab Wiggins' arm.

"Where the hell have you been, shrimp?"

"Out to the Dis doings." Wiggins released himself with dignity and strolled toward the city desk. Wade collared him.

"Well, you're going right back there. Come along." Wiggins halted. "Ain't you got any heart? I got a seven a.m. assignment."

"Hey, Wiggins!" It was Koppel, beckoning wildly. "Get down to Cynthia Fontenay's and make it quick. I'll take care of your other plates. Get along with Wade. Look here, Wade. You've got a deadline at 1:45. I can hold for you fifteen minutes, until two o'clock, but that's all. Get me?"

Wade nodded. "Sure. Call you soon as we get there. Come on, Wiggins."

Wiggins' Graflex was shoved under his arm and he felt himself being dragged ignominiously toward the door. As he scrambled to keep step with Wade's long stride he managed a panting query.

"What the hell is it all about? What's up?"

Wade jerked open the door and rang frantically for the elevator. "They've had a murder down there. Some masker. We just got a tip from Murphy."

The elevator began to ascend toward them. Wiggins looked up at Wade. "Some masker"—so Lucy was all right. He looked down at the

Graflex in his arms. A slow, benign light spread over his stubby features. He stroked his camera with the reverence of a maestro for a beautiful instrument.

"Lord!" said Wiggins of the *Creole*. "Murder and Mardi Gras together! Ain't we *got* fun?"

CHAPTER TWO

WADE of the *Creole* was lean and lank, and so ill-made that he looked as if the Creator had delegated to a clumsy apprentice the task of putting him together. His walk was a long-geared swing and his speech was a drawl, and when he and Wiggins walked side by side the effect was that of a little watch breathlessly ticking away beside the slow pendulum of a grandfather clock. They got into Wiggins' roadster, and as the car started Wiggins glanced from the wheel to the wide-mouthed countenance of his partner. Wade, his long arms wrapped about Wiggins' camera, was staring ahead with an air of abstraction suggesting that this assignment had started a puzzling chain of thoughts.

"What a break I get," Wiggins said savagely. "There I am, right on the spot, and soon as I blow somebody gets shoved."

"Was the party pretty rough?" Wade asked.

"No—just a fancy dress ball with the usual number of drunks and the usual 'you-don't-know-me' crap."

Wade looked from the road to Wiggins. "That's on the level," he assured him. "They *don't* know."

"What's the big idea? So the cute little things can really be devilish?"

"Something like that," Wade returned, more soberly than was his custom. "The Dis revels are supposed to be pretty wild, and if the members are anonymous there's no chance for any kick-backs."

"Then these Dis people really play rough?"

Wade settled the camera to a more stable position on his knees. "Search me. All I know is that Dis has nothing to do with the regular Carnival organizations. Or rather, that the regular Carnival organizations will have nothing to do with Dis. Some people say Dis is made up of French Quarter bohemians, and others say it's a voodoo cult. Then you hear they're just a bunch of uptowners who come down to the Quarter to stage a brawl."

"And there's some talk," said Wiggins profoundly, "that it's part of somebody's racket."

Wade nodded and did not answer.

"There's a lot of dames in it," Wiggins volunteered.

"I understand there are." Wade's wide mouth widened in a somber grin. "And a lot of husbands may find a big surprise in their morning papers."

"Gee, what a story!" Wiggins' small hands paddled the wheel in sudden excitement. "Here's the whole town been wondering who's who in Dis, and now this murder'll blast all the names right out in front of God and everybody!"

Wade gave him a confirming nod. Wiggins swung around a dimly-lit corner with enthusiastic disregard both for laws of traffic and laws of physics. "Big boy, you don't know how good I feel." His voice rose gleefully. "I sure needed some relief from this Mardi Gras blah-blah, so the Lord sends us a nice hot murder. It's swell." He unwillingly pulled up before a red light and let a fleet of trucks go by toward the French Market.

"And that's not all." Wade laughed. "There's another story on the griddle. Up to eleven o'clock tonight the city desk thought sure the Red Cat was going to be raided and Roger Parnell booked as the operator of a gambling joint."

The light turned yellow and then green. Wiggins forgot to move forward.

"What the hell?" he exclaimed—"Parnell and the Red Cat?"

"Keep rollin'," Wade proffered mildly. "I'll tell you about it."

"Sure." Wiggins let in the clutch. "That's a new one—I thought Parnell was in society and all that. What's he doing with a joint like the Red Cat?"

Wade considered a moment. "This is strictly church: they say he owns it. It's been coming along the grapevine. Fritz Valdon is supposed to be his political stand-in, see?"

"Hot stuff," Wiggins commented sagely. "The raid means—"

"—that Fritz Valdon has gone sour and turned on the heat. The police don't bother Valdon's friends unless Valdon orders it."

"Say, listen. I'm still in the dark. Parnell always looked legit. What's he doing running a gambling joint with Valdon?"

"Easy," said Wade succinctly. "Money."

"I thought he was lousy rich."

Wade gave him a philosophical grin. "He was. But I hear he took a big licking last year. This Red Cat is a new gold mine for him."

"And I thought," murmured Wiggins happily, "that this was going to be just another Mardi Gras."

"Well, it would have been, but for this Dis murder. The Red Cat raid was called off. We had the tip, but the headquarters man phoned in to say that Parnell hadn't shown up in the Cat tonight, and that the chief figured it was no go unless they could nail Parnell."

"Maybe he made friends with Valdon again," Wiggins offered shrewdly.

"I don't think so. One thing about Fritz, when he's in, he's in, and when he's out that's the finish. There's no doubt that he was the one putting the finger on Parnell. That was his way of getting even."

"A big murder already and a big raid any minute. What a break for us." Wiggins grinned happily. He and Wade had covered crimes together for a long time.

The car stopped in front of Cynthia Fontenay's wrought-iron gate and they got out. Wiggins picked up his camera, shoved his flash lamps under his arm and made a flourish with his free hand. "The scene of the crime!"

He heard a dance-tune from the house and gave a shrug as he crossed the pavement. "That's a hot one," he remarked brightly. "This Dis crowd certainly ain't letting a little killing spoil their party."

"That is funny," Wade agreed thoughtfully. "Let's go."

"Allez-oop!"

They went toward the gate, Wiggins leading the way.

"Can't go in here," ordered a peremptory voice, and Wiggins blinked indignantly up at the embattled features of a uniformed figure, who stood just inside the gate.

"Oh, I can't, can't I?" Wiggins was beginning, when he heard the lazy drawl of Wade from somewhere behind and above his own head.

"It's only us, Callahan—from the *Creole*."

"Oh," said Callahan, "I couldn't case you in the dark, Mr. Wade. Go in softly. Captain Murphy's here."

"Thanks," said Wade. "Come on, Wiggins."

They walked inside. Captain Murphy of the Homicide Squad was standing by the edge of the fountain peering through the dark in their direction. Murphy was big and solid, with ruddy cheeks and the placid expression of one who has the habit of plodding doggedly ahead to his destinations. His eyes were blue, not a deep violet blue like Lucy's, but a jolly bright blue like the eyes of Santa Claus in a Christmas poster.

"Hello, Wade," he greeted. "You're just in time." He gave his head a business-like jerk toward the five plain-clothesmen who stood around him. "I just wanted to get these fellows stationed around here," he explained. "We'll go up in a minute. I sent the girl to tell Mrs. Fontenay I was ready." He turned to the others.

"Gavaraud, you stay at this staircase and grab anybody who comes down—this one right here. Lehay, you go up on that side gallery and stay there. Wilson, you go back and stand under the rear staircase. Keep out of sight. Good. Dutreaux, you come with me and you too, Matson."

He turned back to Wade and Wiggins and drew them aside. "This," he said, "looks like a mighty tough case. The guy that got it was named Ghent."

"Ghent, eh? Arnold Ghent?" Wade and Wiggins said it together.

Murphy nodded. "That's the one, or so the maid tells me. I'm planting these boys around here so no one gets out, or in for that matter. We'll go up in a minute and see the poor fellow."

The captain was biting at the end of a heavy cigar. "Here's the point that bothers me," he confided. "We got a call at headquarters at 12:42 from the maid here. She said there was a dead man locked up in a room and to come right over. Then she told us there were forty or fifty drunks laying around and not to panic them. Said we'd better sort of sneak in, understand?"

"Good idea," approved Wade, but Wiggins was thinking.

"I'll have to train Lucy better. She ought to call me on murders first."

Murphy was continuing. "Well, when we got here the girl let us in. We had parked our cars down the street a bit. She said no one but her and Mrs. Fontenay knew about this killing, and that she knew no one had come in or gone out since she called up."

Murphy paused to tap his finger against Wade's coat lapel. "Now get this. The body is locked in a room by Mrs. Fontenay. Nobody else knows about it and nobody has left the house for, say, eleven minutes before we came."

Wade and Wiggins signified that they got it.

"Well, about twenty minutes ago, Sergeant Staube over at the Third picks up a guy down near the levee that's almost admitted he did the killing."

"Who?" exclaimed Wade and Wiggins together.

"Well, Staube is doin' a patrol in a police car and he sees a big fellow all dressed up in a monkey suit runnin' to beat hell for the river. Staube calls to him to stop and when he don't stop Staube fires two shots over his head. That stops him."

"A fellow in a monkey suit?" Wade repeated.

"Sure. He's the butler here. Staube asks him what's the matter, where you goin', and so forth, and the man just stands there and shivers. Finally Staube takes him to the Third and gives him a bit of goin' over. The guy says he don't know nothing about trouble, he's just goin' far away."

"So—?" Wiggins suggested.

"Well, this guy's sweating plenty by then, and Staube thinks he'll bring him over. When he arrives, we're here."

"Where's the man?" asked Wiggins.

"I got him on ice," Murphy answered, "he'll keep. But get this, you boys. I ask him who killed Ghent and he pretty near turns white. When he comes to he says 'My Gawd, captain, is he really dead?' 'Dead he is,' I says, 'who killed him?' Then this big fella looks me straight in the eye and says, 'Send me to the jailhouse, captain, my mind is made up to die.' And so help me God I can't get another word out of him."

"Think he did it?" Wiggins showed obvious disappointment.

"How the hell do I know? What I'm interested in is why that girl was so sure no one knew. And just how much this guy knows, and why he was on the lam."

"It's mighty puzzling," Wade agreed. "We'll talk to him later. If you're all set now let's go up."

"And get the picture," finished Wiggins. "Boy, this is like old times. I swear, captain," he turned to Murphy, "I thought this depression was hittin' your racket too."

Murphy shook his head. "I wish to God you were right, boy, but nothing ever stops people killing each other, it seems. Let's go."

He called to the detectives. "All right, men." The two plainclothesmen fell in behind the broad back of the policeman. Wade and Wiggins followed. Without speaking, the five of them went up the staircase.

As they stood waiting for Murphy to complete his instructions to the men, Wiggins beckoned to his lanky companion. "Wade," he whispered, "take a peek at this." He led Wade to the door of the front room and slowly opened it an inch or two. "Look," he said.

The red devils were still dancing against their violent red background, and the orchestra was thumping out its savage tune. Wade softly shut the door.

"Pretty!" he commented under his breath. "This seems like a very nice story."

Wiggins solemnly rolled up his round eyes. "A wow!"

Then he started, half with delight and half with apprehension. For Murphy was coming up to them, and with Murphy was Lucy, very white about the eyes and very stubborn about the mouth. Wiggins went toward her with an encouraging grin.

"'Lo, babe!" he greeted. "Just tell us all about it. Didn't expect me back so soon, did you?"

Lucy smiled bravely and started to answer, but Murphy was eager to get down to business.

"Suppose you take us somewhere we can be private and talk a bit," he ordered.

"Mrs. Fontenay said take you right in here, sir." Lucy pushed back a tapestry curtain and led them into a large dim room with angular furniture in gold and Chinese red. Murphy cast a disdainful glance around and brought his eyes back to rest upon Lucy, who stood uncertainly by a three-cornered red chair with gold markings.

"Now, miss, I'll see Mrs. Fontenay later. First you tell me what's been going on." He scowled as he observed Wiggins brightly tapping his foot to the jazz from the parlor.

"Yes, sir, I'll tell you, sir." Lucy glanced at Wiggins as though for reassurance. He grinned from beyond Murphy's elbow. Wade carefully placed himself upon another of the crazy chairs, and Lucy, apparently relieved at this gesture toward informality, sat down too. Murphy, after a preliminary survey, selected a wide and uncomfortable red bench as the least likely to break under his weight, and produced his notebook.

"First, what's your name?"

"Lucy Lake, sir." She was a trifle awed, but she spoke steadily.

"Lucy Lake." Murphy wrote it down with his stub of a pencil. "You work for Mrs. Fontenay?"

"Yes, sir. I've been her personal maid for three years."

Wiggins sat down and eased his chair as close to Lucy's as he dared. Murphy paid him no attention.

"Where'd you work before that?"

"In the Violetta Beauty Shop on Carondelet Street, sir."

"I see. Now, Lucy, how'd you happen to find the body?"

Lucy shivered. "It was awful."

"Sure, I know, but how'd you happen to find it?"

Lucy drew a long breath. "Well, sir, right after Mr. Wiggins left Mrs. Fontenay told me to go in the china-closet and get some more glasses. The closet is a little room at the back and she always has a lot of extra glasses there when she has a party because people are always breaking them, especially when she has a party for the Dis organization. So I went into the closet, and the minute I opened the door I saw him—"

She shuddered. Wiggins surreptitiously patted her arm.

"—He was lying on the floor. Sort of halfway on his face, with his arms straight out in front of him. I thought at first he had passed out. But it seemed a funny place for him to be."

"Hm," said Murphy. "They often pass out at these Dis parties?"

"O yes, sir. 'Most all of them."

"I get you. So what did you do?"

"I spoke to him, but he didn't answer. So I knelt down by him and spoke to him again, and asked if there was anything I could bring him, and when he didn't answer I thought I could turn him over and straighten him out and open the window and maybe he'd feel better."

"You should have pulled off his mask to give him air," Murphy contributed.

Lucy's blue eyes widened in shocked surprise. "Oh, but I couldn't do that. I wouldn't dare take off anybody's mask."

"Your face is your own private secret at a Dis party, Murphy," Wade interpolated dryly.

"It certainly is." Lucy swallowed and stiffened her spine for the last effort of telling what had happened. "So I turned him over, and then I saw the tiniest little spot of something on his robe—a queer color, as if somebody had spilt a drop of something on him—his suit was all red, you know, and this stain was black, but a funny black—and I don't know why, but I touched it. It was sticky—blood—"

Her lips curled back in a sudden twitch of horror. "Wait a minute, now," ordered Murphy. "Let's get this straight, young lady. The stain is in front?"

"Yes, sir. Just the tiniest spot. But the minute I felt it and looked at my finger I knew it was blood—and then I realized it was right over his heart. I was awfully frightened, and I ran out and called Mrs. Fontenay. I got her out of the party and told her Mr. Ghent was hurt."

"And what did she do?" Murphy inquired.

"For a minute she didn't do anything. She just stood there and looked at me. She had put her mask back over her face, but you know how it is when people are looking at you—you can feel it, and you get all hot and cold. That's the way she was looking."

"And then—?" suggested Murphy.

"And then she said, very quietly, 'Perhaps he's badly hurt, Lucy. I'll go with you and see.' So she went into the little room with me. I was afraid, but she just walked right in. I stood in the door while she knelt down and felt his pulse and stood up. Then she came outside and locked the door. She took the key with her. She said, 'Lucy, he's dead. Somebody killed him.' She stood still a minute. Then she held me by the shoulders. She said, 'Do you think you can be very quiet and do just what I tell you?' So I told her I would do my best. Then she told me to call police headquarters, and tell the police about Mr. Ghent and about all the others that were here and to tell the police to be very quiet when they came. Then she sent me down into the courtyard to wait. So I went down there, and she went back to the party." Lucy looked pleadingly across at the big policeman. "And that's all, sir, really it is."

"And you sure told it straight, honey," said Wiggins softly, scrambling to his feet.

Lucy's smile was grateful, and as she stood up Wiggins noted with delight that her eyes had to look up to his. The trouble with most girls was that they looked down at him.

"There's just a few things I don't get straight, Miss Lucy," Murphy was saying with dangerous affability. "We'll come to those in a minute. Excuse me while I talk to Mr. Wade a bit."

He crossed to where Wade was sitting. Wiggins lowered his voice. "Don't you let that guy give you the jits," he admonished Lucy. "Just stick to your story."

Lucy nodded. "I'm not scared. Honest."

"That's right." Wiggins patted her shoulders reassuringly. "Just excuse me a minute while I see what he's saying to Wade. Murphy and Wade always get clubby when it comes to murders."

He pattered across the room. Wade greeted him with a grin.

"You're right, I'll try it right away," Murphy was saying. "There's no hurry to see the poor fellow. I believe in getting in the groundwork first. If Mrs. Fontenay or anybody else here knows anything it's a good plan to keep them worrying about how they're going to hide it. A little uncertainty works wonders sometimes."

Wade agreed. "But don't forget my deadline. Give me a chance to get to a phone before you go into action. Koppel is probably going nuts now waiting for a flash."

"Sure, boy, I'll see to that all right in just a few minutes. There's a phone in the hall just outside. You go to it." Murphy wrinkled his forehead. "Hurry back."

Wade nodded and went out to the telephone. Murphy crossed back to Lucy. Wiggins sat on the arm of a chair and gave his attention to Lucy, who was standing obediently in front of Murphy, looking very tiny and fluttery before his authoritative bulk.

"Yes, sir?" she said. She had laced her hands tightly, but her voice did not quiver.

Murphy did not appear to be in any haste to come to the point. He looked her up and down, taking in all the details of her frivolous little uniform. He put his big hands into his jacket pockets.

"Now, young lady," he rumbled, "maybe we can get finished here in just a minute."

Lucy tried to smile. The effort was a failure. Murphy's smile did for them both. It was a smile of stubbornness and triumph and command.

"Why didn't you take the false face off the man and give him air, Miss Lucy, when you first found him?"

Lucy sighed. There were exasperation and despair in her voice when she answered.

"But I *couldn't* do that! I'd lose my job. Don't you understand? Nobody knows anybody else at the Dis parties. They never take off their masks. It's all a secret."

Murphy's face turned a brickish red. His eyelids tightened around his eyes as though pulled in by drawstrings, and his eyes fastened themselves on Lucy with threatening concentration.

"That's a very—good—answer, young lady," he told her deliberately, "and you've made it twice."

Lucy drew back into the big chair. Her little figure seemed to shrink smaller. Her eyes stared into his, and her lips opened and shut, and opened and shut again, as if a thousand answers had rushed into her throat and had paralyzed one another as they came, so that she could say nothing at all; Murphy's big person towered over her and his thick forefinger pointed at her accusingly.

"Now think up another good answer to this one," he demanded, stepping closer. "If nobody knows anybody else at this party, and if you didn't take off the false face that Ghent had on—how did you know it was Ghent that was killed?"

Lucy's hands fluttered aimlessly about her face and she stared at him helplessly, as if her constitution were too frail to master the terrible task of speaking.

"Think up a good answer for that, now," Murphy was ordering, his indignation burring his words, "for unless you do, I'll arrest you tonight, so help me God, and let you tell a jury what you know about the murder of Arnold Ghent."

CHAPTER THREE

WIGGINS bent over Lucy and patted her shoulder.

"It's all right now," he said, "he's gone. Stop crying."

Lucy looked up. Her tiny handkerchief dabbled inadequately at her eyes. She curled herself farther back into the big armchair.

"What's he going to do with me?" she asked helplessly. Her sobs broke her voice into little dips and rises.

"Nothing." Wiggins smiled confidently. "Listen," he said. "Murphy's a cop, see? His job is to get the guy that killed Ghent. In the meantime he's gonta try to make everybody in the place feel like they're in a big jam."

Lucy drew a long choking breath and then another. Her blue eyes appealed to Wiggins between tear-laden lashes.

"Will he really—arrest me?" she asked.

"What for?" Wiggins spread out his hands to emphasize by their emptiness the equal emptiness of Murphy's charge. "Did you kill Ghent?" His voice and face were blank. "No. Did you have any reason to kill Ghent?" He shook his head ponderously. "No."

Slow comprehension crept over Lucy's face. "Then he was just trying to scare me?"

"Sure." Wiggins drew up a chair opposite her and sat down. "Now look, Lucy. I know about murders. I know the way Murphy works. He ain't got so many brains, so he just hammers away, see? He ain't gonta arrest you. He might hold you as a material witness and he might not. It depends on how hot he burns and if the case is tough, see? I'll tell Wade you're a big friend of mine and Wade'll take care of you."

Lucy listened in respectful silence. "Thank you," she said softly. "Thank you so much." Then with a sudden new tremor she asked, "What will they do with me now?"

Wiggins puckered up his lips and considered a moment before replying. "Well, Murphy'll talk to the others. Then unless he gets a lucky break that pins the job on somebody, he might bother you again, but it won't be much. Tomorrow Farrell—the district attorney—will be on the job. He's out of town tonight."

Lucy had drawn back again, stiff with fright. "The district attorney? But he'll—"

"Say, you been going to the movies too much." Wiggins could not help laughing. "Farrell is a good egg. Me and him are big friends, kid."

"But it'll be awful—I'll be questioned and in the papers—"

"Don't you lose your nerve. Murphy's a lot worse than Farrell. You see, finding the body puts you in the grease the first day. After that they forget you."

The handle of the door turned. Wiggins heard Wade's and Murphy's voices. He had only time to whisper to Lucy a warning to buck up before the other two walked in. They both looked serious, and Wiggins sensed that this was no time for him to interrupt by protesting that Murphy had been rough with Lucy.

"Say, captain," he said instead, "this little lady says she won't pose for a picture unless Mrs. Fontenay says it's all right. Tell her it won't do no harm, willya?"

Murphy grinned shortly. "So that's what you're after. Well, far as I'm concerned it's all right."

Wade came to the rescue, smiling. "How about it, Lucy? We haven't got much time, and we'd like the people who read the paper to see what a nice girl you are."

Lucy was sitting on the arm of the big chair. Her eyes moved from Murphy and rested on Wiggins, who was screwing a flash bulb into the socket. He cocked an eager look over his shoulder. Lucy slowly began to smile too. "All right," she said. "But I guess I look awful."

"You look beautiful," whispered Wiggins as he set up his camera and turned to pose Lucy in the chair. There was a rush of light and Lucy was safe on the plate. Wiggins hurriedly scratched on a piece of copy-paper, "Lucy Lake, personal maid, as she tells how she found Ghent's body."

"And now," Captain Murphy was saying, "we'll see Mrs. Fontenay. In the meantime," he added to Lucy, "you'd better make up your mind to answer a lot more questions. I'm not through with you yet. Come on."

"Yes, sir," said Lucy demurely, and she caught Wiggins' eye and smiled. "Mrs. Fontenay's in her room, sir. I'll show you the way."

She led them across the passage and opened a door. A zephyr of perfume brushed past them and they entered Cynthia Fontenay's bedroom.

The room was sleek with lavender satin and glowing with mauve-shaded lamps, which threw their reflections from many mirrors in little spots of light that created rather than dispelled the illusive dimness. The satin draperies hung in deep folds from the bed, drooped over the windows and ruffled lusciously around the scented disorder of jars and flasks on the dressing-table. A negligee and little discarded under-garments bubbled on the chairs as though a gay hurry of dressing was just now over. The room was soft, inviting and intimate; Wiggins felt as if he might have blushed when he entered it and hoped he hadn't. He caught Wade's eye, and Wade's bony shoulder lifted in an infinitesimal and expressive shrug, and then their glances parted and changed swiftly to the focus of their interest, where Cynthia half lay on a low chaise-longue.

They saw her face and figure in profile, and apparently she did not hear the opening of the door, because she did not look up as they entered. She still wore her red devil-costume, and one black-gloved hand hung over the arm of the chaise-longue, dangling her painted mask. She had pushed back the headdress, so that the black and scarlet hood with its fantastic horns lay on her shoulders, and her bright golden hair was rumpled above her forehead as though the headdress had been pushed away in a hurried gesture for freedom. Cynthia looked like one of those women who at one time have been exquisitely beautiful. She was still very lovely, but it was a loveliness crystallized as though in ice; her hard mouth and tired eyes suggested that she had had too much of everything, and that now, though she was still young and still charming, she had arrived at the desert place where life held no more promises.

Wiggins wrinkled his nose inquiringly in Murphy's direction, but Murphy, after one disapproving look at his surroundings, calmly toed a pink satin mule out of his way and cleared his throat. Cynthia looked up with a start.

"Good evening, ma'am," said Murphy stolidly.

Cynthia stood up. "You're from police headquarters?" she asked. Her rich, husky voice had a suggestion of tiredness, as though she dreaded what was before her and was wearied by what was behind her. But there were no traces of tears around her eyes.

"Captain Murphy of the Homicide Squad, ma'am." Murphy shook his head at the damask-covered chair Lucy was indicating, less in refusal than in disapprobation of such expensive flimsiness.

"You'll want to see the body," said Cynthia. She was regarding Murphy and his companions with a severe politeness, such as she might have given a delegation from an orphan asylum who had come to ask her for a donation, which she did not want to give but which she feared she might be cajoled into giving. Murphy answered genially.

"Yes, ma'am. Wise move on your part to lock up the room, ma'am. The coroner'll want to see the body just as you found it."

She nodded. The coroner. The Homicide Squad. The body. It was with almost visible shocks that the strange words struck her consciousness. Murphy got out his notebook.

"What's the full name of the murdered man?" he inquired.

"Arnold Ramsey de Clifford Ghent." Her voice did not quiver.

"Now this little lady with the red hair—" Murphy jerked his head toward where Lucy stood like a Dresden figurine in front of a lavender-curtained window—"told us about how she found the body. She said you went and looked at it."

"Yes." Cynthia sat down again on the chaise-longue and began pulling off the black gloves that hid her hands. "I—I thought he might not be dead." She shivered.

"But he was dead?" Murphy prompted.

"Yes. His pulse. His hands. He was dead." She held one hand tightly clenched in the cup made by the other. "He was dead," she repeated.

"You didn't take off his mask?" Murphy was still making notes.

Cynthia threw down her gloves and pushed her hand through the bright rumple of her hair. "No. I thought it best not to touch him. To wait for the police."

"And quite right, ma'am," said Murphy, snapping his notebook shut with a satisfied air. "And now, ma'am, I think we'll go in."

Cynthia's hands slipped slowly down to grasp the seat on each side of her as though it were only with a great effort that she could force herself to stand. She gestured to Lucy.

Lucy opened the door, and the men stood aside for Cynthia to go out. Wiggins, at the tail of the party, paused to whisper.

"You ain't scared, are you, Lucy?"

She smiled and shook her head. The shaded lights of the room behind her glowed graciously on her hair. "Not very much," she whispered back. "You made me feel lots better." She closed the door and followed the others.

Cynthia led them down the passage to the door of the china-closet. She handed Murphy the key.

Murphy beckoned the two detectives he had left waiting. "Dutreaux, you come with us. You stay in the hall, Matson, and keep everybody out of here."

He fitted the key into the lock. The bolt rasped softly as he turned it, and the door to what Wiggins called the scene of the crime swung open.

Lucy pressed back against the wall as though to get as far as possible from the figure that lay in front of her.

The beat of jazz came merrily from the room down the passage. Cynthia stood in the doorway, her hands locked in front of her, her eyes fixed tensely on the body. Murphy and Dutreaux stood over the dead man, carefully studying the position of the body and the arrangement of the closet.

It was a small room with built-in drawers and cabinets holding china and crystal. The single window, opening on the back gallery, was closed, and the outside shutters drawn. In the space in front of the window lay the dead man. Over the heart was a small queer-colored stain, at one side of a swell in the red robe.

The arms were flung wide on either side, and the devil-mask poked its long nose toward the ceiling.

The horns stuck arrogantly out from the head, and the eye-holes with their black silk pointed eyebrows were hideous in their suggestive emptiness. The whole figure was repulsive, almost loathsome, with its ugly mockery of death.

It seemed so to Wiggins, and he guessed from the morbidly fascinated eyes of Lucy and Cynthia that it seemed so to them, but Murphy's powers of analytical observation were not marred by any flaw of sensitiveness. He got briskly to work.

"Look him over, Dutreaux," he ordered.

Dutreaux got down on his knees and lifted one of the black-gloved hands. He rolled back the full sleeve and felt for a pulse. His fingers felt carefully about the high collar of the robe. He dropped his head to the chest and listened, then looked back at Murphy.

"He's dead," he said.

Murphy nodded agreement. Dutreaux felt around the mask.

"Don't touch that," Murphy admonished. "We'll wait for the coroner. Can you get us some chairs, miss?" he asked Lucy. "Help the little lady, Dutreaux." As Lucy and Dutreaux went out he turned to Cynthia. "Coroner ought to be here in a minute," he assured her.

She nodded and did not reply. A draft from the open door blew the edge of her red robe to touch the edge of the red robe on the floor; she snatched it back as though the body were that of a leper. Lucy brought her a chair, and she sat down mechanically. Murphy took the chair Dutreaux set for him, facing Cynthia across the mute accusation of the body. Dutreaux and Wade leaned against the gallery window.

Murphy looked across the body to Cynthia.

"You can help me if you will, Mrs. Fontenay," he said.

Cynthia wrenched her eyes from the dead man and looked at him. Her eyes were hazel, large and limpid, and they seemed strangely dark under her golden hair.

"I'll do all I can, Captain Murphy," she answered.

It was the first time she had spoken since they had left her bedroom. Her voice had an evenness that suggested not resignation nor resentment nor self-control, but an odd combination of all three, as though Cynthia was not yet sure of her position but was confident that whatever it was she would be mistress of it.

"Thank you, ma'am." Murphy crossed his legs and leaned back as though to settle for a long conversation. "Now here's what I wanted to ask you about, Mrs. Fontenay. This party you're having—it's the regular party, ain't it, that you're accustomed to give the night before Mardi Gras for the people that belong to Dis?"

Cynthia's eyes narrowed ever so slightly. "Yes."

"And I gather, ma'am, that they're all mighty careful not to be recognized?"

"Yes."

"Seems to me I've heard somewhere that they're so careful that everybody comes to the party in a hired car. That right?"

"Yes."

"And everybody, men and women alike, dresses just like everybody else? Like you're dressed now?"

"Yes."

"I see, ma'am. Now those people in there—" he jerked a thumb toward the source of the jazz—"what time do they unmask?"

"They don't," said Cynthia.

Her frozen little monosyllables affected Murphy's determined magnanimity as little as chips of ice thrown against a brick wall. Murphy gave her a smile that she might have thought amiable, but which Wiggins recognized as a threat of wrath to come.

"Then there's just one little point I'd like to have cleared up, Mrs. Fontenay. If nobody could possibly know who anybody else was, how do you suppose the person who did the killing knew who to kill?"

A shiver ran through her whole slim body. Then she recovered herself and smiled back. It was a studied and eloquent smile. In the instance before she answered the smile said quite plainly, 'I am in a deplorable situation. You are here because it is your business to be here, and therefore I shall not be rude to you. But as to my private and personal thoughts upon this occasion, those I shall keep to myself.' And so plainly did she convey this to Murphy, and to Lucy and Dutreaux and Wade and Wiggins, that it was like putting a needless epilogue to a speech when she said,

"I'm sure I don't know, Captain Murphy. That's what the police are for, isn't it?"

Murphy clasped his big hands around of one of his big knees and rocked himself gently to and fro.

"Yes, ma'am, that's what we're for, and that's one of the things I guess we'll have to find out." He ceased rocking and reached into his breast-pocket for his notebook, pursuing his train of information with the steadiness of an expert following an old trade. "Now everybody in yonder is masked, ain't they?"

"There is one girl unmasked," Cynthia answered readily. "But she is not a member of Dis. Her name is Esther Morse."

Murphy wrote it down and put the book back into his pocket. There was an airy reassurance of finality in the way he did it, a suggestion of

'We won't need to make notes on what's coming. Not at all. It's just between friends.' He looked benignly at the ceiling. "Now, Mrs. Fontenay, before I go into the question of who you think might have wanted to kill Mr. Ghent, suppose you help me clear up this other question about everybody's name being so secret. Seems to me if nobody knew anybody else, and everybody took such pains to keep his face hid, any guy that wanted could get himself a devil-dress and crash this party. How do you see about that?"

Cynthia smiled again. "We don't usually like to make the plan of our organization public, Captain Murphy, but I see why you will have to understand it." She hesitated, as if uncertain as to how to satisfy Murphy and at the same time divulge the fewest possible secrets of Dis. Wiggins felt a little bit sorry for her. Wiggins was an amiable soul, and he had the newspaperman's paradoxical quality of combining a genuine sympathy for people who got into trouble with a naive eagerness to put their trouble in the paper. This lady, now. She really did seem to be trying to be nice. But of course she'd had a big shock, and of course she wasn't used to talking across the body of a dead man, and of course she didn't know how to handle the cops.

"It's like this," Cynthia explained after a moment. "Each member of Dis is given a seal ring at the time of his initiation. When we have a meeting, he is admitted on showing this ring and on giving a password. We have a different password for every meeting. Tonight it was 'Persephone.'"

"Ma'am?" said Captain Murphy.

"Persephone—queen of Hades."

"Yes, ma'am," said Murphy, with more confidence, for he had surreptitiously glanced at Wade, who had indicated by a nod that he could both spell and remember 'Persephone' for future reference.

"But this is what I don't see, ma'am," continued Murphy. "There must be somebody who knows the names and addresses of all these people, or how do they get the passwords and things like that?"

"Oh," said Cynthia. "I'm sorry. I'll explain." Her eyes fell suddenly on the dead man at her feet. She started and caught her hands together as though to stop a gesture of hysteria. But after an instant she spoke again, and her voice was low and rich as before.

"Nobody has a list of members," she explained. "I'm the only member whom everybody knows, and I have never made any attempt to violate the anonymity of Dis. I'll try to make it clear.

"Dis was begun seven years ago by—by Mr. Fontenay. Mr. Fontenay invited me to join—that was before we were married. I invited another member, and so on. So you see, each member knows only two others: the one who invited him and the one he invited. The membership is limited to fifty.

"At every annual party at my house I pass around a tray containing fifty numbered slips of paper; each guest draws a slip, and this number is the one by which he is identified at every Dis meeting during the ensuing year. I also give a password, which is used for a year. A member unable to attend any meeting notifies me in advance, signing his number; if any member is unaccounted for at a meeting, his number is eliminated from the rolls. Announcement of this is made, and the person who invited him is told to get his ring and return it to me. Then the newest initiate, who is identified by an X on his costume, is given the ring and is told he may invite a friend to join. When he invites a friend he sends me the friend's measurements and I have the costume made.

"We have regular meetings in the den where the floats for our Mardi Gras parades are built, and any message that must be given between-times is inserted in the personal columns of the newspapers. We have never had any trouble with gate-crashers—our tellers stand at the doors and check as the members come in. We know, you see, that there are fifty people to be accounted for, and we have the list of numbers being used each year. A gate-crasher would either use a number not on this year's list or would duplicate the number belonging to a legitimate member, even if he had managed to find out the password and get a robe and mask and ring exactly like ours. If he used a number not on the list he would be denied admittance; if he duplicated the number of someone already present they would both be asked questions about the minute detail of our ritual, and if we could not tell which was the gate-crasher that way, the accredited member would be given his choice of unmasking and being identified by the person who had invited him, or of resigning. But we have never had this happen."

Murphy ran a hand through the heavy white hair that crowned his disapproving face. The goings-on of some people, especially rich people, left Murphy puzzled, for Murphy knew very little about the state of boredom or the devices created to banish it.

"And so," he summarized, "everybody knows just two members. And they don't even know those two members when they get all dressed up for a party."

Cynthia's smile had become patient. "That's the idea, captain. I can't promise that some members haven't recognized others or told others who they were."

Murphy nodded again. Cynthia's answers had been given readily, too readily, thought Wiggins, who knew Murphy's oft-voiced distrust of people who seemed to be coming more than halfway to meet the police. But Murphy was evidently determined not to be outdone in politeness. He spoke with expansive geniality.

"Now that's a very nice clear account, Mrs. Fontenay. I think I understand just how it is. I hope what I'm going to ask you won't be unduly embarrassing, because we know you've had a big shock and all that, but I believe Mr. Fontenay ain't living with you any more, and don't he know some of the members of Dis?"

Cynthia sighed as if her patience was being sadly strained. "Mr. Fontenay has been living in Europe, captain, for about two years."

"I see, ma'am, thank you." His eyes studied Cynthia narrowly across the body on the floor. He looked her up and down, from the shining disorder of her hair to the tip of the red satin slipper that showed under the hem of her robe. Then he asked, "Mrs. Fontenay, did you invite Arnold Ghent to join Dis?" Wiggins looked at Wade. He met Wade's eyes, and the look was a mutual agreement that this was an episode to be watched. Wiggins glanced at Lucy, and saw that her eyes were fixed on Cynthia with something very like fear.

"No," she said quietly.

"All right." Murphy stood up. "Then maybe you can tell me, Mrs. Fontenay, how you are so sure that this murdered man—" he pointed to the body on the floor—"is Arnold Ramsey de Clifford Ghent." For a moment Cynthia did not move. She simply sat there, very still, and suddenly every trace of expression sank out of her face and it became as vacant as the mask she had been wearing, as if she had withdrawn herself far away and was looking at Murphy from an infinite distance. Then she drew herself slowly to her feet.

"Why—"

"Never mind any 'whys.' Tell me how you know. Everybody came here masked. Everybody is dressed like everybody else. And yet you and this girl—" he pointed his thick forefinger from the body to Lucy—"without taking off the mask or the gloves of this man, tell me Arnold Ghent has been murdered."

Cynthia was tense with anger. For an instant Wiggins thought she was about to break into a tirade of fury. Then she shook her head ever so slightly. Her hands clenched with bitter resolution.

"Because he told me who he was—about two hours ago," she answered briefly.

Murphy wheeled on Lucy.

"And you? I suppose he told you too. You don't belong to Dis, do you? But you knew it was Arnold Ghent who was dead."

Lucy took a step forward. She looked straight into Murphy's eyes, her hands defiantly on her hips.

"You can't scare me like that again. I knew him because Mrs. Fontenay told me. Early this evening she said 'Mr. Ghent is number 47. He doesn't seem to be well. Sort of look out for him, Lucy.' When I came in he was lying on his side and I saw the number. That's how I know."

Wiggins' grin was an ovation.

Murphy had turned again to face Cynthia. "Is that true?"

"Quite true." Cynthia had regained her self-mastery. "If you will turn that body over you'll see a number 47 on the back. Mr. Ghent did seem strange tonight. That's why I told Lucy to take care of him."

Murphy shrugged incredulously and slowly took out his black notebook. Wiggins, standing on tiptoe, saw Murphy's pencil mark a big cross on a page headed 'Identity.'

There was a knock on the door. Dutreaux opened it.

"It's Doc Emerson, captain," he said.

"The coroner," Wiggins whispered to Lucy. She glanced up with frank curiosity.

"That Murphy gives me a big pain," she whispered.

"Sorry I kept you waiting," the coroner was saying as he came in. He was a big man with a ruddy face, dressed in a dinner-jacket that bore testimony to the party from which he had been summoned to attend to business. Wiggins noted with disgust that behind him came Kennedy of the *Telegram* and McFee of the *Star*, with a couple of photographers. He and Wade exchanged looks of resignation.

"We haven't moved the body, doc," Murphy was saying.

"Good. I'll be done in a minute." Emerson opened his small black satchel and dropped to his knees. He made his measurements of the room and the position of the body and put a few routine questions to Lucy as to the body's position when she found it.

"Want the mask?" he asked, taking out a pair of surgeon's scissors.

"Sure," nodded Murphy. "But don't cut it unless you have to. The d. a. may need it."

Cynthia turned away. She looked toward the door and back at the curious huddle of reporters and policemen, and then at the door again, but she did not try to leave. Wiggins felt a new rush of sympathy for her. Funny, he thought, how what's just business for some people is life and death for others.

Emerson fumbled impatiently with the mask. His fingers found the hook and zipper that held it closed. There was a soft ripping sound as the hook slid over the metal catches. He took the ends in his hands and pulled carefully.

There was a scream from Lucy and a muffled choking cry from Cynthia. Wade muttered a low "Hell." Wiggins put out a hand to steady Lucy and looked at Murphy's dazed expression and then at the dead face on the floor.

"That's not Arnold Ghent," said Wiggins quickly.

"You're damn right it's not," said Wade. "It's Roger Parnell."

CHAPTER FOUR

WADE put the telephone back on its stand and glanced over his shoulder toward the locked door of the ballroom. The music was still blaring, mingling with sounds of voices and snatches of songs. So far it appeared that nobody but Cynthia and Lucy knew the police were in the house; and it appeared also that nobody was likely to inquire till morning. He tiptoed back into the china-closet.

Cynthia and Lucy were not there. Murphy and Emerson were leaning over Parnell's body. They had loosened the red robe and unfastened the belt, and Emerson was looking at the body with a bewildered scowl. Wade went over to Wiggins, who was leaning against the window-sill watching the proceedings.

"What'd you do with the girls?" he inquired.

"Murphy sent 'em to Cynthia's room. Told Cynthia she'd feel better after she'd had some rest. I guess he wanted a chance to talk things over kinda private, this guy being Parnell and all that. Coupla cops looking out for Cynthia."

Wade glanced at Emerson. "What's on your mind, doctor?" he asked, but as he spoke Emerson emitted a low expletive.

"I knew it," he added half under his breath. "Here, Murphy, take a look at this."

Wade leaned over; the reporters from the other papers came closer to watch. Emerson slipped down the shoulders of the robe and pointed. Protruding from the dead man's shirt-front was the hilt of a pearl-handled knife—a knife that had not pierced through the red robe.

"By all the saints," Murphy exploded softly, "he was dead when they brought him here."

"Wait a minute," said the coroner. He was on his knees examining the bloodstain on the red robe. "Get this right: the knife pierces the body in the cardiac region, probably through the heart. It hasn't gone through the robe. The robe hasn't a sign of a tear, and no opening either—it was fastened close up to the neck. With the robe fastened, the only indication of the knife was the little swell of the cloth over the hilt." He paused and thought a minute. "I guess you're right, Murphy—he must have been dead when they brought him here."

"You mean they killed him first and dressed him afterwards?" Wiggins asked incredulously. Disgusted disagreement was all over his stubby features.

"That's just one supposition," said Emerson. He was still crouching by the body, the center of the ring of puzzled listeners. "You remember when we first saw the body, with the robe fastened, the only evidence of violence was the little splotch of blood on the robe—and of course the rise where the hilt of the knife was covered."

Murphy was paying close attention. "I think I get you, Emerson," he assented. "The fellow that did this job figured if he could stab the man and dress him up in one of these outfits—maybe stab him some place else and bring him here—anybody who saw the body pitched over on its face the way it was would figure it was just another drunk, and not bother about it much."

"You're right," exclaimed Wiggins, grabbing Murphy by the arm to add emphasis to his next remark—"and if it hadn't been for that girl out there that you were just manhandling a minute ago, all the Irish cops in town wouldn't know anything had happened till yet."

"I guess that's right," Wade agreed. "Lucy's noticing the bloodstain and discovering so soon that the man was dead does rather spoil the play, doesn't it?"

"Yeah," said Murphy, "if he was killed here."

"Huh," Wiggins added grandly. "And if she'd acted like some girls I know would have acted, busting in on that bunch of drunks screaming bloody murder, you'd have had a riot and they'd be all over town by now and nobody would ever know who was here tonight—and instead she just stepped out quiet-like same as if finding bodies was all in the day's work, and so you've got your suspects all locked up in one room. Me, I think you oughta give her a medal or something."

"As a matter of fact," Wade said with a grin, "Wiggins is perfectly right. That's probably what the murderer planned too—that when the body was found there'd be a panic and the police would never know who'd been here tonight, let alone who might have killed Parnell."

Wiggins scratched his head. "Then I guess," he contributed, "all this makes it pretty clear that the murderer knew all about how this Dis business was run. He knew nobody knew who was here, and that once they made a run for it the cops couldn't prove from now till doomsday that any of 'em had been near the place. Me, I think Lucy was pretty damn smart."

"Not to speak of Mrs. Fontenay," added Kennedy of the Telegram.

"Come to think of it," said Wade suddenly, "Cynthia might have done this job herself, figuring just along those lines. If she had given the alarm and they'd all made a bolt, she would have been the only person we could interview. As it is, we've got about fifty possible murderers."

"Yeah," said Murphy again, "if he was killed here."

Wade lifted the heel of one turned-up slipper. "Doesn't look as if he were dragged."

"What about being carried?" asked Murphy.

"He'd make a pretty big load," Wade objected. "Must weigh a hundred and seventy-five pounds."

"At least," agreed Emerson. Wade paused to think, and Kennedy asked, "About how long d'you think he's been dead?"

"Hour—hour and a half—certainly not over two hours."

"Wait a minute," said Wiggins. "Look at the back of his head, doc. See if there ain't a bruise on it."

"That's an idea," exclaimed Emerson. He turned over Parnell's body. "Yes, right below the base of the skull—it's more than a bruise—it's an abrasion. Right up here toward the hairline."

"Smart boy, smart boy," approved Wade out of the side of his mouth.

"Wait," went on Wiggins excitedly. "I'm just trying to get the picture for you. He was knifed here—" he pointed toward the enamel-topped table—"and he fell back and hit his head here—" he pointed to the table-edge. "He must've been dead when he hit the floor. So he must've been killed in this room."

"I think you're right," said the coroner after a moment. "But I'm puzzled to know how he was stabbed from under the robe."

"Couldn't they get the knife up through the sleeve?" Wiggins asked. "Reach in? Are the sleeves wide enough?"

Emerson tried it. "No, that won't go."

"Sure, and what would this fellow be doing while they were sticking the knife up his sleeve and pulling it down?" inquired Murphy. "Brushing his teeth? There's no signs of a struggle in here."

"No," nodded Wiggins, "but there's something else. Somebody shoved this stool after we came in." He indicated a pantry stool. "It was over here. Now look." He placed the stool back in front of the cupboard. "You see, you step on the stool, then on this cabinet counter here, then up here." He illustrated by hopping up. "Now suppose this guy was up on the cabinet ledge, looking for something, and suppose the murderer was standing on the floor. He coulda slipped the knife up under the robe and drove it in just when this lad stepped down."

The coroner considered, then asked suddenly, "What about the belt?"

"Well, you can't think of everything." Wiggins looked crestfallen. "I forgot the belt."

Murphy turned to Wade. "What do you see in it?" he asked.

Wade shook his head. "Not much. All I can see is, he was killed here and banged his head on the table, or he was killed some place else and planted here. Either he was dressed for the Dis ball when he was killed or he was dressed for the ball later. One guess is as good as another." He pulled out a cigarette, tapping it on the face of his wrist-watch, and slowly touched a match to it. "I know that doesn't seem to make sense, Murphy, but here's what you're up against. Mrs. Fontenay and Lucy saw him alive—or at least they saw someone wearing this costume alive—that means he was here in full regalia. Now they thought it was Ghent.

Remember, it might have been Ghent, and he might have killed Parnell, who was hidden back here without a costume, and then Ghent might have dressed Parnell up in this stuff and left in plain street clothes."

"You're all wet," Wiggins insisted. "This guy must have been here in costume and he must have been killed here."

"Why?" asked Murphy.

"Because," said Wiggins, looking up confidently, "if he was carried in any position but flat the blood would have streaked down. That's why."

Dr. Emerson looked up. "That's right, Wiggins." He pointed to the shirt-front. The bloodstain around the knife was almost a neat circle. He considered a moment. "Didn't you tell me, Wiggins, that when you took the pictures Mrs. Fontenay told you there were forty-nine Dis members present and one guest?" Wiggins nodded.

"Well, Murphy said she told him there were just fifty members of the organization, so that's all but one accounted for."

"Wonder who the absent guy is?" Wiggins murmured. "I'd kinda like to talk to him."

"We'll find him," the coroner promised. "Meanwhile, get this. As Wiggins says, if Parnell had been stabbed somewhere else and brought in, the blood would have trickled down and there would be a point to this circle. And if he had been thrown over a man's shoulder and brought in here the knife would not be upright—I mean by that, if the knife had been pressed upon by the carrier's shoulder you would see some post-mortem evidence around the edges of the wound. Wiggins is right. He must have been killed here."

"All right," acquiesced Murphy, impatient to be at his work. "You can take charge of the body, coroner." The coroner carefully extracted the knife from the wound. It was a sharply-edged stiletto with an eight-inch blade that tapered down to a fine point. The handle was mother-of-pearl. Murphy inspected it carefully. The fine steel of the blade was bright where it showed through the blood.

"It's a good knife," he observed as he folded a handkerchief over it and handed it to the coroner. "You'll give it to the Bertillon men for us, will you? I believe mother-of-pearl don't show fingerprints, but tell them to be careful, and to look for a trademark." He turned to the reporters. "All right, fellows, clear the room now. I'll take Wade as representing all of you while I have a talk with Mrs. Fontenay and that girl again. I don't want too many of you around and he'll give you anything he gets. That all right with you fellows?"

"Suits me," said Kennedy with a grin at Wade, "but no finaglin'."

Wade grinned back. "No more than the law allows," he said.

"All right, boys," concluded Murphy. "You wait here and we'll be back in a minute."

"Okay," put in Wiggins. "Let's go."

Murphy stopped. "You can't—" he started, but Wiggins interrupted.

"Listen, you. We photographers got to have a representative too, don't we, fellows?"

"Sure," agreed the chunky round-faced boy from the *Star*. "If we don't that guy Murphy'll never get on a plate of mine again."

"Mine neither," chimed in the *Telegram* photographer, putting down his camera. "Besides, if it hadn't been for a photographer you apes would have been looking all over to find out where this guy was killed." He winked significantly, and then, in an undertone that could be heard all over the room he added, "*That* ought to hold him."

But Murphy had already barged out into the hall with Dutreaux. Wade followed him, and Wiggins, carrying the whispered injunction of his colleagues to "show that red-necked camera-louse where to head in," was already on his way.

CHAPTER FIVE

CHARACTERISTICALLY, Murphy did not pause to knock at Cynthia's door, but grabbed the knob and walked smartly into the scented lavender privacy of her bedroom. Cynthia had curled herself up on the bed, two lavender satin pillows behind her shoulders; she held a cigarette between the fingers of one hand and with the other she was idly turning the pages of a fashion magazine. An empty highball glass stood on the bedside table.

She barely glanced up as they entered, and dropped her eyes again to the contemplation of the page, but Lucy, who had been clearing up some of the more intimate details here and there, stopped short, a flask of perfume in her hand and a bit of blue crepe lingerie over her arm. The two policemen Murphy had sent in, who had been laboring to make themselves at ease in a pair of spindle-legged chairs near the door, jumped gratefully to their feet. Lucy glanced uneasily from Murphy to Cynthia, then hurriedly thrust the step-ins into a drawer as Murphy strode over to where Cynthia was reclining.

"You can go, boys," he jerked over his shoulder to the two policemen by the door. Cynthia laid down her magazine, tapped the end of her cigarette and raised her limpid eyes to his as he halted by the side of the bed.

"You wanted to speak to me, captain?"

Murphy thrust his fists into his jacket pockets and regarded her with resolution. Murphy was not brutal, but his twenty years on the force had taught him that a cop on the Homicide Squad usually chalks up a defeat for every softening of his program of ruthlessness.

"Now, Mrs. Fontenay," he announced, "we know where we are at."

She frowned questioningly. Murphy continued.

"Roger Parnell was killed in this house less than two hours ago. He was alive in this house. You saw him here. I want to know how you got him mixed up with Arnold Ghent. I want to know if Ghent's number is 47. I want to know what Parnell's number was. And I want to know if Ghent is inside there and whether he's got Parnell's suit on."

Cynthia moistened her lips.

"Roger Parnell never was a member of Dis to my knowledge," she answered, slowly and clearly. Wiggins caught himself in the middle of an odd emotion—wondering how much she was covering up, and determining to find out, and at the same time admiring the courage with which she was facing them. She was quite steady as she went on. "How Mr. Parnell got a costume and a ring, and who gave him the password, I can't tell you. And I don't know now whether or not Mr. Ghent is here tonight."

Murphy turned to speak over his shoulder. "Dutreaux, get to the phone and ring Arnold Ghent's apartment. Don't tell him anything, but if he's at home ring headquarters and have them send a man to bring him here. Got that? Now, Mrs. Fontenay, if Ghent's a good friend of yours seems like you'd have known him well enough to know Parnell wasn't him, even with a false face on."

"You weren't engaged to him, were you?" Wiggins interpolated.

"Certainly not," she retorted crisply.

"But you are gonta marry somebody, ain't you?" Wiggins insisted.

Cynthia's great hazel eyes turned to rest on his small figure. The corners of her mouth twitched in the ghost of a smile.

"Frankly, Mr. Wiggins," she returned, "I don't think that's any of your business."

"Well, ma'am," insisted Murphy, who had no patience with people who strayed from the point at issue, "what made you think Mr. Parnell was Mr. Ghent?"

"The man with the 47 on his back told me he was Mr. Ghent, Captain Murphy. I told you the man I thought was Mr. Ghent had been behaving strangely tonight. He seemed to be making pointed efforts to avoid me. His attitude was so unusual that I thought he couldn't be feeling well—I said so to my maid, as she told you."

Lucy nodded valiantly. "And Mr. Ghent and Mr. Parnell are about the same size," she added.

"Yes," said Cynthia readily, "they are both six feet one."

"Huh," grunted Murphy. "You're mighty sure. I guess you knew Parnell pretty well then, even though he didn't belong to your lodge?"

Cynthia started. A slow dull red crept up from her throat and over her cheeks. For a moment she did not answer, and when she did her voice was uneven, as if every word came with a separate effort.

"I knew him—rather well. But he—has been in this house—to my knowledge—only once or twice—before tonight."

"Ghent's phone don't answer, captain," reported Dutreaux from the other side of the room.

"No? Well, I guess we'll have to find him." Murphy returned his attention to Cynthia. "So you knew him rather well, eh? Tell us about it."

The instant's interruption had given her time to recover her poise. "We were in college together," she said evenly.

"Oh, in college, eh? Where was that?"

"Chicago."

"Chicago, eh?" Murphy's ruddy face expressed simple exasperation. Wiggins leaned against the wall and scowled thoughtfully. He was beginning to see that Murphy was dealing with a lady of audacious though variable temperament, and that it would take a finer instrument than Murphy possessed to pry out her secrets. Wiggins was not versed in linguistic subtleties, and he would have been hard put to it to frame the sort of questions he thought Murphy ought to ask, but he had a feeling that somebody ought to get busy and pull the facts out of Mrs. Fontenay. He glanced at Lucy. She stood with one hand on the foot of Cynthia's bed, like a small defiant bodyguard, watching the effect of Cynthia's last statement with implacable eyes.

"Uh-huh," said Murphy eloquently. "Uh-huh." He rocked back and forth on his heels. "When's the last time you saw Parnell before tonight?"

Cynthia's eyebrows, plucked into two thin arches, drew together in a polite little frown. "Let me see. Several days ago. I went into the Palm Gardens restaurant, and he was lunching there."

"Did you lunch with him?"

"No."

"Was he alone?"

"No. He was with a friend."

"With who?"

"A friend—Mr. Valdon."

"Oh—I get you. Fritz Valdon?"

"Yes."

Murphy rocked on his heels, his slow nod suggesting vast comprehension. Cynthia regarded him with poisonous sweetness.

"Did you speak to Parnell?" he demanded.

"Briefly."

"What did you say?"

Cynthia's demureness was almost absurd. "I said, 'Good afternoon, Roger. How do you do, Mr. Valdon.'"

"Is that all?"

"Every word, captain."

"Humph."

Wiggins looked at Wade, and saw that Wade like himself was far from satisfied with Murphy's questionings. Wiggins was puzzled. There ought to be another factor in this inquiry—he was not sure what was lacking, but he was sure that so far Cynthia had all the laurels.

"So you didn't speak to them long, eh?" Murphy's cold blue eyes were drilling at Cynthia's. But it was like diamond meeting diamond. "Now, Mrs. Fontenay, you see I don't know much about you, and this affair makes it necessary that I ask you some personal questions. Do you mind?"

Cynthia smoothed a fold of her voluminous red robe and looked up with an air of resigned exasperation. "My dear Captain Murphy," she answered sweetly, "I wouldn't mind anything if I could just have a drink."

Murphy's flushed face creased into a half-smile. "That you can, ma'am," he said affably, "if you can get it." As long as there was no sign of rebellion, Murphy was quite willing to keep a witness in good humor.

Lucy was already opening a scrolled rosewood cellarette that stood in a corner near the dressing-table. She brought out a decanter and several glasses, and offered the tray to the captain.

"No thanks," he said, rather brusquely. "We don't need any."

"Oh, speak for yourself, Murphy." Wiggins reached out to detain Lucy. "I need lots of it."

"Mr. Wade?" asked Lucy. Wade gave the captain a sidelong smile and accepted.

As they nodded to Cynthia and lifted their glasses they could see that she had filled her own nearly to the brim. She drained it and took another. Then she reached for a fresh cigarette.

"All right, captain," she said smiling. "I'm a fortified woman. Do your worst." Her smile was confident.

But Murphy was serious. "I'm going to start on the assumption that you want to help me, ma'am," he said to her. "And I'm going to start off with the most important question. Who do you think killed Parnell?"

Cynthia took a deep draw from her cigarette. She looked down as she blew out the smoke, as if she was pondering his question. "I don't want to seem trite, captain," she said after a pause, "and I don't want you to misunderstand me. I know before this case is over there will be lots of grief in it for everybody concerned, myself included."

She paused to pour another drink. "This is my house; you say you are certain Roger Parnell was killed here. Those people in the other room are as much a mystery to me as they are to you. I don't know who five of them are. I can't possibly say, then, who killed Mr. Parnell—but I can say this: that from what I've heard there are only two dangerous things that Roger Parnell ever played with."

Murphy nodded. "Yes. Two things?"

Cynthia finished her drink and set down the glass. "Two things, Captain Murphy, either one of which might have led to his death. Perhaps I shouldn't tell you this, but I'll gamble it's true—that behind the murder of Roger Parnell you'll find one of these two. Maybe both."

"What are they?"

Cynthia smiled. "Two very old man-baiters, captain. Women, and money."

Murphy was interested but not convinced. "That fits almost every murder that's ever been committed, Mrs. Fontenay. What makes you think it's unusual in this case?"

"You asked me what I thought." Cynthia shrugged. "I'm simply telling you what's been told me."

"Sure, I understand that." Murphy stood looking down at her, as she half reclined against her cushions, and Cynthia slowly turned her great eyes full upon him, in a fashion that suggested serene detachment from the affairs of Roger Parnell and wonder at Murphy's importance. Wade would have called it tantalizing; Wiggins mentally termed it "giving Murphy the full works."

But Murphy was determined. "What I want to know," he insisted, "is some of the things about Parnell that people aren't talking about. What people don't like him? Who might want him out of the way? What do you know about his ambitions? Whose toes has he stepped on? That's what I want from you."

Cynthia's expression changed—subtly, but definitely. It was plain that she disliked this switch away from the generalities she had advanced.

"I'm sorry, Captain Murphy," she said clearly, "but I know very little about Roger Parnell's personal affairs. I have already told you our acquaintance was casual."

"Listen, sister." Murphy had suddenly begun to thunder. "Quit this damn stallin' and fiddlin'. You knew Parnell. You knew him pretty well. Now I want to know what you know about him. And I ain't staying here all night."

Cynthia sat up straight. "Don't be absurd." She slipped off the bed and stood up, facing him across it. "I won't be talked to like that by you or by anyone else. Please leave my room. All of you. At once. Get out."

"Sit down," barked Murphy, "and shut up."

Their eyes met. Cynthia's were dark with anger; Murphy's showed a curious mixture of menace and hopelessness.

"You listen to me, Mrs. Fontenay," he threw at her, in a voice that had become low and threatening.

"I don't want any foolishness. You've got the right not to say anything if saying it is going to incriminate you. Because whatever you say is going to be used against you if you're charged. Don't say I didn't warn you of that. But—"

Wade smothered a smile; Wiggins wanted to chuckle. Murphy was observing the letter of the regulations with practised skill. They both knew that his tactics meant he thought he was on a trail worth pursuing.

"—but if you don't tell me now the things I know you can tell me I'll make it plenty rough even if you are a lady. Who hated Roger Parnell? Why?"

"I don't know," said Cynthia.

"O yes you do, sister. Who hated him?"

They could see her wavering between rebellion and acquiescence. "I tell you," she parried, "I don't know."

"Listen," said Murphy. "Maybe you don't understand that I mean business. What do you know about Roger Parnell?"

"I don't know anything about him, but—"

"But what?"

"But—why do you make me say this?"

"Come on. Who hated him?"

"Oh, Captain Murphy—lots of people hated him—I suppose."

"Who were they? Who do you know? Quick now. Who?"

"Please—!" she exclaimed. "I don't know—but if there's anyone who does—there's a girl—"

Murphy's face betrayed surprise. He leaned closer. "Take your choice," he said. "Tell me or take the consequences. She won't know you said it. Who is she?"

Cynthia's gesture across the bed toward him gave a tinge of melodrama to her surrender.

"Esther Morse. She's in there. With a white dress on. Now leave me alone."

"Esther Morse. What does she know about him?"

Cynthia sighed. "Do you remember last year a boy named Dick Barron nearly went to jail for stealing his employers' money to pay his gambling debts?"

"Sure. What's that got to do with Esther Morse and Parnell?"

"He lost the money at the Red Cat. People say—anyway, his father paid back the money and kept him out of jail, and then died. The papers said heart failure. You remember. Esther Morse was engaged to Dick. After she broke the engagement she became very intimate with Roger Parnell. They say—you ask her." She stopped. "Now let me alone, will you?"

Cynthia sat down on the edge of the bed opposite him. She poured a drink.

Murphy's jaw set. "Now answer some more. Where's your husband?"

Cynthia turned her glass up before she answered. She smiled.

"Paris, or somewhere on the continent. If you mean Mr. Fontenay, but he's not my husband."

"Divorced?"

She nodded smiling. "Thoroughly."

Murphy grunted.

"You'd been married before, hadn't you?"

"Yes."

"Where is he?"

"Washington, the last I heard of him. He's an aviator." Her answer was maliciously polite.

"Divorced from him too?"

"Yes."

"His name?" Murphy demanded.

"Davenport—August Davenport."

Murphy put it in the notebook.

"Any others?"

Cynthia reached for the flask of perfume Lucy had set on the bedside table when Murphy entered, and held it delicately to her nostrils. "That," she answered, "is my entire case history. There were no others."

Wiggins' head bobbed up abruptly. He looked at Lucy. She had turned away and was emptying an ash-tray into the wastebasket. Wiggins scowled. He remembered that when he and Lucy had sat in the courtyard discussing Cynthia's next bridegroom and he had held up three fingers, Lucy had shaken her head and held up four. Wiggins puckered his lips and studied his shoe-laces.

Murphy had closed his notebook and was replacing it in his breast pocket. "Let's look over the rest of them. You'd better come with us, sister."

Cynthia stood up. "All right, but for God's sake stop calling me sister!"

Lucy, still avoiding Wiggins' searching eyes, opened the door. Cynthia went out and Murphy followed with Wade and Dutreaux. Wiggins hung back, and stopped where Lucy stood by the door. He held up three fingers.

"How come?" he asked.

Lucy blushed. She looked down.

"Gee, Tony," she said finally, "I always was dumb at adding things up."

CHAPTER SIX

"Nothing like it since the battle of the Marne," Wade exclaimed joyfully into the telephone. "Murphy calls for a riot squad and they pile down in about twelve police cars. There's a cop at every twist in the place and fifty red devils and one little girl in white all lined up for them to work on. Dr. Emerson took Parnell's body to the morgue."

He listened for a second or two.

"It's going to be worth holding up the city edition. Murphy swears he's going to make them tell their real names."

He paused again.

"Now look, Koppel. Send down one of your bright young men to stand by for pictures. We'll send the plates in as soon as he gets here. Charlie can get the pictures out for you. Wiggins says send some more flash lamps. He's all set to break the world's mug-making record tonight. This place is a madhouse—I'll give you a new lead in a half hour. So long."

Wade replaced the telephone on its stand and lit a cigarette. His lean face creased with a slow placid smile. Everything was jake so far. This was a big story and Koppel knew it. Wade lounged happily down the hall.

His placid smile still illumined his countenance as he greeted the policeman on guard at the door of the ballroom.

"What say, hots?"

"Okay, pops. Go on in. The old man is going to make a speech."

"Wouldn't miss it for a farm," Wade assured him.

The room was a jambalaya of terrified confusion. The jazz had given place to scared voices and the dancing to jerky little movements of protest; the red devils were huddled into groups, talking and gesticulating incoherently. At every door there was a policeman, and in front of every policeman was a group praying, demanding, offering bribes to be let out. Murphy stood on the steps leading up to the throne, and flanking him was a cluster of reporters and headquarters men. Over in corners the photographers were adjusting their cameras and chattering in pleased whispers. Wiggins peered around a clamorous masker and gave Wade a cheerful grimace that told him plainly, "*This* is what I was born for."

Lucy was not in sight. As Wade entered Cynthia Fontenay detached herself from a frantic red group and came toward Murphy. Her face under her bright golden hair was strangely composed; there were shadows under her eyes and a hard little line at each corner of her mouth that looked as if it might have been put there with a pencil, but there was nothing to indicate fear—her whole manner suggested simply tiredness and exasperation. She stood quietly at Murphy's elbow, watching as two policemen came in. They carried between them a small Chinese-red table, which Murphy indicated that he wanted in the center of the room. He advanced a step. The clatter of voices slowed, hesitated and under Murphy's pitiless glare died down.

"It pains me to tell you," boomed Murphy, his syllables rumbling in the corners of the room like thunder, "that Roger Parnell was murdered in this house within the last two hours and that you are all detained for questioning."

There was a muffled shriek as Murphy paused to let his announcement sink in. The devils buzzed impotently and huddled closer together. Murphy looked around with lordly assurance and caught sight of Wade. He beckoned.

"You can tell the rest of the boys," he said in a low voice as Wade reached his side, "that this murder is going to be investigated here and now and that all these people are going to answer questions."

Wade chuckled. "I'll tell them. Looks as if we'll be here all night."

Murphy's right fist smacked the palm of his left hand. "I don't give a damn if we're here till Easter morning," he retorted. "Mrs. Fontenay has been blathering about how impossible it is to shatter all the regulations of Dis. What the hell?"

Wade glanced involuntarily at Cynthia. She was sitting on the steps of the throne, her hands laced lightly around her knees, her hazel eyes lifted to Murphy's back with enigmatic calmness. Her lips had curved gently into a smile, a slow, baffling smile, as if it hid a secret triumph.

Wade looked back at Murphy. "Good boy," he applauded in an undertone. "But for God's sake do it in time for us to get it in the paper."

"Very well—" Murphy made the announcement to the room in general in answer to Wade's plea—"we'll start taking the names right now."

There was a wild cacophony of protest. Cynthia stood up and came toward him, and her husky voice cut clearly across the confused babble in the room.

"Captain Murphy," she said, "I'm sure if I explain to you that for an hour before Mr. Parnell's body was found, no one but the four members of the Dis Council and the tellers left this room, you will not embarrass my guests."

Murphy shook his head. He surveyed Cynthia with his blank "what-do-you-think-you-are" appraisal.

"Sorry, sister, but this is just my job." He raised his voice. "I'll have to have the name, and I mean the real name, of everybody who was in this house at the time of the murder."

A masked figure, betrayed as masculine by its height and walk, came over to them.

"I don't think you've given this careful consideration, Captain Murphy," he said. His voice was muffled by his mask, but the words were plain. "What Mrs. Fontenay said is true. We had our own tellers—sergeants-at-arms, if you will—lock the doors, and only four of us left. I was one of them. The others could not possibly have gotten out."

Murphy ran his hand over his bush of white hair.

"Who were those?"

The masked man answered evenly. "I don't know their names. Mrs. Fontenay has their Dis numbers."

Cynthia had reached into an inside pocket of her robe. She held out a slip of paper. Murphy glanced at the numbers listed on it.

"Bring them up here," he ordered.

Cynthia walked away. Wade saw her moving from one group to another with a poise that amazed him; he was beginning to wonder at such rigidity of temperament, and then suddenly he surmised that it was not rigidity. It was simply callousness. Cynthia's whole life had been a series of dramatic climaxes, till now she was so bored that a houseful of policemen presented simply another nuisance to be dealt with as speedily as possible. Wade caught himself making a grimace of puzzled distaste, then he recalled himself to the business in hand as he heard Murphy address the masked man.

"Well, mister, and you? If you're so anxious not to have all these folks bothered, I guess you'll pull off that false face and let us have a look at you. You were one of them that got out, I think you said?"

"Yes—I was." The masked man hesitated, then, as though yielding as readily as he could to the inevitable, he raised a hand and unfastened the mask. "I'm Dick Barron," he said to Murphy. With the mask off, his voice was deep and pleasant.

Murphy looked him over with complacent recognition. Wade studied him too, but with more thoughtful attention than Murphy—the tight stubborn lips, the eyes that habitually narrowed as though they had learned to look suspiciously at the world, the aquiline nose with its thin, sensitive nostrils. It was an odd, contradictory face, a face crossed with conflicting characters like a palimpsest. Wade found himself involuntarily recalling Dick Barron's narrow escape last year from a sentence for theft—an escape made possible by the relinquishing of virtually all the family property—and his father's death, which the coroner out of consideration for his family had agreed to call heart failure. He met Dick Barron's scornful dark eyes with the impersonal pleasantness that ten years of newspaper contacts had taught him.

"I'm glad to know you, Barron—I've heard of you. I'm Wade of the *Creole*."

Dick did not seem to be much interested. "I've heard of you too. I suppose I'll hear more of you before I get out of this—yes?"

Then suddenly, before Wade could answer, he had turned away and was standing with his back to them; and at the same time that Wade saw his movement he saw the reason for it; Esther Morse had come toward them.

"Please," she said, "are you Captain Murphy?"

Her voice was low and childish; her dark eyes, as they lifted to meet Murphy's, were appealing in their simple bewilderment and fear. Murphy turned to her with an unpremeditated smile.

"Sure I'm Captain Murphy, miss. What can I do for you?"

Esther pushed back her flowing dark hair, and her hands twisted together in helpless fright. "Won't you let me go home?" she exclaimed. "Won't you please? I'm Esther Morse. I don't belong to Dis—I don't know why on earth I ever came here tonight—I don't know who any of these people are—won't you let me go home?"

Murphy's ruddy face had resumed its grimness. He shook his head. "Can't do that, miss. Can't let anybody leave."

She smothered a little helpless cry. "But I'm so frightened—Cynthia said I should speak to you—she said you wanted to see everybody who left the room while the initiation was going on—I thought perhaps you were going to let us go home—"

There was a muffled inarticulate sound from the man whose back was turned. Esther raised her head to look at him, and she drew back with amazed recognition as he slowly turned around.

"Dick!" she exclaimed, and then for an instant neither of them spoke; they simply stood staring at each other, and the look between them was so intense and so utterly self-forgetful that Wade felt as if he was shamefully spying. Then Dick Barron spoke to her, in a manner that tried to be matter-of-fact and was not.

"I'll look out for you, Esther."

His voice recalled her. As though she had suddenly remembered that she stood in a room full of people, she swept back her hair with a little self-conscious movement and took a step away from him.

"Thank you, but I'll be all right."

"Sure, miss, you'll be all right," said Murphy hastily, and as Dick gave a hopeless shrug Esther moved further away from him toward the throne. Murphy turned his attention to the masked devils marshaled up to him by Cynthia. "These are the ones that left the room, ma'am? I see. Matson!—take all these people in the other room. Get the maid, and I'll be right in. You go too, Miss Morse." Esther obediently went out with the others. One man in the group waited by Murphy's side. Wade saw the number 31 on his back.

"I want to see you privately before you start," Wade heard him say. Murphy grunted an impatient assent. The members of the Dis Council filed out. Murphy glared suspiciously at the policeman on guard at the door. "That door closed?"

"Sure, sir."

"Right. Connelly! That door by you closed? And all the windows?"

"Yes, sir."

"All right." Murphy resumed his embattled posture and looked over the remaining members of Dis, who stood uncertainly in front of him, whispering and edging out of range of the photographers. "Now look here, you" he announced. "There seems to be a little bit of misunderstanding about what I want, so I'm going to tell you again. I want your names and addresses. I know you think I'm unreasonable, but this is murder. You get me? A man has been killed. Killed here. Get that, now? Murder. It's a serious thing." Murphy paused.

"And so," he resumed, ignoring the exclamations of protest that popped like little rockets around him, "I'm going to have to use serious methods. Get that? Serious methods. And so all of you will please go peacefully with the officers and do like they tell you. Until your names are given and verified you're all under technical arrest."

The protests became a howl of rage. Murphy paid as much attention as he would have paid to a dripping faucet. He beckoned to a sergeant.

"Take them to the Third Precinct, Harry, and check up on the names. Keep them there till you hear from me. No paroles unless in the custody of a lawyer with affidavits on identification. Let 'em use the phones and make 'em comfortable." He shrugged toward Wade. "And that, my boy, is that."

Wiggins and two other photographers were elbowing their way through the furious throng of Dis. "What's up?" Wiggins chirruped to Wade.

"Booked at the Third."

"Suits me." Wiggins was out of the door, camera, tripod and flash. Wade grinned. He could write the caption for the picture without seeing it. "From Dis to Dismay." "Party Ends in Jail."

The room was wild with protesting confusion. Several persons sat on the floor, refusing to be moved. Others rushed up to appeal to or to threaten Murphy.

"I'm Mrs. de la—"

"Captain, this will ruin—"

"I'm a friend of—"

"Please, captain, my wife will—"

Murphy was unrelenting. "Tell it to the clerk at the Third. Boys, see if you can't carry those ladies and gentlemen that seem unable to walk." He turned to the reporters, his hands spread out. "What else can I do?" he asked. "We got to know who's here."

They nodded with enthusiasm. The morning paper men hurried off. Wade saw McFee of the *Star* beat him to the phone on the hall table. Then he caught sight of Lucy, who was chattering brightly with one of the detectives. Wade beckoned to her.

"Any other phones?"

She nodded comprehendingly. "One in Mrs. Fontenay's bedroom—but you'd better not use that; one in the kitchen downstairs, for marketing."

Wade smiled his thanks. "Keep it a secret," he urged. Then, diplomatically, "I'm with Wiggins on this story."

Lucy returned his smile. "So am I, Mr. Wade."

In the courtyard Wade saw Wiggins and his confreres joyously attending to their jobs. Every time a flash bulb glowed somebody screamed. Every time somebody screamed another flash bulb glowed. Wade found the kitchen door and lit a match. The phone was on a shelf. He took it down and called Koppel.

When he walked back into the courtyard it was cleared of maskers, and Murphy was standing by the fountain smoking a cigar. He was alone.

"I've been waiting for you, my lad," Murphy said glumly. "Who do you think is upstairs dressed up in one of them suits?"

Wade laughed. "You tell me. Peggy Joyce?"

"No. Listen, this is serious." Murphy eyed him severely. "Fritz Valdon."

"You mean it?" Wade had lost his languor. "Valdon? That's funny—"

"No it ain't," said Murphy. "He says unless I let him take a sneak there'll be big trouble, and I'll be in the middle of it."

Wade peered at Murphy's ominous face through the dark. He and Murphy had been friends for a long time, and Wade knew that Valdon was a powerful politician in or out of office. Right now he happened to be out, but Wade knew that his devious alliances still made him a dangerous man to antagonize.

"Well—?" he asked at length.

"I told him a reporter had already recognized him and had sent his name to his paper. His number's 31. Will you go through for me?"

"Oh, sure," nodded Wade. "Go on back. *The Creole* and Valdon never have been friends. I'll make your story stand up when I see him."

Murphy patted his shoulder. "You're a good boy, Wade. That damn—" The rest of his words were smothered with the incoherence of honest wrath as he climbed the stairs. Wade waited a minute or two and followed.

The members of the Council were gathered in the dining room, all of them, except Cynthia and Esther, still masked. They were seated, waiting in angry resignation, while Murphy scratched something on his pad. Kennedy and McFee, in a corner, were talking things over in low tones. Wade caught sight of a black 31 on one of the red suits. He walked over to the man who wore it and bent over his chair.

"Anything you'd like to say about this, Valdon?" he asked. "I'm Wade of the *Creole*."

"No—not a thing." The voice from under the mask was muffled and flat. "How did you know me?"

Wade laughed softly. "Never forget an old friend, Valdon. I knew you in there the minute you spoke."

Number 31 got up and moved further away from the others. "So," he said when they were out of earshot. "Smart, aren't you?"

"Just so-so."

There was a moment's silence. "Smart enough to use ten grand?"

"Meaning?"

"First—how did you recognize me inside?"

"When you were talking you kept rubbing your thumb like this." Wade illustrated by rubbing his own thumb across the third joint of his forefinger. It was, he remembered, one of Valdon's characteristic gestures.

"Rubbed my thumb, did I? Well, can you rub out that recollection with ten grand? That's what I mean."

"Oh, I see." Wade nodded thoughtfully.

The other man's voice dropped. "That's only one kind of a rub—forgetting things."

Wade returned whisper for whisper. "Nuts, Valdon. Just because you bullied Parnell, don't get a swelled head. Anyway, you're too late. The office has your name." He prevaricated glibly.

His companion shrugged. "Too bad," he said. "We might have done business. And don't misunderstand me. I meant if you wouldn't take money you might do it, say—for friendship's sake. I'm a—good friend to have."

Wade smiled. "I don't misunderstand, Valdon. I just saw a friend of yours go to the morgue for an autopsy." He turned to walk away.

A gloved hand on his arm detained him. "No. Don't go off on the wrong track, Wade. I didn't kill Parnell."

Wade drew his arm away. "That's your story. Let's make it unanimous. I didn't either."

There was a low laugh, a cocky, arrogant laugh that crystallized Wade's dislike for the man behind the mask.

"Figure me for anything but a sap, Wade," he said calmly. "If I had known Parnell was here I shouldn't have been here myself. If I'd known Parnell was dead I shouldn't have stayed. But if I had wanted him out of the way—that way—he'd be out."

Wade studied the slant-eyed mask with cool interest.

"And on top of that," the calm voice went on, "you should know me better than this. If I had killed Parnell I wouldn't call attention to the fact by offering chumps like you and Murphy a big score like ten grand to lam."

Wade smiled admiringly. "Keep it up, Fritz. You've got a good case."

The other man reached back and loosened the catch on his mask. The zipper slid up and he pulled at the edges. Still muffled, his voice came through.

"And this clinches it," Wade heard. The mask fell. Wade started.

The man he had spoken to was not Fritz Valdon.

"It's a peculiar thing, Mr. Wade," the man said, "how you newspapermen remember things you've never seen." He rubbed his thumb and forefinger together slowly. "But please remember me. I'll be seeing you again. My name, Mr. Wade, is Conroy—Con Conroy. A great many people say I'm Mr. Valdon's secretary."

CHAPTER SEVEN

Con Conroy leaned idly against the wall, his eyes traveling with languid attention over the indignant confusion of the other members of the Dis Council, who were whispering and protesting and putting off as long as possible the inevitable moment of unmasking.

Wade, his hands plunged into his pockets, studied Conroy while interest began to displace his angry astonishment. In the instant that he had seen Conroy's face he had realized that his own foolish position would provoke mirth from Fritz Valdon's friends when it was recounted, but in that same instant he was intrigued by the cool impudence of Conroy's tactics. Conroy pushed back his horned headdress and stood smilingly attentive.

He appeared to be about thirty, and looked, Wade thought, like an overgrown cherub; his face was round and rosy, and his arrogant little smile was accompanied, of all things, by a dimple; his eyes were the mild china-blue that one is accustomed to associate with innocence, and his fawn-colored hair fluffed over his head like a baby's. For an instant neither he nor Wade spoke; Conroy stood calmly twirling his mask, his manner plainly indicating that the next move was not up to him, while Wade's hands, clenched in impotent wrath in his pockets, gradually relaxed, and then Wade said,

"All right, Conroy. I don't say I'm delighted to make your acquaintance, but at least it's advanced my education. Since when—"

He was interrupted by the approach of Murphy, who came up red-faced and thick-voiced, to demand "Who the hell are you anyway?"

"Why, captain!" Conroy's reply was offered with elaborate suavity. "Just a working man enjoying his night off."

Murphy's thick fists rested on his hips. "What the hell do you mean by saying you're Fritz Valdon? Think that would get you anywhere?"

The blonde eyebrows of Mr. Conroy lifted. "I thought it might get me outside," he answered mildly.

Murphy glared. Wade heard a chuckle in the neighborhood of his elbow and glanced down to behold Wiggins, who was observing the altercation from the rear. As he met Wade's eyes Wiggins gave his head an expressive movement to indicate the space behind Murphy, where Wade saw the others, absorbed by this new promise of adventure, coming nearer to listen to the dialogue. Kennedy of the *Telegram* had edged in at Murphy's elbow.

"What's all this about?" he inquired with interest.

"This chiseler," foghorned Murphy, "told me he was Valdon—said he wanted to make a sneak. He tried to high-pressure me, that's all."

Murphy's violent contempt had not, however, the slightest effect on the equanimity of Mr. Con Conroy, who was playing with a cigarette he had produced from the voluminous folds of his red robe. An ebony lighter flicked in his gloved hand, the cigarette met the flame and Conroy's meek blue eyes studied Murphy calmly through a veil of smoke.

"That's his story," said Conroy. "What happened was that I told this copper Valdon was here and would appreciate a private quizzing; just a request for ordinary official courtesy. And then," he continued gently, but with the ironic smile of the man who presents a sure case, "the said copper did address me as the aforementioned Valdon and did inform me tenderly and with apology that I had already been recognized by this member of your noble profession." His cigarette indicated Wade. "The reporter then came over and tried to make Murphy's play good." Conroy smiled benignly over Murphy's shoulder at the policemen and the red robed figures who had closed in to listen. "He told me I was Valdon, and I, being a meek person, said 'yes' and 'yea' and 'verily I am.' Then I made a liar out of myself, the gentleman from the police and our journalistic friend, and introduced Mr. Cornelius Augustine Conroy, in person."

There was an instant's pause, broken only by a rustle of whispers from the group behind Murphy. Conroy continued to smoke with amused unconcern. Murphy turned livid with rage. Wade glanced uneasily toward the others.

Dutreaux and Matson stood just beyond Murphy, looking as if they only awaited orders to grab this nuisance and trundle him off to face any sort of work-out that Murphy's wrath could devise, and the other policemen who guarded the doors and windows regarded the flippant

Mr. Conroy with equal dislike. The robed figures who had not removed their masks—Wade judged by their comparative sizes that two of these were men and one a woman—were standing in a little group apart, as though enclosed in their shell of anonymity. Cynthia Fontenay sat on the arm of a chair, one hand flung over the back for support. A flicker of amusement lit the bored cynicism of her face as she watched Con Conroy's performance, and she glanced up at Dick Barron, who stood near her, as if inviting him to join in her appreciation, but Barron was staring at a picture on the wall with a black hopelessness that was strange to see on his sensitive features.

Lucy was standing uncertainly by Esther Morse, who had sat down on a footstool; Esther's face was so drawn and white that Wade thought she might faint, and he was glad Lucy was keeping close to her. He was beginning to admire the saucy competence of Cynthia's maid, and was glad of her presence.

He looked back at Murphy, whose white knuckles suggested that his fists were eager to strike. But Murphy gave an angry movement of his shoulders and spoke but one terse line.

"Take him down and sweat him."

The ready hands of Dutreaux and Matson closed on Conroy's shoulders. His look of patient astonishment was met only by a low growl from Dutreaux, and in another instant he would have been whisked out of Cynthia's red and gold apartment into a police limbo from which he might have had considerable difficulty returning, but as the concerted strength of Murphy's assistants gave him a first shove a voice cut in with peremptory command.

"Just a minute."

The order came with paradoxical authority from behind one of the grinning masks. The man who gave it was reaching for the zipper on his headpiece with a grimness implying that his identity would epitomize his threat. There was a soft ripping noise as the mask came off and revealed the sharp, hard features of Fritz Valdon.

Valdon's was an arresting face, with small eyes and a long thin mouth, the face of a man who talks little and is accustomed to being listened to and obeyed. The two policemen hesitated and Conroy smiled.

"This man is my secretary," Valdon was saying incisively. He threw his mask toward the chair Cynthia was occupying. The mask glanced off her knees and fell on the floor, but neither Valdon nor Cynthia noticed.

She was watching him with interest that held a trace of concern as he addressed Murphy.

"You're very high-handed, Murphy. It's time for you to pull up."

Murphy cleared his throat. "I'm enforcing law and order, Mr. Valdon, and investigating a murder." His big voice boomed in indignant self-defense.

Valdon's small eyes looked him over. "Well, keep within your bounds." His eyes slid away from Murphy as from an object of slight interest and he turned to face the reporters. "I'd like you all to take notice that Murphy is mixing a little practical politics with his police job. He has been annoying Conroy because he thought I might want to leave. He framed it with one of you men to say that I had been recognized as the man wearing robe number 31. When he found it was Conroy, that irritated him, and he trotted out all the bullying tactics. Very well, Murphy, now that that's over—" he switched his attention back to red-faced captain—"what is it you want to know?"

Murphy rocked on his heels, his fists still planted on his hips.

"Search them both," he ordered gruffly. His voice rose. "Everybody else unmask. Matson, take their names."

Two sergeants, glad to have something definite to do at last, began an energetic frisking of Valdon and Conroy. Conroy smiled tolerantly; and Valdon submitted with an insolent acquiescence. Matson had started an imperious argument with the last two maskers in the room.

"Come on, now, there ain't no use stalling. Take 'em off. You ain't got nothing to be scared of, but I got to have your names. That's right, mister—" as a hesitating hand went up to rip one zipper—"take it off. We don't want to cause you no trouble."

The zipper ripped and the thinned gray hair of an egg-shaped head emerged, followed by a furrowed brow and two small green eyes with reddish lids, a pointed, thin-tipped nose and a weak but cheerful mouth. There was no chin to speak of, and the whole face suggested a fussy and irritated gentleman.

"I am Mark Oliver," he said.

"The toy man?" Matson scratched the name in his book. "Right, I know you. What's the address?"

Oliver stood up, wiped some beads of perspiration from his forehead and gave an address in the Metairie section of the suburbs. Wade, who had watched his unmasking, was puzzled. This Dis party seemed foreign to the interests that Oliver was known to have. Oliver's toy shop had given him a widespread reputation, colored by stories of his hermit-like life. Wade remembered perennial Christmas anecdotes about this man who with no children of his own devoted his life to making other people's children happy as an inventor of the amusing trickeries that enliven playrooms. His patterns and patents were the basis for the entire programs of numerous manufacturing plants, for Oliver himself did only a little manufacturing. He was said to be worth a good deal of money, and his retreat was a lordly-looking house with his toy shop behind it.

Cynthia, Wade observed, was looking away from where Oliver and Matson were standing. Oliver walked over to her.

Wade could not hear his words, but he saw that Cynthia responded with the slightest of formal nods and turned away again. She walked over to where Matson was interviewing the last masked figure, and watched as the last zipper was pulled open and the last hidden face came to view with the announcement,

"I'm Mrs. Sophie Hildreth."

Matson wrote it down. "Mrs.," he repeated. "Your husband here, madam?"

Sophie Hildreth gave him a quick, bright, brittle smile, like that of. a hostess who must be pleasant though she is suffering agony from a corn. "Yes, he was somewhere here before Captain Murphy sent all those others down to the police station."

"Somewhere here," Matson echoed dutifully as he recorded the information. "He belong to this outfit that you're sure of?"

"O yes, I know," said Sophie. "He is a member of Dis—in fact, it was he who invited me to join. But I haven't seen much of him tonight."

"What's his first name, ma'am?"

"Ross."

Sophie was answering with alacrity as if to emphasize her eagerness to be of service. She had a little voice with a faint rasp in it—a voice that matched her appearance, which was at the same time young and faded: her face was a trifle pinched and her expression almost vinaigrous, and when she pushed back her headdress Wade saw that her hair was faded too, and was of a drab indefinite color. He judged that she was one of those women who are radiant at sixteen and wilted at twenty-five, and he found something pathetic about her stale beauty. She was politely telling Matson that she lived on Chartres Street.

"Your husband arrived here the same time you did?" Matson asked her.

"I really don't know." Sophie's thin lips parted in another of her bright artificial smiles. "You see, my husband and I don't live together."

"No?" Matson's lean cheeks creased and his mouth widened, and his whole expression betrayed simple exasperation at these women who couldn't keep their minds made up. "You mean you're divorced?"

"Not yet," said Sophie sweetly. "But we will be soon. When he gets home you'll find him at his apartment—it's on St. Peter Street, facing Jackson Square."

There was another zephyr of laughter at Wade's elbow and he felt Cynthia's hand on his arm. She beckoned him into a corner.

"Please," she whispered, "get me a drink."

He hesitated, glancing to where Murphy and Valdon were exchanging laconic opinions of each other and then to the whispering cloud of people at the other end of the room, who were regarding one another as if in fear of the intimacy their position had forced upon them.

"There's some liquor in the bottom of the buffet," whispered Cynthia, the corners of her mouth twitching with suppressed amusement, "and if I don't get a drink soon I shall laugh out loud at that Hildreth woman. Can't you see how she's glaring at me?"

Wade got a bottle, suddenly remembering that Sophie had sent a glance at Cynthia when she told Matson that she and Ross Hildreth occupied separate apartments. He found Lucy beside him with a tray of glasses she had taken from the top of the buffet. He set the decanter on the tray.

Cynthia took a drink, and then a second, with an eagerness that crystallized in Wade's mind a suspicion that had been forming itself since he first came into her house. He excused himself and drew Wiggins aside.

"That woman," he said in an undertone, "is going to be blotto before long."

Wiggins nodded solemnly. "She sure is."

"Ask your friend Lucy if Cynthia is in the habit of getting tight every evening."

"I done asked her," Wiggins informed him in a sepulchral whisper. "Lucy says not every evening. Not more than three or four nights a week."

"I thought so." Wade glanced again at Cynthia and then went back to where Matson was still questioning Sophie Hildreth. Sophie's determined sweetness had become tart.

"I tell you," she insisted sharply, "my husband is a free agent. I don't keep up with his comings and goings."

"Yes, ma'am." Matson was unhurried. "But you can swear he was at the party, can you? Remember nobody took off their masks."

"I can swear it, yes."

"How do you know?" Matson was slyly searching the list of names that had come over from the Third Precinct. He scowled as though his search had been in vain.

Mark Oliver edged a step closer. The others were listening with interest.

"How did you know?" Matson repeated.

Sophie beckoned him closer. He leaned over.

"I—er—recognized him," she said in a low voice.

"Oh," said Matson, "then you aren't sure he was here—you just thought you recognized him. You couldn't swear it was him."

She lifted her head and put her lips close to his ear. "I don't want the others to hear," she said. Her voice dropped. She whispered.

Matson started. "You're sure of that?" he said.

Sophie had dropped back into her chair. She shook her head in birdlike nods that meant yes.

"I see," said Matson.

He said nothing else, but put up his notebook and walked smartly off to where Murphy was occupying his attention with Valdon and Con Conroy, then scratching a quick message, he tore the page out of his notebook and gave it to the corporal at the door.

"I've got to duck out of here for a few minutes," Wade heard him say. "Just as soon as the old man gets through talking to Valdon slip him this, and don't forget because it's important."

As Matson slipped outside Wade followed and plucked his sleeve. "What's the excitement?" he asked.

Matson hesitated. "Well, don't print it unless the old man says you can. But that lady in there—that Mrs. Hildreth that ain't living with her husband—she never saw Parnell's body, you know. But she says she knows her husband was here because her husband's suit was number 47."

CHAPTER EIGHT

WADE strolled back into the room, where he saw on a table the collected belongings of Fritz Valdon—money, keys, a cigarette-case, a folder of matches and a couple of handkerchiefs. Murphy was obviously chagrined.

"You were pretty smart, Fritz," he was saying, "damn smart, and I fell for it. But we ain't through yet." Murphy's jowls creased in what might under pleasanter circumstances have been a grin. "We ain't through. I guess it may be mighty interesting to find out why you were so anxious to get away and wouldn't take a chance on coming up and trying to arrange it for yourself."

Valdon gave a laugh of arrogant tolerance. "Hell, Murphy, you can't mix me up in this. Since you're so bent on knowing, I just wanted to get away because I thought it would be a bad thing for me with the people. I joined Dis a good many years ago. I don't come to these doings very often."

Valdon took his case from the table and got out a cigarette. His beady eyes flicked from Murphy to Dutreaux and from Dutreaux to Wade, with sly satisfaction.

Murphy growled a greeting to Wade and whisked his attention to Conroy. "What'd you find on this fellow?"

Dutreaux grinned and extended both his hands. In one was a 38-caliber automatic; in the other a brown leather wallet, open to show ten new thousand-dollar bills. Conroy had rested his elbows on the back of a chair and was blandly watching this display of his property. Murphy wheeled upon him.

"What're you doing with a gun, Conroy?" he demanded.

Conroy sighed and shook his head as if the stupidity of the police was something designed to try the souls of citizens. "License to carry firearms issued by a judge of the courts of the State of Louisiana will be found in the wallet along with my driver's license."

Valdon laid a hand on Conroy's shoulder. "There won't be any trouble about that, Con," he assured him. Then to Murphy, with emphasis, "This man works for me. I arranged the license for that gun."

Wade took his hand out of his pocket holding a dilapidated cigarette. "Here's a match, pal," said Wiggins alongside of his shoulder, and as he accepted the light Wade asked, "How long have you been employed as a secretary, Conroy?"

Conroy's gaze was guileless. "You may tell your readers, Mr. Wade, that secretarying is a comparatively new vocation for me. I engaged in it principally for the sake of my health—it brought me to your delightfully mild climate."

Wiggins smothered an appreciative chuckle, and Wade caught himself smiling. But Murphy was not amused.

"Where d'you live?" Murphy asked curtly. Conroy bowed. "I live in, sir, with Mr. Valdon."

"Where d'you come from?"

"O, yes, that's a good question." Conroy tapped his forehead, ruminatively. Valdon's thin lips were curved in a smile of supercilious enjoyment. Conroy considered and then spoke to Wade. "Now *you* should have asked that, reporter. It's always interesting for newspaper readers to get the background on people. Shows why and wherefore on certain of their actions."

"I'm listening," said Wade. He was studying Conroy with more interest than he had yet vouchsafed to any of the other actors in the scene surrounding the murder of Roger Parnell. Conroy's cool effrontery had not surprised him, for a henchman of Fritz Valdon had little to fear from ordinary police activities, but Conroy's assurance had an indescribable and yet definite difference from that of the ordinary bodyguard of a political racketeer. He was keeping them all at bay in a manner that was not explained by calling it arrogance or defiance—it was like the attitude of a veteran politician being annoyed by a cub reporter.

"I came from a great many places," Conroy was saying, "and if it ever becomes necessary and I really think you're interested instead of just being curious, I'll tell you, and perhaps we'll find some mutual friends."

"You're from up North, ain't you?" inquired Wiggins. "You talk like it."

Conroy's mien expressed a dignified grief. "Ah me," he sighed reproachfully, "if my old father, Colonel Conroy, could hear you say that, young man, he'd lift the headstone off his grave."

His heels clicked and he made a pretty bow. "I, sir," he said, "was born on the broad acres of Conroy's Plantation. We raised a fair amount of cotton and a great deal of hell up in my country, sir, and what—" his eyes narrowed and his words began to come like little snaps—"what the hell do you care where I came from, shrimp? Screw!" He faced Murphy. "Now, copper, I'm not talking until a lawyer tells me to talk, see? Anything else you want to know, ask me at somebody's trial."

He and Valdon exchanged smiles. Valdon turned to Murphy. "Inspect that gun, if you please, captain. See that the clip is full and that there's one bullet in the chamber."

"I'll turn it over to the district attorney," Murphy answered, but Valdon clipped his answer short.

"No, you aren't going to frame this kid. You'll inspect it now—here—see?—*then* you can turn it over."

Murphy deliberating turned his back. "Dutreaux, take that gun. Put a tag on it saying it belongs to Mr. Conroy."

Valdon gave a low snort that reiterated his suggestion that the police department would hear more from him before long. Wade slipped over to Matson.

"Let's see your list," he said. "I want to be sure that I've got everybody who has been detained for questioning."

Matson proffered his notebook. Wade caught a look of appeal from Esther Morse and the persistent little glimmer of triumph in Cynthia's eyes. Resolutely ignoring Esther and noting with relief that Cynthia had set the flask on the window-sill, he repeated Matson's list of names.

"'Mrs. Sophie Hildreth, Dick Barron, Mark Oliver, Miss Esther Morse, Mrs. Cynthia Fontenay, Fritz Valdon, Con Conroy, Miss Lucy Lake. All to be questioned immediately by Murphy; Arnold Ghent not yet located, but will be questioned as soon as possible.' I guess that's all, Matson, except that I'll remind the office that the dead man wore Ross Hildreth's costume and was passing himself off as Arnold Ghent, so a little pleasant chit-chat with both those gentlemen should be illuminating. Thanks—I'll go phone." Then, seeing Wiggins at his elbow, he added in an undertone, "Try to frame a picture of the bunch. Cover for me—I'm going to call Koppel."

Wiggins slipped him a couple of plates. "Okay. And get these out for me, will you? That Murphy is a big dumb donkey—I knew he'd get you in a jam."

Wade grinned and mumbled "Nertz" as he went out to phone.

He called the city desk, dispatched Wiggins' plates and came back to discover that Murphy by the simple process of having a little table and an understuffed leather put in the middle of the inferno-like ballroom, had established an impromptu office. He had left the members of Dis in the red-and-gold room across the hall to await his pleasure. A police stenographer sat in a straight-backed chair next to Murphy's and two uniformed men guarded each door. Wiggins, who having made a picture of the scene and sent it through to the office felt that he had done his duty for the present, had ensconced himself on the lowest step of the red throne for a breather.

Empty of devil-figures and with the full lights on, the ballroom had a morning-after look. It had become simply a room draped in red silk and decorated with red and black paint, with shoddy details easily apparent—just a room fixed up for a rather silly party that had been raided by the cops. Murphy glanced up and nodded as Wade entered, then resumed his instructions to Dutreaux.

"Sure, I'm going to question 'em all. Valdon and Conroy and Oliver, and that Barron kid and all those women. I've had headquarters check up on Ross Hildreth. They say he went to Baton Rouge Sunday and ain't known to be back yet. I want you to see to it—"

There was a confused noise beyond the door that led to the balcony. Matson, in response to a gesture from Murphy, hurried over to slip the bolt and put out his head.

"Here's a new one," he called over his shoulder.

With two uniformed men behind him, another red-robed figure walked into the room. His mask was off and his hood with the horned head-dress had been thrown back. He glanced queryingly around for a second, then walked directly up to Murphy. Wade and Wiggins exchanged glances of recognition, for Wiggins' boast to Lucy earlier in the evening had not been idle. Every news photographer in town knew Arnold Ghent.

CHAPTER NINE

"Good evening, Captain Murphy," he said. "I am Arnold Ghent."

Murphy lay back and his eyes slowly traveled up and down Arnold Ghent, and for a moment he did not speak, as though he felt it necessary to readjust his mental equipment to meet a new and baroque personality. Ghent stood waiting for recognition, impatient, but not apparently self-conscious, and he returned Murphy's examination with a scrutiny that was equally detailed, and which, Wade felt as he watched, would be likely to prove more penetrating.

Ghent's naturally dark face had been sunburnt many shades darker, and he walked with the long firm stride of a man who is accustomed to do most of his walking out of doors. Even in his crazy devil-suit he had a hard, muscular look, and one could have guessed his famous athletic triumphs even if one had never heard of them. He was the sort of man who cannot be lost in a crowd: his look was piercing, as if his eyes at once stripped the object of his attention of all subterfuges; his voice, as forceful as his appearance, was the sort that simply cannot be reduced to an undertone. As he waited for Murphy to speak his attitude suggested neither irritation nor annoyance—nothing but a good-humored endurance before an incomprehensible series of events. It was with a queerly defensive brusqueness that Murphy finally said:

"Well, how do you do, Mr. Ghent? Have a seat."

Ghent accepted the chair Dutreaux was offering him, and smiled.

"They tell me I'm pretty lucky, captain—that I'm supposed to be dead."

"You sure are," volunteered Wiggins, who had wriggled over to a better point of vantage. "Your obit was already in type when my partner Wade called up to say Mr. Ghent wasn't dying this evening." Ghent regarded him with humorous indulgence. Murphy looked grimly at his new acquaintance.

"You were at this party tonight, were you?" he started.

"No, I was ready for the ball, but I was—er—prevented from attending." Ghent had stretched his long legs in front of him and looked at his red satin slippers as if in apology for his whole fantastic attire.

"Prevented, were you?" Murphy jerked a thumb toward one of the policemen who had come in with Ghent. "Where'd you find him?" he asked.

"At his apartment, sir," the man answered. "Tied up."

"Tied up, eh?" Murphy turned on a leg of his chair to face his subordinate. "Tied up, was he? In his own house? Well, tell me about it."

"Sure, cap'n, sure. We went from headquarters, you know, soon as the call came from here to find Mr. Ghent. We knocked on his door and nobody answered, but we heard some sort of moving around inside, so I says to Lalland here, 'Let's go in,' I says, so we tried the door and it wasn't locked, so we went right in. There wasn't nobody in the front room, but we heard noises like somebody bumping around, and we went into the next room which was the bedroom, and there was this gentleman with this red dress on, tied up to the bed with a rope, and blindfolded, and gagged with a towel, fighting like a bull to get hisself untied. Part of the bedclothes was burned like somebody'd tried to set fire to the house. So Lalland holds a gun in case he's violent, and I take the towel off and he says he's Arnold Ghent and for God's sake to get him loose. Which I do, and I tell him a guy named Parnell is dead which everybody thought was him, and we bring him here to talk to you."

"Huh," Murphy said expressively. "That right, Ghent?"

Ghent gave a slow nod of confirmation. "Entirely right, Captain Murphy."

"Suppose," said Murphy, "you tell us what happened to you."

Ghent considered an instant, absently chafing one wrist, where a red circle showed the recent presence of a rope. He glanced at the reporters.

"I hope you understand, Captain Murphy, that I'm still in the dark about a good deal of what's been going on this evening, and I'm still pretty badly shaken up. So if I don't make myself quite clear don't hesitate to interrupt me."

"I won't," Murphy promised shortly. "Who tied you up?"

Ghent did not answer directly. "I suppose I'd better begin with what happened before I was tied up. The beginning, as far as I was concerned, happened about ten o'clock. I was getting dressed for the Dis ball when I got a phone call from Roger Parnell."

"Parnell, eh?" Murphy muttered.

"O yes, I had known him for years, though we were never very intimate friends. We were in prep school together. He said he wanted to see me. I asked him if tomorrow wouldn't do, for I didn't want to be seen in this Dis outfit—I suppose you know that we don't like to make public our connection with Dis."

"Sure, sure, I know," Murphy nodded with easy carelessness suggesting that he had learned the mysteries of Dis along with the alphabet.

"Parnell insisted that he had to see me at once," Ghent continued. "He sounded pretty excited, so I told him I could see him in about twenty minutes. I thought I could slip out of this robe and put on a dressing-gown before he got there, but I don't think it was more than two minutes later that he walked in."

"Your door wasn't locked?" asked Murphy.

"No—I live in the Pontalba apartments on St. Peter Street, and they aren't very modern. I know most of the occupants of the apartments near mine, and we rarely lock doors."

"I see." But Murphy's nod was impatient, for like most practical folk he had little understanding of bohemian vagaries. "What happened?"

"Well—something that perhaps you can explain better than I can." Ghent was frowning. "When Parnell opened the door I was surprised to see that he had on a Dis costume. He was carrying the mask in his hand. I thought he must be considerably agitated, for I'd never known a member of Dis to reveal his identity. It's just one of the things we don't do. I was annoyed, too, that Parnell should have come so soon after his call, for I'd had no time to get my own costume off, so I probably wasn't very enthusiastic when I greeted him. He sat down in the living room. I asked him what was on his mind. He said, 'Ghent, I'm in a hell of a mess. I'm desperate, and you've got to help me.'

"I told him I'd do anything I could, though I thought it strange that he should come to me, for as I said, we were never on very intimate terms and I knew he had some powerful friends. I asked him if it was money he needed. 'No,' he said, 'not money.' Then he asked me for a pencil and paper. I got them for him, and he stood up and began to sketch a rough map of Jackson Square."

Ghent paused a moment. "I was bewildered by his actions. He was nervous, but he seemed perfectly sane."

Murphy's face was expressionless, but his eyes were on a straight line with Ghent's, and he was listening closely. Ghent pushed back his chair and stood up.

"Here's what he did. He laid the paper on the table like this—" Ghent drew Murphy's notebook toward him and bent over as though writing in it. "Then he handed me the pencil and asked me if I would mark an X where each of the park entrances was. I took the pencil and leaned over to mark the positions of the park gates, and he must have stepped back, for the next thing I knew a rope had dropped past my face and bound my arms, and Parnell had a knife against my back."

"Did you put up a fight?" Murphy asked with interest.

"Lord, no. I'd not have hesitated with the chances even, but I wasn't going to try it against that knife."

Murphy nodded in agreement, and Ghent went on.

"Parnell told me that if I turned around he would kill me. Then he slipped a blindfold over my face, held the rope tight around my arms and shoved my head down against the table-top with his elbow. In another instant he had a rope around my legs, then he dragged me into the bedroom, threw me on the bed, trussed me up like a turkey, gagged me with a towel and took off my Dis ring."

"Took your ring, did he?" Murphy leaned toward him with increasing interest. "Just what kind of knife was it that he had?"

"I never saw it. After he trussed me up he took the blindfold off me only for a minute."

"What was that for?"

"Why, when I was safely tied up and couldn't move, I heard him say that he was going to take off the gag but that if I put up a howl he'd kill me. Then he slipped it off, that and the blindfold, and asked me to tell him what was the password for the Dis ball." Ghent glanced at the group of reporters. "I told him to go to hell."

"You knew he wasn't a member of Dis?" Wade asked.

"Not until then. When I saw him wearing a Dis costume I assumed that he was a member, and during the performance that terminated with his taking my ring I wasn't doing much reasoning of any sort, but when he took off that gag and demanded tonight's password I understood of course that all this was just a way of getting himself into the Dis ball. Why he wanted to get in I didn't know, but I figured that he couldn't have any good reason."

"And—?" prompted Murphy.

"He did something that sent my blood cold." Ghent rested his elbows on the table and looked over his crossed arms directly to Murphy. "He picked up an edge of a sheet on the bed and lit his cigarette-lighter and set fire to the sheet."

"Must have been crazy," Wade commented.

"No, he didn't seem crazy," Ghent demurred. "He seemed even to have lost the nervousness I had noticed when he first came in. He was perfectly sane and very much in earnest. He looked down at me, as I lay there helpless as a baby with that sheet burning close to me, and said, 'I told you I was in a hell of a fix, Ghent, but so are you. You'll either tell me enough to get me into Dis tonight, or so help me God I'll burn down this house and you in it.'"

Ghent reached among the folds of his robe and got out a cigarette and a packet of matches.

"I told him the password was 'Persephone.'" He smothered the flame with the hearthrug.

"Then he left?" Murphy asked.

"Not right away," said Ghent. He hesitated, then went on. "Under ordinary circumstances, Captain Murphy—I mean if nothing serious had developed from Parnell's visit to the Dis ball—I might have kept this to myself. I know that whatever it was that turned the easy-going chap Parnell always was into the cold-blooded proposition he appeared tonight must have been something pretty desperate."

"Go on, boy," Murphy permitted himself a gleam of understanding. "I know how you feel."

"Well—Parnell made very sure that the fire on the bed was out. He opened a window, asked me if I felt all right, put a pillow under my head, sat down on the edge of the bed, and put a cigarette into my mouth and lit it for me." Ghent's sunburnt features contracted. "I'll never forget it. His face was almost green and his eyes looked like a man's when he is going down into the water for the third time, and yet there wasn't a shake in his hands or a tremor in his voice. I'll try to remember exactly what he said. It might be important."

He paused for a moment, thoughtfully.

"Here's as nearly as I can remember, and I think it's pretty accurate. He said, 'Arnold, I know you're a sportsman. I'm depending on that. I realize of course that you don't understand my actions here tonight, and I realize too that if you broadcast them I'm finished in New Orleans. But I want to get into Dis tonight worse than I ever wanted to do anything else in my life. I'm desperate, and it's my only way out.' He looked straight at me. 'If I find,' he said, 'that I can't get in, that you've fooled me about the password, I'm coming back and kill you, because you will be responsible for my failing in a last attempt to save my personal honor and the honor of someone who means more to me than anything else in the world.'"

"Is that all he said?" Murphy asked when Ghent paused.

"No. He told me that he had to leave me trussed up so I couldn't possibly get to the ball, because he knew that every member was accounted for and one extra guest might cause Cynthia to start an inquiry. Then he added that he would give me one more chance to tell him the truth. I took it that he meant I was to tell him if I had given him a false password. I told him to go ahead to the ball, and even promised him, I'm afraid, that if he could justify what he had done I'd say nothing about it. He didn't answer. He got up and put the blindfold and the gag back on me, and I heard him walk toward the door. He spoke just once more after that. As I heard him turn the doorknob, he said, 'Frog'—that's a name they used to call me in prep school—'Frog, I may never get a chance to explain this. But if I don't, please try to remember that it was something I had to do.'"

Ghent reached again into the folds of his robe for a handkerchief and wiped a little frost of perspiration off his forehead. "And that," he finished, his voice curiously low and taut, "was the last time I saw Roger Parnell."

CHAPTER TEN

"So that's the last time you saw Parnell, eh?"

"Yes. I didn't see anybody else until your men came in and untied me."

Murphy stroked his rubicund cheeks and looked musingly at the reporters and at Wiggins perched on the steps of the throne. "When's the last time you saw him before tonight, Mr. Ghent?"

"A day or two ago. I met him on the street and he asked me to come up to his apartment for a drink. I didn't stay long—not more than half an hour."

"What was he like then? Seem to have anything on his mind?"

Ghent considered. "I shouldn't say so. You understand, Captain Murphy, that I was never a close friend of his, and I don't think he'd have confided in me."

"I thought you said you'd known him since you went to school."

"I had, but we never were good friends."

"Didn't think much of him, eh?"

Ghent's stern face relaxed into a deprecating smile. "After all, captain, Parnell's dead, and that was years ago. It can't mean anything now. He just struck me, when I was a boy, as a fellow who was a little too sharp and too wise, and I never made any effort to make friends with him."

"I see. How long's he been in town?"

"Two or three years. I didn't know he was living here till I ran into him on the street one day."

"I get you." Murphy crossed his big arms over the table and leaned forward. "Do you know what his business was?"

Ghent shrugged. "I suppose there's no harm in saying it now—he was the money man at the Red Cat over in Jefferson Parish."

"That's what I thought," Murphy affirmed with a satisfied nod. "Now, Mr. Ghent, when he came to see you tonight, do you really think he'd have killed you if you hadn't told him how to get into this party?"

Ghent raised his black eyebrows and lowered them slowly, as though to imply that there might be doubt in some minds but not in his. "He seemed pretty desperate, Captain Murphy."

"But you said you wouldn't have borne him any hard feelings if he'd been able to explain it later. Is that right?"

"Well—" Ghent laughed shortly—"I like to think it is. Of course I was mad. Maybe it's just a conclusion I arrived at after I heard he was dead."

Murphy thumbed the pages of his notebook. "What time did he leave your house?"

"I should say about eleven o'clock."

"How long would it take him to get here?" asked Murphy, scratching down the figures.

"About five minutes in a cab."

"Oh, he had a cab?"

"He called one after he tied me up. I forgot to mention it."

"And he didn't say anything to you but what you've told us?"

"Not a thing."

"Just that stuff about it being an affair of honor. A woman, you think?"

"It might have been. He always had plenty of women friends. But I don't know."

"Mhm." Murphy sighed. "Well, I think that's all for the present, Mr. Ghent. You can go outside now, but I wish you'd kind of stay around. There might be a few more things I'll want to ask you. I'm much obliged."

"I'll be outside if you want me, then."

Ghent rose, and Murphy walked to the door with him, followed by Wiggins, who trotted placidly off for a photograph. As he closed the door Murphy turned to face the reporters. "What do you think of that guy, boys?"

"If he's lying," said Kennedy of the *Telegram*, "he's a mighty straight liar."

"He sure is. He don't seem to overdo it any. Of course, he may be crooked all the way through, but he looks straight, and unless we can find out some sort of motive for him killing Parnell, I guess we might as well believe him." Murphy sat down.

"Let me see," ruminated Wade. "You've got his address?"

"Sure."

"Ross Hildreth lives at the same place, just above Ghent. Parnell had on Hildreth's costume when he was killed. I figure Parnell called Ghent from Hildreth's apartment and came down right away."

"That's reasonable. I'm kind of itching to talk to that guy Hildreth. I'm having him brought down from Baton Rouge."

"His being in Baton Rouge doesn't give him an alibi," Wade reminded. "Anybody can drive here from Baton Rouge in two hours, and a man set on getting himself an alibi for murder could do it in considerably less."

Murphy leaned glumly back on the hind legs of his chair, looking up without interest as Wiggins bounced in, beaming.

"Get the picture?" Wade asked.

"Sure. Say, do you think that guy Parnell was killed over a woman?"

"I don't know," said Wade. "But here's something we might remember: I sort of picked it up that it's Cynthia's fault that the Hildreths are separated."

"Rats," said Wiggins, "I coulda told you that. I seen Cynthia and that guy Hildreth together a lot, around the racetrack. When Lucy told me Cynthia was gonta get married again, I guessed the next husband was Hildreth and she sorta shied me off."

"Probably because the Hildreths aren't divorced yet," Wade surmised. "Still, I'm inclined to think there's something else in this business besides some man's liking some woman."

"F'r instance?"

"I wish I knew. But I don't. Ghent's story fits. If it's not true, it's been cut to fit. The men did find him tied up, the bedclothes had been burned, and we can check up on whether there was a taxi called from that address at that time."

"I'll have Matson do it right away," said Murphy. "I wish we knew exactly what time Parnell was killed. This rigor mortis stuff is all right, but sometimes it throws you a couple of hours off."

"Hell!" Wiggins sprang up. "Why didn't you ask me?"

"Ask you? Were you there?" Murphy's scorn was profound.

"No, but—" Wiggins slapped his knee. "Lord, I forgot something." He jumped back to where his camera was and swooped upon it. "Look, Murphy. If that cop at the door will tell Lucy she's got to come with me, I'll maybe bring something back."

CHAPTER ELEVEN

MR. WIGGINS of the *Creole*, like most young gentlemen who take photographs for the daily press, had attained eminence in his vocation not only because he could handle a camera but also because of his smallness of stature, which enabled him to wriggle unobserved through a crowd of hostile humanity or through half-open windows of guarded dwellings. So it was no subject for surprise that Wiggins got out of Cynthia Fontenay's garrisoned house and into his roadster without being observed by anybody but the single policeman who stood at the gate and who had received orders to send Lucy with him.

Wiggins opened the car door and grandly assisted Lucy inside, then ran around and slithered himself under the steering-wheel. "You okay, honey?" he inquired.

Lucy nodded. She had put on a coat, and had exchanged her bit of organdie headgear for a little dark hat. Wiggins examined her approvingly by the light of a street-lantern. "You warm enough?"

"I'm plenty warm," said Lucy.

"Let's go, then."

Wiggins slipped in the clutch. He turned off Royal Street and into St. Peter, chugging at a leisurely rate along the dark side of the Cabildo toward Jackson Square. Another turn headed them downtown toward the old cathedral.

"Well," said Lucy at length, "what's the big idea?"

Wiggins grinned at the stubborn profile outlined by the lanterns. "Just going bye-bye for awhile."

Lucy turned sharply. "Where are you taking me?"

"Now don't get all excited, babe," said Wiggins soothingly. "I just had to go by the office a minute and I figured you might like to get away from that place a little while, so I asked Murphy to let you come with me."

"Humph. To let me come with you! To order me to come, you mean."

"Now don't be sore, baby. Didn't Murphy say it would be okay?"

"You listen to me. I don't have to have the police department make my dates. *Where are we going?*"

Her back was straight and her blue eyes blazing. But Mr. Wiggins of the *Creole* was not disturbed. He had the smiling audacity which is rarely found except in young children, movie stars and reporters with a nose for news.

"Say, you're like all women. Any time you try to give a girl a break she thinks you're putting something over on her."

Lucy shrugged. "A break? Thanks."

"No foolin', babe," he exclaimed, "I was beginning to worry about you, and I figured I'd get you out of the place. Tell the truth, ain't this thing getting on your nerves?"

"Well," she admitted grudgingly, "I never saw so many policemen in one place before. When they took Mr. Parnell's body out to the morgue it kind of gave me the creeps. Gee, I wish it was all over."

Wiggins let Lucy think about this a moment before he answered. "So do I, babe," he told her solemnly. "Murphy's really on the warpath."

He turned back into Royal Street and started up-town. Lucy snuggled further into her seat and looked silently out at the dark old walls of the Quarter. The white blaze of light at the end of Royal Street widened, and they entered Canal Street, glaring and enormous, and empty save for the few persons waiting at the car stops and newsboys calling headlines about the murder at the Dis ball. Wiggins went on.

"You know, I wanted to talk to you about something. That's why I got you out."

"I thought there must be something on your mind," she answered coolly. "This is a queer time to have a date. What did you want?"

Wiggins pulled up to the curb and stopped. "Well you're trying to give me the old runaround, see, and I don't like it." His manner was that of a man with a grievance. "I don't like it," he went on, "because I think you're doing the wrong thing."

"I'm not doing anything." Lucy's voice expressed a fine degree of puzzlement. "I don't know what you mean."

"Look, babe," Wiggins started seriously. "I'm working this story for my paper, y'understand? I know I'm only supposed to make the pictures, but I got some authority too. I work with Wade and Murphy all the time when a story like this breaks."

"So," she interrupted calmly, "what's that make me? Front page stuff or something?"

"No," he said vehemently. "But I want to take care of you."

"Thanks," she retorted with good-natured irony, "but I've been doing that little job for myself very well."

Wiggins became stern. "Yeah? Is that what made you lie about that Fontenay woman's marriages?"

Lucy leaned back. "Oh, you're still talking about that. I didn't lie to you I just made a mistake. I shouldn't have talked to you about it anyway."

Wiggins shook an unbelieving head. "You know you lied. *Why* don't you get right? You know Mrs. Fontenay lied too. She said she'd been married twice and you said you counted wrong. Malarkey. It was three, wasn't it?"

Lucy drew herself up. "Say, Tony Wiggins, what is this? The third degree or something? I'm going to get out of this car and you can think anything you please." She opened the door.

"Sit down." Wiggins snatched her back and banged the door shut. "You ain't going no place till we get right, understand?"

Lucy sat down. She drew herself as far as possible from him and eyed him scornfully. "I understand," she said hotly. "You're a punk that wants to be a cop. Well, you're wrong trying it on me. 'You got a lot of authority; you help Murphy and Wade.' You make me laugh."

"So that's what you think." He was plainly indignant. "You think I'm trying to be a big guy or something." His face was poked close to hers and his fists clenched on his knees. "You think I wanta be a cop? All right, go ahead and be a chump. Go to the front for that old biscuit you work for. Go ahead, give me the bird. And where'll you wind up? Where'll you wind up?" His voice was taunting. "I'll tell you. You'll wind up in the can making aprons for orphan asylums."

Lucy laughed. "That's a swell line. You'll make a lovely detective when you grow up. But I got scared once tonight and I'm over it now, see?"

Wiggins' hands opened in a gesture of finality. "All right, babe." His voice expressed baffled resignation. "Let it go at that. You go through for that dame and she'll put you in the grease any minute she thinks it's gonta help her."

"No she won't. You don't know her."

"I know her plenty. Now tell me. How many times has she been married?"

"Twice."

"Cripes," groaned Wiggins in wrathful helplessness. "You're hopeless. No matter what I tell you you're gonta be a dummy and take the rap on this thing. I guess you better get out and walk."

"Tony, I can't tell you—All right, I'll go."

She reached for the door.

"You stay here." Wiggins grabbed her arms. "I ain't gonta let you take any rap. Before I went up tonight to make that first picture you told me Cynthia's next husband would be her fourth. Now what do you want to lie about it for? Tell me you can't add up. It's no trouble to add up one and one and one. Why don't you give yourself a break?"

Lucy drew a long breath. She turned around and faced him.

"Listen, Tony. Maybe there's some things you don't understand. Mrs. Fontenay's been good to me. She's treated me like a human being. And now when she's in trouble I'm not sneaking out and talking about her, see?"

"Yeah. I see. I figured she'd be like that. She'll be nice to anybody as long as it don't bother her none. But when she gets in a hole—you saw what she did when Murphy was giving her the quiz, didn't you? She tried to hang this job around that Morse girl's neck. You saw that."

"Yes," Lucy retorted valiantly, "but she didn't want to."

Wiggins laughed. "Didn't want to—you must be nertz. Sure she wanted to. Otherwise she'd have kept her face closed."

Lucy did not answer.

"Listen, Lucy, let me ask you one question. Do you think Cynthia killed Parnell?"

Lucy shook her head.

"All right then. Why did she say she was only married twice?"

Lucy considered. "I guess—" her voice was low and troubled—"She didn't want it in the papers. Nobody knew it."

Wiggins felt something click inside him. He'd been sure he was right. There *was* a husband that Cynthia forgot.

"But don't you think she's crazy to try and hide it?" he demanded. "They'll start checking up on her story and find it out."

"That's her business," said Lucy. "Not mine."

Wiggins waxed persuasive. "Listen, babe, I'm giving it to you straight, so help me God I am. Holding back won't get her anything. The more she lies the more she'll have to lie and when they trip her up it'll look lousy. You're in the same fix. I wouldn't mind if she was your kind of person—on the level and decent—but she ain't. Murphy's bound to ask you a lot of questions. Tell him the truth. You got nothing to hide. Why did she say she'd had only two husbands? What's the lowdown? Please tell me, honey, and I'll see that she don't find out where I got it."

Lucy considered. "You won't fool me, Tony? You won't let her know I told?"

"Of course I won't."

"She's going to marry Mr. Hildreth as soon as he gets a divorce. Mrs. Hildreth has been holding it up."

"And he'll be the fourth, won't he?"

Lucy nodded. "Pull up under the light."

Wiggins started the car. As it stopped under a street-light Lucy opened her pocketbook.

She hesitated, and looked up at the street-light. In the thin river-fog it looked like a flame shining through cotton. She looked back at the pocketbook in her hands.

"One day last week," said Lucy, "—it was the time she told me she was going to get married again—she got out her bond box and tore up a lot of old papers. One of them looked like a marriage certificate. There were a lot of letters too. She burned them up in the grate. Well, there was a little bitty box. She threw that in the fire on top of the letters and it must have rolled off. She was drinking pretty hard and getting kind of a crying jag on. She told me never to get married. Said she had done it three times and wouldn't be doing it again except that she was a damn fool. Then she went to sleep. I saw the box on the edge of the fireplace. It was just burned a little bit. I thought maybe she had thrown it in by mistake because she was drinking. I opened it and found something I thought she might regret putting in the fire because it was valuable. Here it is."

She opened her hand. Wiggins saw that she held a wedding ring.

"Look inside," Lucy prompted.

He held it down to the dashboard and switched on the light. The inscription, engraved in tiny letters, was one that he knew he had been half-consciously expecting.

"Cynthia Ludlam—Roger Parnell
December 19, 1916."

CHAPTER TWELVE

Wiggins spent nearly a quarter of an hour in the photographers' rooms of the *Creole* building before returning to where he had left Lucy waiting downstairs behind the want-ad counter. She came out to meet him questioningly.

"What have you been doing, Tony?"

"Just looking over some negatives they put through the tanks for me."

"What are they for?" she asked as they went out.

"Don't know yet," Wiggins said. "I got a couple of 'em here in the envelope. We gotta see." He climbed into the car.

Lucy looked anxiously at him through the dark as he pressed the started. "Tony, do you know anything that's going to put Mrs. Fontenay in a jam?"

"I don't know, babe. Honest I don't." Wiggins shut his mouth tight and leaned over the wheel. He was driving fast. Lucy caught her breath as the wind whizzed past her and spoke vehemently.

"Tony, if you do anything to get her in trouble I'll never forgive you, or myself either."

For a moment Wiggins did not answer. But as they entered the Quarter and the narrow street forced him to slacken his speed, he replied with earnest conviction.

"It's this way, Lucy. I got a coupla negatives. She used to be Mrs. Parnell. That either puts her in or out. If she's not right for the job this dope can't hurt her and if she's right for it she oughta be hurt."

Lucy sighed. Wiggins hurriedly parked his roadster behind a big police car and bidding her stick around inside and see what happened, he went upstairs. At the door of the ballroom he almost collided with Fritz Valdon. Wiggins looked up innocently.

"Howdy, Mr. Valdon," he greeted.

"Hello," said Valdon. His satisfied expression suggested that he was well pleased with his interview with Wade and Murphy. "Keeping you busy?"

"They sure are," Wiggins replied non-committally, and went in. He hurried over to Wade and Murphy. "Well," he said, "whatcha know?"

Wade grinned and shook his head. "Nothing much. Valdon has decided to be nice, so he told us about the Dis meeting tonight. Murphy's trying to make out a time-table to determine just when Parnell got it."

Wiggins pulled up a chair and chuckled as he glanced at Murphy laboring over a list of figures. "What did Valdon say?"

"Well—" Wade's forehead puckered in a series of lines—"he told us that this initiation shindig took place at about a quarter of twelve. First there was a lot of business about honoring the guest of honor and that sort of thing. Then, at a quarter of twelve, they sent her out—told her to wait in Cynthia's bedroom while they had the real ceremony which only members could witness. It's really quite a performance, with lighted devils' heads and solemn proclamations of the dreadful consequences to anyone who tells the secrets of Dis. Most of it is done with the lights out. Valdon says the room was dark for ten or fifteen minutes. It seems reasonable that somebody who was smart enough to slip past the teller at the door might go out and kill Parnell and get back in without being noticed."

"About a quarter to twelve, you say?" Wiggins scowled and tried to remember. "You mean he'd go out and go back to the china-closet? Look—I was here about that time, and the butler told me I'd have to wait. When I finally went up Cynthia said they'd been having a meeting."

"And what's that prove?"

"Nothing much—except that when the butler left me in the courtyard he walked upstairs and went around the gallery to the back. Now ain't that where the china-closet window opens? On the back gallery?"

"Fine!" Wade exclaimed. "That's one of the things we wanted to know. Listen to this, Murphy." He hastily recounted what Wiggins had pointed out.

Murphy was grateful. "Good boy. We'll just jump down and see that fellow in a little while. He's safe where he is, and the more we've got to tell him the more liable he'll be to talk."

Wiggins pouted his lips in a disdainful grimace. "Yeah. Well, if I got to do all the police work here one of you guys might just as well learn how to make pictures. Look what I got."

He took out the negatives and prints he had brought from the office. "Here's your time-table, Murphy," he announced grandly, and as the other two bent closer to see he went on. "This is the picture I took of the party before anybody knew anything was wrong. I know it was about twelve, because the cathedral clock struck twelve while I was waiting down there in the courtyard, and when I went up Cynthia said I'd been kept waiting because they'd been having a meeting. Just before I shot the bunch I asked her how many there were. She said forty-nine Dis members and one guest. You can see the guest—she's Esther, in the middle of the front row in a white dress. And Cynthia said forty-nine others, see?"

They nodded.

"Well," announced Wiggins, "count the heads. There's forty-eight."

Murphy's fist banged the table. "Then that settles it, boys."

"You bet it does," Wiggins assured him. "Look. Parnell left Ghent all tied up at about eleven. He musta spent some time in the ballroom because some people saw him. Let's give him twenty minutes doing his stuff in here. That would give him time to get out to the pantry before the lights-out meeting, wouldn't it?"

They assented.

"Then I figure he got the knife while the room was dark, and the guy that did the killing came back in here while it was still dark, because he was here when I made the picture. Now it ain't possible that I left one figure off the end, because I made two pictures just in case one was blooey, and there's forty-eight devils in each of 'em."

Murphy had been counting heads with a thick forefinger. He looked up. "Pretty good work, boy," he said with rare generosity. "You better let me keep these plates."

"Sure." Wiggins found himself a cigarette and began to blow smoke rings with the nonchalance of the expert who really doesn't want to brag. "Something else you might like to know, Murph. Just a cute little bit of evidence." He eyed Murphy with a fine air of mystery. "I sort of looked through some old, old papers down in the files at the office, and I found out that our girlfriend Cynthia went and forgot one of her husbands."

"What's that?" Murphy demanded. "I thought as much. Anybody we know?"

"And how," said Mr. Wiggins with lordly assurance. "She forgot the first one. Roger Parnell."

Murphy started up, his blue eyes snapping. "I knew it," he raged, poking his cigar at Wade's face. "I knew that dame was fishy." He glared at Wiggins. "All right, me laddybuck, we'll see what she has to say. I'll get her myself."

Emitting an uncomplimentary monosyllable, he strode to the door. Wiggins trotted after him, and Wade followed. Murphy banged his way into the dining-room.

Cynthia and Arnold Ghent, chattering vivaciously, were the center of the group. They were all talking, with a bright artificial gaiety and determined little interpolations of laughter, except Esther Morse, who sat on a sofa at one side of the room, her forehead resting on her hands. As they entered, Con Conroy stopped in the middle of a drawling speech and threw a quizzical glance at Wade, and the police officers nearby snapped to rigid attention.

"Let everybody go home," said Murphy shortly to Matson. He looked at nobody else, as if saving his contacts with the others for a more fruitful time. "Give Valdon and Conroy a receipt for that junk you took off them and bring it to me in the other room. Then I want to see Mrs. Fontenay."

He stamped out again and took up his position by his table in the ballroom. Wade surveyed him with a grin, but said nothing. A moment later Matson came in with the black wallet he had taken from Conroy and laid it on the table.

"Have they gone?" Murphy demanded.

"They're going, sir."

"Fine. Send in that Fontenay female."

As Matson left, Murphy took out his badly bitten cigar and motioned vigorously toward Wade and Wiggins. "Now look here, you two. If I have to get rough with this dame you keep your faces shut, get me? This is business."

It was several minutes before Cynthia came in. She entered and walked up to them without a suggestion of fear or timidity in her manner, and her smile was graciously apologetic. She had utilized the delay to change her Dis robe for a pair of black velvet pajamas with trailing trousers and puffed sleeves, and her bright golden hair framed her face with ripples of such exquisite faultlessness that Wiggins suddenly felt for Lucy the involuntary reverence he paid to anyone who was particularly good at his job. In one hand Cynthia held a cigarette in a long jade holder, and in the other a highball; but nothing but a faint glassiness of her eyes betrayed the effect of the liquor she had been drinking all evening. Wiggins caught himself trying to calculate how much she must have had, and confirming his own earlier opinion that the trouble with Cynthia Fontenay was that she had always had too much of everything, so that now she was glassy inside and out, and he wondered if there was anything on earth that could get her really upset. Certainly she did not appear disturbed at the prospect of this interview. She was cool and ever so slightly patronizing as she accepted the chair Wade offered her, and said smilingly to Murphy,

"I'm so sorry I kept you waiting, captain. But I had to speed the parting guests." She sipped her drink and looked archly at him across the rim of the glass. "And even you must agree, Captain Murphy, that it has been a *very* trying party."

"Yes, ma'am, I suppose it has." Murphy's voice was bland, but there was menace in his eyes. "There's just a few things I want to talk over with you, ma'am."

"Certainly," said Cynthia. "Can't I offer you a drink first? There's some whiskey on the stand in the corner."

"No, that's all right. I wanted to ask you—"

"Oh, just a minute," she interrupted pleasantly. "I suppose I ought to tell you that we decided outside that since Mr. Parnell was not a member of Dis, and since we're sure he couldn't have been killed by anyone who was a member of Dis, we would have the Dis parade anyhow tomorrow." She smiled. "The floats are all ready, and it seems a shame to disturb the order of Mardi Gras. Nothing has ever interrupted a Mardi Gras program except the World War, you know, and this isn't as serious as that. We decided, you see," she added as though explaining as politely as possible something he could not be expected to understand, "that Mr. Parnell was probably killed by some prowler who climbed into the closet to steal the spoons. I hope you aren't shocked, Captain Murphy."

"No, Mrs. Fontenay, I'm not shocked." Murphy shook his head. "But I guess I'm just a little bit old-fashioned. There's some things I don't get about the world in general as it's being run today, but a cop's life is made up of plenty of things he don't understand. He gets used to not being shocked at anything." He paused, and watched her delicately tasting her drink.

Cynthia's smile had not altered. "Then you don't think—"

"I ain't thinking," said Murphy rudely. "It ain't any of my business about your parade. I'm just concerned right now with you."

"With me?" Her thin arched eyebrows lifted inquiringly. "Do I shock you?"

Murphy folded his big hands on the table in front of him and looked at her with a straight hard stare. "Mrs. Fontenay," he said, "I've seen all kinds of women and I've seen them do all kinds of things. But never in my life have I seen the widow of a man who'd just been murdered carry on like you do."

Cynthia had put down her glass with a rattle before his sentence was ended. For a moment she said nothing. She simply stared at him. Her whole expression had changed; it was like what happens when a painter removes the false face that has been laid on over the real portrait on a canvas. The gay banter of her look had become hard, bitter, furious; her voice when she spoke rasped like a rusty wire.

"Damn you!" she said. "Why didn't you tell me you knew?"

Murphy's jaw had set grimly. His thick forefinger pointed at her in inexorable challenge.

"Mrs. Roger Parnell," he said, "who killed your husband?"

Cynthia's hands gripped the sides of the little table as though she would have liked to feel it break. She began to laugh. "Mrs. Parnell!" she repeated. She laughed as though she found the name bitterly ridiculous. "Are you trying to make me do an Enoch Arden?" She laughed and laughed. "Because you can't, you know. That marriage was annulled. I was too young. I'll show you the papers if you don't believe it—I've got them somewhere."

"Who killed your husband?" Murphy demanded.

"I don't know!" she sprang up. She was almost screaming. "I didn't kill him, and I can't be frightened into saying I did by any damn fool of a half-witted cop. You've found out I was married to him—all right, I was. But I didn't kill him. Do you hear me?—I didn't kill him."

"Sit down," barked Murphy.

She did not move. She looked down at him, one corner of her mouth curling in angry contempt.

Murphy pushed back his chair and stood up. "Mrs. Parnell," he exclaimed, "you're a hard and unchastened woman. You've lied to me tonight, lied and lied. Now I'm going to give you one chance to tell the truth. I want it and I'm going to get. Get it out of you here, right now. Who killed Roger Parnell?"

"You go to hell," said Cynthia.

For an instant she stood quite still. Then, suddenly, she crumpled up into her chair, her head on her out-crossed arms, sobbing. Her words came brokenly, muffled and hardly understandable, between her sobs.

"What in God's name are you trying to do to me?—I haven't done anything!—Do you want me—to tear myself—up—into little pieces—for you? *Why* don't you let me alone?"

The rest was disjointed syllables. Wade silently got up and tiptoed around the table to where Murphy was still standing, looking down at Cynthia's bent golden head.

"Let me talk to her," said Wade in a low voice.

Murphy hesitated. He looked down at Cynthia's quivering shoulders. "Think you can do any good?" he asked. "Me, now, I'm in favor of sweating it out of her here and now."

"I'm afraid," Wade demurred in a half-whisper, "that won't get you anywhere. Let me try."

Murphy looked down at Cynthia again, and across at Wiggins. Wiggins nodded vigorously. Wiggins had had enough experience of Wade's police work to feel assured that Wade was a more adequate questioner than Murphy in a situation of this sort. Murphy looked back at Wade, and yielded.

"Okay," he said briefly, and beckoned to Wiggins. They went to the far end of the room, behind Cynthia's back, and sat down. Wade slipped over to the buffet and got a decanter of whiskey. He waited till Cynthia's wild sobs had quieted.

"Mrs. Fontenay," he said.

She looked up.

"Where's that idiot policeman?" she asked.

"He's here, but he won't bother you now." Wade poured out a drink. "Take this. I think it will help you."

She drank it gratefully. "Thank you," she said. Then, "Can I go now?" She spoke like a whipped child.

"I'm afraid you can't, not yet." Wade sat down. "That is, of course you can if you want to, but I think you'd prefer to stay and talk to me if you knew what it meant to be taken down to police headquarters for questioning." As she started to retort he shook his head to enjoin silence. "Mrs. Fontenay," he said, "I don't want to threaten you, but that's what will happen in the morning if you won't talk to me tonight."

Cynthia wiped her eyes and looked down at the flimsy little handkerchief in her hand.

"But why do they torment me so?" she exclaimed. "I didn't kill him."

"But you didn't tell the truth about him," Wade reminded her.

"No." She poured another drink. "I've been a fool all my life," she said wearily. "I've done a lot of silly things, but I've never killed anybody. Why should I?"

"Mrs. Fontenay," said Wade, "why didn't you tell us you'd been married to Parnell?"

She swallowed the drink. It seemed to restore her confidence. She smiled. "Why, because I didn't want you to know. It wasn't any of your business."

He smiled back. "I'm afraid it is, now. You see, when you told us you'd been married only twice, it made it pretty obvious that there was a good reason why you wanted us to think Parnell was only a casual acquaintance of yours. Why were you afraid to tell us you had been married to him?"

"Because he'd just been murdered," said Cynthia. "I think that's a fairly good reason. And because—" she hesitated, and flecked a speck of dust off the black velvet across her lap—"because I told him once I wished I could kill him. But that was a long time ago."

Wade leaned nearer, and spoke earnestly to her. "Won't you tell me about it now? Believe me, it's got to come."

"He's dead," she said in a low, tired voice. "He can't hurt anybody any more. I think if the police knew how many people he had hurt—perhaps they wouldn't say killing him was such a crime."

"Don't you think," he urged, "that you might let the district attorney decide that? The district attorney is a very fine man, Mrs. Fontenay. He has been my most intimate friend for a good many years."

Cynthia was looking down. "What do you want me to tell you?"

"All you know about Roger Parnell," he answered.

"I don't know all about him," she said after a pause. "But I do know so much that I can't be very sorry he's dead." She stopped, and he did not interrupt her. After a moment she looked straight up at him.

"I met him when I went to college in Chicago," she said. "I was sixteen years old. I was what they used to call boy-crazy. I was forever slipping out for dates and dancing all night and cutting classes to sleep the next morning and making a general little idiot of myself, the way some girls do when they're first away from home. Roger was a junior. He was good-looking and a beautiful dancer. I thought he was marvelous. My parents were wintering in the South. Roger and I were both invited to a house-party for the Christmas holidays. He asked me to drive up from college in his car. We stopped on the way and got married and spent the holidays at a hotel in Evanston."

He nodded, sympathetically. "I understand. One of those things that kids do when they're too young to be turned loose, and spend the rest of their lives being sorry for."

"It was just that." Cynthia tied a knot in the corner of her damp little handkerchief. "Of course I thought then it was one of those grand romances I'd read about. He told me not to say anything about it, and I didn't, because I knew how angry my parents would be. I planned to keep it a secret till I was eighteen or so, and then get married all over again—a big beautiful church wedding with bridesmaids and ushers and lilies and a table full of presents for guests to gasp at—oh, I was such a fool!"

For an instant it looked as if she would break down again. He was relieved when she steadied herself and went on.

"It didn't take me very long to find it out," she said. Then she stopped abruptly.

"What do you mean?" he asked her at length, as gently as he could.

"Money," said Cynthia briefly. She looked back at him. "My parents weren't precisely rich, but father had made a lot of money—it was during the war, and prices were high—and I had everything I wanted. I knew Roger didn't have anything, and at first I thought it was very romantic to write home for money and give it to him. It got tiresome after awhile, but I might have gone on for a long time without realizing that that was why he had married me, if something hadn't happened in the spring. Roger was asked to leave college because he was found to have been blackmailing the wife of one of the businessmen in town. It was pretty bad.

"I stayed on at college, praying nobody would find out about us, until my father appeared one day and took me home. Roger had gone to him—father was back from Florida by that time—and had told mother and father that he was their son-in-law and that it was up to them to get him out of this mess. Father paid him to get out of the way and then had the marriage annulled because I was under age."

She smiled wanly. "I don't suppose the rest of my biography is of any special interest to you. I told Captain Murphy the truth about the other two men I'd married. They haven't anything to do with this."

"What about Parnell's coming to New Orleans?" Wade asked her. "Why was that?"

"I don't know. I suppose because he'd made friends with Fritz Valdon, and Valdon is so powerful here. When he found I was here he came and wanted to borrow some money. I told him I'd let him have it if he'd never tell anybody I'd been married to him. It was with my capital that he started the Red Cat."

"Did you share the profits there?"

Cynthia hesitated. "Yes," she said finally, then with a snatch of defiance, "That's probably illegal and all that sort of thing, but one must do something! Money hasn't been easy to get in the past year or two. I'm not immune from the depression."

"That's all right," he assured her. "I think the district attorney is going to be more interested in Parnell's murder than anything else now. Is there anything more we ought to know?"

"I think maybe there is," she said after a moment.

"I'm sure Roger wasn't a member of Dis, because he asked me to get him in and I refused. I told Fritz Valdon I didn't want him in, and Fritz said he was sure he hadn't a chance. That was just before Fritz and Roger split. Fritz told me later he couldn't stand the things that were being said about controlled wheels at the Red Cat. Things seemed to be tightening around Roger. He asked me to do him a favor. He said Esther Morse had lost a lot of money in a private game and that she had promised the house manager to pay him off in installments. He had told Esther she could leave the money with me, and Roger asked me to give it to him instead of to the house manager."

"And you let her leave it with you?"

"Yes. It was a lot of money. She gave me eighteen thousand dollars in small payments, and last night she came to me with ten thousand more. Of course I know Esther can afford to lose that much, but all the same it seems a lot for a child like her to lose in a gambling game. Roger wanted to come to the Dis ball tonight and get the money, and I told him he couldn't. I said he could send somebody else. When he said he knew no one who was a member of Dis, I violated a rule and told him Arnold Ghent was a member. I told him he would have to arrange his own transaction."

"And you gave the money—" Wade began, and she finished,

"—to Parnell, thinking he was Arnold Ghent. He came up to me and slipped a typewritten note into my hand. It just said 'I'm Arnold Ghent. Have you got a package for me to take to Parnell?' I told him I'd pass it to him when the lights went out."

"And you did?"

"Yes. There was a lighted devil's head in one corner, and by the glow from that I made out the number on his suit and passed him the money."

Cynthia smiled slowly. "Don't you see the point I'm making?" she asked.

Suddenly Wade glanced at the black wallet lying on the table. Their eyes met.

"Why, yes," said Cynthia. "I saw the policeman taking ten thousand dollars from Con Conroy. Why don't you ask him where he got it?"

Wade nodded. "Thank you," he said. "I will." He considered a moment. "Do you really think Esther lost twenty-eight thousand dollars gambling at the Red Cat? She doesn't look like the sort of girl who'd go there at all."

Cynthia drew a long breath. "I don't know, Mr. Wade. All I can tell you is that after the ceremony, when Esther asked me if I had sent the money to Roger, she said 'I loathe myself, Cynthia, every time I do this. Thank God tonight is the last time.' About that time Lucy came and called me into the china-closet."

"And that's all?"

She shook her head. "No, Mr. Wade. That's not all, but you know the rest. Roger Parnell is dead. And I suppose," she added bitterly, "that before long you'll see to it that I wish I were."

CHAPTER THIRTEEN

MURPHY sat facing Con Conroy in a cubbyhole on the second floor of police headquarters. It was a dark little place, one of a succession of cubbyholes used for similar purposes, with lights ingeniously arranged so that the policeman behind the desk sat in shadow, while the light blazed full upon the person facing him. But no blaze of light could be called revealing when it illumined the person of Fritz Valdon's secretary. For the expression of Con Conroy, as usual, revealed precisely nothing.

Wade, who occupied a chair near the door, within the shadow that blurred the features of Murphy, watched Conroy and the captain with interest tinged with a shade of involuntary amusement. His association with Murphy as the district attorney's unofficial assistant in several crime cases had given him respect for the lumbering but rarely foolish processes of Murphy's reasoning, but he had his doubts about the efficacy of Murphy's methods when matched with the placid subtleties of Mr. Conroy. He waited.

Con Conroy leaned back in the big oak chair and smiled. It was not a taunting smile. It was simply a pleasant, good-humored smile, the smile with which one man might invite another to have a cigarette or a drink. His cherubic face was serene, and his round china-blue eyes met Murphy's with blank cheerfulness.

"You've no right to expect me to answer that question, Captain Murphy," he said. He said it with the same gentle politeness with which he had agreed to come to police headquarters to talk things over.

"Maybe you're right, my boy." Murphy was dangerously genial. "But unless you answer it here, I'm going to push this and force your going to trial."

Conroy's blue eyes did not shift, and his smile did not alter.

"Meaning," he said mildly, "that I'm to take the fall."

Murphy nodded, poking the ashy end of his cigar at a burned match in the ash-tray. "Just that, Conroy."

Conroy's chubby forefinger pushed back a vagrant lock of his blond hair. He gave a little sigh of resignation.

"You're going to feel very foolish about this, captain," he observed, "but I suppose you're used to that."

"I'm used to being told that I'll feel foolish, boy," Murphy answered. He laughed, a low, appreciative chuckle.

Conroy gave an expressive lift of his golden eyebrows, and got up. "Well, I've got to be going." His fingers tapped a long slow yawn. "It's past my bed-time," he explained with a glance at Wade.

Murphy shook his head. There were determination and a suggestion of regret in his manner. "No, Conroy," he said, "don't go yet." He gave Conroy a bit of a smile. "You can't do it that way," he added. "You've got to come through." His voice rose. "I'm going all the way on this thing, and I don't give a damn if it's Valdon or yourself that's hurt. Now answer me. *Where* did you get that money?"

"I won it in a dice game," said Conroy.

His voice was patient, almost sweet. He stood with one hand on the back of his chair, smiling at Wade. The fingers of his other hand smothered another yawn. Wade observed irrelevantly that there were dimples where the knuckles ought to be.

"All right, then," snapped Murphy. "So that's your story." He pressed a black buzzer on his desk. "We'll see what we have to do with you in just a minute."

A night orderly came in, and Murphy motioned to him with a crook of his blunt forefinger. "Bring her in," he ordered.

As Murphy sat back, Wade stepped over to Conroy, who still stood leaning on the back of his chair.

"This is bad medicine coming up, Conroy," Wade advised in a low tone. "Murphy'll be more decent about this thing if you'll tell him beforehand where that money came from."

Murphy got up and walked to the door to wait for the next arrival. Conroy studied his broad back.

"I don't like him well enough to tell him," he answered coolly.

"What's the matter?"

Conroy shrugged. "He's likely to put a monkey wrench in the works if he gets half smart."

"Meaning?" Wade was puzzled.

"That what he doesn't know may not hurt anybody."

Wade shook his head. "I'm still in the dark."

Conroy tossed him a smile that had an odd suggestion of tantalizing friendliness, and just then Murphy turned around. The door had opened. Esther Morse came in.

She wore a dark blue hat and a big coat of Persian lamb, and her face looked small and white above the great collar. As the orderly closed the door behind her she stood for an instant just across the threshold looking at Wade and Conroy and Murphy, with a look that was half pleading and half defiant. Murphy offered her a chair. "Thank you," Esther said in a low voice, and sat down.

For a moment Murphy watched her without speaking. Esther waited quietly, one hand smoothing down the fur of the tiny muff she carried.

Wade looked at her with sympathetic interest. In the flowing white costume she had worn at the Dis ball, with her hair loose on her shoulders and the wreath of poppies above her forehead, she had looked, not like Persephone, but like a child dressed up for a party. But now there was an odd suggestion of maturity about her, as though in putting on street clothes she had put on a new courage. She slipped her other hand out of her muff, threw back her coat and addressed Murphy in a clear, steady young voice.

"What did you want to see me about, Captain Murphy?"

Murphy came directly to the point. "Miss Morse, what denomination were the bills making up the ten thousand dollars you paid Mrs. Fontenay tonight?"

Esther started. Her hands slipped inside the muff again, as though she were afraid they might tremble.

"Why—they—" her voice steadied again. "Who told you I gave ten thousand dollars to Mrs. Fontenay?" she asked.

"We know about that," Murphy told her stolidly. "What we want to know is, what denomination were the bills?"

Esther looked down. Wade could see a convulsive little rumpling of the muff, as though the hands inside it had clenched.

"Ten one-thousand dollar bills," she answered.

"Now, Conroy—" Murphy wheeled upon him—"where did you get them?"

Conroy stood watching Esther, intently, as though his mind was busy with a problem of his own. He did not answer.

"Where did you get that money, Conroy?" Murphy repeated.

"I beat a dice game," said Conroy. He looked directly at Murphy. "A man's dice game," he said. "There were no women in it."

Murphy gave vent to something as near a snort as a controlled explosion of temper ever gets to be.

"All right," he jerked out. "Let it go at that." He pressed the buzzer on his desk. The orderly came in.

"Take this guy to the Ninth Precinct," Murphy directed shortly. "Hold him as a dangerous and suspicious character. Don't let anybody get to him if you have to dig a hole to hide him in."

Esther bit her lip. One of her small gloved hands went up and twisted a point of her collar. She said nothing.

Conroy smiled tolerantly. He picked up his hat and went toward the door. As he passed Esther's chair he winked at her broadly. She frowned, as if she did not understand.

"I had a nice little thingamajig all fixed up, Miss Morse," Conroy said to her pleasantly, "and you made it look as if I were wrong. Now I know it's right." She smiled, a little puzzled smile that tried to be friendly, and Conroy turned to Murphy. "Have your little party, captain," he added with smooth good-nature. "Maybe you don't know it, but you've done me a big favor by asking me here. I may do as much for you some day." He followed the orderly, and his eyes fell on Wade, who was standing by the door.

He paused a minute. "Come and see me sometime, Wade," he said distinctly, and as their eyes met Wade understood that the summons was real.

"Fine," he answered, smiling. "Tea is four-ish, I suppose?"

"Four-ish," Conroy nodded. "That will be excellent."

Murphy had watched them without comment.

"Have fun while you can, Conroy," he advised with a grim smile. And then to the policeman the orderly had summoned, "Take him away, and don't let them book him."

Conroy smiled back, but his smile was not grim. "Come on, hots," he invited the officer. "Let's see what kind of a place I'm to have for my Mardi Gras headquarters."

They went out, and Murphy sat down again behind his desk. He grinned contentedly at Wade, and Wade grinned back, wondering how a night at the Ninth was going to affect the placid Mr. Conroy.

The Ninth Precinct station house was an old one, and a favorite place for stowing away recalcitrant suspects, who were charged, as Conroy had been, with being dangerous and suspicious characters—a charge better known as 1436. Ordinance 1436 was the police loop-hole for men who could be proved to have committed no particular crime but who looked ready to commit one as soon as circumstances made it possible, or who the police felt sure had committed a crime but against whom nothing could be adduced as evidence. Local members of the half-world called a night at the Ninth "taking the cure." As a cure it was pretty effective, for unless one was already inured to crime and its penalties a night in the dripping, rat-ridden, unlighted depths of the old station cells caused one to think twice before entering upon any fresh transgressions; and even the toughest of gangsters had been known to confess with teary appeals for mercy after two days on sparse fare among the rats.

"Think he'll like it?" Murphy asked Wade with a wink.

Wade glanced meaningly at Esther, who was again looking down at her muff.

"It's pretty medieval," he said smiling. "But it ought to make him talk."

"Well, ain't that what we want?" Murphy demanded. He returned his attention to Esther. "And now, young lady, I want the truth from you. What about that money?"

Esther sat up as if she had been struck. "I gave it to Mrs. Fontenay," she said stiffly. "I don't know how that man got it."

"What did you give it to Mrs. Fontenay for?" Murphy persisted.

Esther was silent.

"Now look here, Miss Morse," said Murphy, and his manner was as persuasive as he could make it. "We don't want to get you into any trouble undeserved. You play fair with us, and we'll play fair with you. I mean it. But we've got to have the truth."

Esther hesitated. She looked at Wade, as if taking courage from the fact that he was not in uniform. "I'll tell you—all I can," she said breathlessly. "I've been giving it to him—to Mr. Parnell—for about four months.

He promised me tonight would be the last time. He said he was leaving town tomorrow and wasn't ever coming back. I brought the money to Cynthia. She said she would give it to him."

"Why were you paying Parnell?" Murphy asked.

Esther shook her head.

Wade moved his chair a bit nearer hers. "Miss Morse," he said quietly, "You must understand that we don't like to do this. But before we can look for the murderer of Roger Parnell, we must have all the facts we can get about his life. We're asking you for a statement that may involve personal embarrassment for you, but believe me, what you say here will be kept as confidential as it is possible to keep it. Won't you tell us?"

Esther's dark eyes met his. "Mr. Wade," she said with a faint smile, "if this was something I could have asked the police to protect me from, do you suppose I'd have paid money to that man?"

"But he is dead," Wade urged her. "He can't hurt you now."

"No, Mr. Wade, he can't." Her voice was low and steady. "But you can."

The quiet suggestion of tragedy in her answer made him wince. He wished it was possible for him to tell her how deeply his sympathy had gone out to her, and how much he would have liked to shield her from the terror she was accepting so bravely. He asked his next question as gently as he could.

"Then it was blackmail?"

"Yes," said Esther. Suddenly she leaned toward him, her hands stretched out to him in desperate appeal. "Please don't let them know that!" she cried. "He promised me he would tell Cynthia it was a gambling debt. I don't think she believed it, but she pretended she did—it's easier that way." She twisted her fingers together as though the words were wrenched from her with dreadful pain. "I—I've got a lot of pride," she whispered, "in spite of the things I've let happen to me."

Suddenly Wade remembered Dick—Dick's thin, sensitive face, with its overlaid look of bitterness. He thought how like Esther's that expression was. Impulsively he stood up and leaned over her chair, shutting out Murphy's accusing presence from her eyes.

"How old are you, Esther?" he asked gently.

"Nineteen."

Wade set his jaw. This was difficult, but it had to come. He had not realized how difficult it was going to be till his mind began to form the question. He looked down at Esther, and saw her against the incongruous awfulness of her surroundings—a young girl fresh from school and coming-out parties, here in police headquarters at four o'clock in the morning, despairingly defending herself with the stern barricade of her innocence. He felt himself cruel, almost inhuman, to be the instrument that would strip her of her last defense. But he knew also that Murphy's hands would be less tender than his.

"Esther," he said, and did not realize till after he had spoken that he was calling her by her first name, "you've got to believe me when I say this. We don't want to create a new tragedy for you. You are very young, and we know that you might be helpless before the machinations of a man like Roger Parnell. We know that he might drive you to absolute desperation. If you should tell us now that he had been blackmailing you till you could endure it no longer, and that you killed him, I'm not even sure the district attorney would make you stand trial. But before we can stop, we've got to know why."

He paused. Esther was listening with a heartbreaking intensity that almost unnerved him. She said nothing.

Wade went on. "In asking you why you were paying blackmail to Parnell, Captain Murphy is only doing what you and the rest of the decent people in town pay him to do. So don't think I'm being too cruel when I ask you—was Parnell blackmailing you because of something he knew about Dick Barron?"

Esther started up. Her hands gripped the arms of her chair. She stared at him from eyes that were dilated with anger and terror. For an instant he thought she was going to faint, and he had put out an arm to catch her if she fell; but after the shock of the first instant was over she slowly stood up, and faced him with a challenge that dared him to go further.

"I don't know what you hoped I would say to that," she exclaimed scornfully, "but I'm not going to say it, because I shan't answer." She turned away. "Are you going to arrest me?"

Murphy pushed back his chair and came quickly around the desk to her. "Of course not, macushla. You can go home now."

"Oh—thank you!" she exclaimed. "Thank you so much."

"Did someone come with you?" Wade asked hastily. "You won't have to go alone?"

She looked up at him with an odd expression. "I came alone," she answered. "You don't think I want Uncle Claude to know I'm being dragged down to police headquarters, do you? I have my car."

"I'll send one of the boys along to take care of you," Murphy offered. "Just come with me."

He went out with her. Wade sat down wearily. He was glad that much, at least, was over.

CHAPTER FOURTEEN

"MARK Oliver shot."

Wade settled back against the leather seat of his taxi and tried to resign himself to the slow maneuvering of the driver.

This *was* a story—Mark Oliver, the hermit toy manufacturer, shot in his own house after leaving the Dis ball. Wade did not know how serious the wound was, but as the car backed and turned on the uneven road in front of the Ninth Precinct station, he surmised that a word or two from him now would make Oliver amply able to talk.

He looked over his shoulder at the gloomy station-house, black against the pink dawn, where he had gone to visit Con Conroy shortly before the news of Oliver's injury had reached the police. The officers at the Ninth had taken Murphy at his word, and had shown Conroy no courtesy because his clothes were brushed and his English good, but had summarily tucked him away in a pitch-black cell with damp crawling walls. Conroy had greeted Wade with his habitual cheerfulness and had suggested that their talk be brief, "because," he had said, "I'm going to fool that red-necked so-and-so Murphy."

Wade had looked around the cell by the light of a candle he had been permitted to bring with him. He grinned at Conroy with undisguised admiration.

"Sit down?" that gentleman offered, indicating the hammock swung along one side of the wall, which was the cell's only furniture.

Wade took a glance at the walls and shook his head. "No thanks."

Conroy laughed placidly. "I suppose you're right. That is, for yourself. As for me, I'll sit down. You see, I'm going to sleep here."

Wade laughed in spite of himself. "I doubt it," he said.

"Young man," said Mr. Conroy, "I've slept in a great many places. Not of my own accord, as I'm not here of my own accord. But the point is, I've slept. And I shall sleep here. Also, as I observed before, it is past my bedtime. Therefore your visit must be brief."

"I'll go with pleasure," Wade assured him. "But what did you want to tell me?"

Conroy got up and came a step closer. His ironically meek blue eyes studied Wade.

"I only wanted to suggest, in my humble way," he said, "that it might be wise for you to pay some attention to Oliver. The kind old gentleman who makes the toys."

"Oliver?" Wade called up a mental picture of Oliver's irascible but apparently harmless manner. "Why?"

"Because," said Conroy smiling, "a little bird is whispering to you that before I had that ten grand—Oliver had it."

Wade started to exclaim, but Conroy shook his head. "Good night," he waved smiling. "I shall see you again. Good night."

Wade saw that his dismissal was final. He set the candle down on the floor. "All right, and thank you. I'm going to leave the candle. You aren't supposed to have it, but we'll say I forgot and left it here."

"Thank you," said Conroy politely. "By the way, nothing of this to Murphy. He might mess up something that's on the way."

Wade agreed and went out. His heart was thumping. Oliver—of all men. He wondered how far the enigmatical Mr. Conroy could be trusted. At any rate, he planned to go out to Metairie and interrupt Mr. Oliver's slumbers.

He had followed the doorman who had come with him to Conroy's cell block and they had gone up to the sergeant's room. The sergeant had met them at the door.

"Just going down to get you, Mr. Wade," he had exclaimed. "Look what came over the teletype."

Wade snatched the paper from his hand and read the report.

"Mark Oliver, 7915 Metairie Lane, shot and wounded at about 4:20 this a.m. All-station message to pick up any suspicious characters, in Metairie neighborhood especially, for questioning."

Wade grinned to himself now as the cab bounced along the side streets. Wiggins, he knew, had gone to sleep on a table in the photographers' room at the *Creole* office, and Murphy was already at home in bed. As the cab bore him along Tulane Avenue toward the emergency entrance of Charity Hospital he debated whether to call Wiggins at once or to let the picture wait till later. But he rather enjoyed the prospect of razzing his little cameraman for being asleep while things were going on, so ordering the cab to wait he swung through the side entrance of the hospital.

Passing an orderly in the ambulance driveway, he hurried inside. A nun in a blue habit and a broad white coif was talking to the registry clerk, and a brace of patrolmen from headquarters waited in the anteroom. Wade touched his hat.

"Hello, Sister Lucille. How's everything?"

Sister Lucille started and then smiled. "Oh, Mr. Wade. We haven't had you here in a long time. What are you doing up so early in the morning?"

"Usual thing. Fellow named Oliver this time. Shot. Where is he?"

"Oh, and sure I thought that would be the one!" Sister Lucille laughed. "He's out by the door, talking to a friend of yours. Not badly hurt."

Just then a bright, bright light flashed on and off, and Wade heard the scrape of shoes on concrete and the soothing voice of Wiggins.

"'Stoo bad for a fact, Mr. Oliver, but you're plenty lucky."

Wade grinned and hurried outside. By the door he saw Mark Oliver, his head dressed in a big bandage, and Wiggins happily putting up his plates. Wiggins looked up with surprise.

"Hi, big boy, where you been? You sure were a time getting here. Pictures all made. You know Mr. Oliver—well, the bogey man tried to get him with a roscoe and he wound up here seein' the birdie."

Oliver was wiping his watery eyes and replacing his thick-lensed glasses. He smiled weakly.

"Yes, Mr. Wade, a close call it was, a mighty close call."

Wade grinningly acquiesced Wiggins' victory and spoke to Oliver. "That so? It's too bad. Hurt much?" Oliver stepped under the doorway light and pointed to the bandage running from the back of his neck up the crown of his head. "Just nicked me," he said, in what was meant to be an offhand manner, "just nicked me. A few inches more, and I suppose it would have been all over. But as it was, just a nick."

Wade was sympathetic. Wiggins, on his knees by his camera, rattled off details. "Got it in the neck," he began, slipping in a plate. "The slug took an upward course and just about creased him. No concussion, slight contusion marking path of bullet. Report and treatment by Dr. Finch. How's that, pal?"

"Fine. Where's Murphy?"

"He ripped his way outa his nightshirt and I guess he'll be along in a minute. The flatfoots said we'd better wait for him." He looked up at Oliver. "You know, the cops say Murphy thought at first you were killed."

"It was close, young man." Oliver was mopping his brow and dabbing at his eyes. "Very close."

"Sure, but they tell me you put up a great fight." Wiggins scrambled to his feet and turned to Wade. "Our friend here, he dug out a gun from under his pillow and chased the other guy with five chunks of lead. That takes tonic—" he turned an approving eye on Oliver—"but it's too bad you didn't have your glasses on. You mighta got some place with all that blooie-blooie."

Oliver cleared his throat. "I'm afraid I only broke a window or two. I—well, I must admit I was quite nervous."

"Yeah, sure—who wouldn't be?" Wiggins agreed knowingly. "You there in the middle of the room pumping that roscoe of yours and the back of your head playing Niagara Falls with claret. Say—" he looked Oliver over with fresh approbation—"if it hadda been me, I'da stayed right on the floor after the first brodie."

Oliver gave a cackling little laugh. Wade said nothing. He had watched Oliver thoughtfully, as the nervous little man kept mopping his forehead and pushing back his glasses to dab at his red-rimmed eyes, a perfect picture of a bashful man ill at ease because circumstances had made him a cynosure. Wade was relieved to observe Murphy coming down the ambulance drive.

"What's all this?" Murphy demanded energetically. "How d'you feel, Mr. Oliver?"

"All right, captain, all right, quite all right," Oliver assured him. "Just a bit—er—shaken up, of course. Shall we—shall we go indoors?"

"Sure." Murphy pushed back the door. He was as brisk as though being grabbed out of bed after an hour's nap was part of his health program. Swinging across the threshold he beckoned to Sister Lucille.

"Bring this gentleman a bit of brandy, sister, if you'll be so good. And let us use one of your offices."

The good sister smiled. "You can go in here, captain."

She led them into an office on the side of the emergency corridor, and they sat down by the white table. Murphy pushed aside several rolls of gauze and got to business.

"Now, Mr. Oliver, what the devil's been happening?" Oliver cleared his throat and wiped his eyes. "It was all quite unexpected, captain," he started.

"Sure, sure." Murphy glanced up as Sister Lucille came in with a bottle of brandy. "Thanks, sister. I hope we won't trouble you again. Here, Mr. Oliver." He poured Oliver a drink, and Wiggins reached for the bottle. He made a gesture to Wade, who shook his head, and Wiggins tilted the bottle back for a big swallow.

"Hey," roared Murphy, "that's for the sick."

Wiggins grinned. "Boy, but you're a great doctor, Murph. Nobody but you and me knows how sick I am."

Murphy grinned back, in spite of himself. Then turning to Oliver, "You feeling better now?"

"Quite all right, captain."

"Then tell us what happened."

Out came the handkerchief and up went the glasses. Wiggins made a face and cleared his throat. "I got ants from this ape," he whispered to Wade.

"After you told us we might leave Mrs. Fontenay's house," Oliver had started, "I got a cab and drove to Metairie."

"Direct?"

"Well, no. There were several of us in the cab, and we stopped at Mr. Valdon's house to have a drink with him. I got to my house." He stopped and looked around and coughed. "I'm afraid I'm not telling this very well." He cleared his throat, wiped his forehead and fitted his glasses again. "Perhaps I had better begin over."

Wiggins sighed. Wade and Murphy waited attentively.

"After you released us, we all telephoned for taxicabs and went down to the front gate. Mr. Valdon invited us all to stop at his house for a drink. Mr. Ghent said he would not be able to come, and Mrs. Hildreth also refused. When the cabs came, she and Mr. Ghent took one. He had offered to see her home. Miss Morse—I believe it was Miss Morse—yes, I am sure—Miss Morse also refused, and took a taxicab alone. She declined our offers to escort her, though we objected to a young lady's going home alone at that hour. So the other two of us went off. Mr. Valdon and I."

"What about Dick Barron?" asked Wade.

"O yes, Mr. Barron. He was with us. I forgot to mention him." Oliver paused. Wiggins took out his own handkerchief and wiped his forehead.

Oliver rubbed his handkerchief between his hands and cleared his throat. "Yes, Mr. Barron went with us. But he asked to be let out at Canal Street. Mr. Valdon and I went on to Mr. Valdon's house."

Wiggins reached over and lifted the brandy bottle. He threw an expressive glance at Wade, and took a drink. Oliver coughed.

"I—I am afraid I am extremely nervous. Could I—could I have the privilege of making a statement in the morning?"

"Are you going to stay here all day?" Murphy asked. "In the hospital, I mean?"

Oliver shook his bandaged head. "I'd rather not. I'm not really hurt— just distraught. A little weak, perhaps."

"Then you'll have to make the statement now," Murphy ruled.

Wiggins shoved the bottle toward him. "Take another shot of Murphy's Famous Remedy," he advised. "You might feel better."

Oliver took a drink eagerly. "Very well, then I'll be as brief as I can. I must have left Mr. Valdon's house about three-thirty. I went home. I went immediately to my room to prepare for bed. The running water in the bathroom might have made it impossible for me to hear anyone enter the room; at any rate, I walked into the bedroom from the bath drying my face. My glasses were on a bathroom shelf."

Wade and Murphy sat as still as mummies.

"I was fully dressed." said Oliver, "except that I had taken off my Dis robe and my shirt. When I reached the side of the bed I stooped to feel for my slippers, which I knew were usually placed there." He paused and explained parenthetically, "My eyesight is very bad, you know. Without my glasses I am seriously handicapped. As I bent over I heard a report behind me and felt a stab and a burning sensation at the back of my head. The force was not great, but I fell to the floor."

He brought out the ubiquitous handkerchief. "The bed was between me and my attacker," he went on. "I could not see him. I slid my hand under the pillow for a gun. I always sleep with a gun there—the house is some distance from any other house, you know, and I live alone."

He took another drink of brandy. "On the other side of my bedroom are three French windows that open on a balcony. They were closed. I fired in the direction of the windows, and I heard sounds as if someone were running along the tiled porch. I hurried out, and could see a figure, very dimly. I emptied my gun at it.

"Then a neighbor came. I had tried to stop the flow of blood with a towel. My neighbor, Mr. Dwight, got my car and drove me here. We told a policeman about the affair when we got into town. Mr. Dwight went back to the house with him and two other officers."

Out came the handkerchief and up popped Wiggins with the proffered bottle. Oliver made use of both.

"You couldn't see this fellow?" Murphy asked.

"No. That is, I could make out some sort of moving outline in the dark. My eyesight, you know."

"Could it have been a woman?" suggested Wade.

"Possibly. My impression is that the figure was taller than the average woman, but I could not swear to it."

Wade reached for his hat, which he had hung on the back of his chair. "Well, you're to be congratulated on a narrow escape, Mr. Oliver. If it hadn't been for the slippers, I'm afraid you'd have been done for." As Oliver nodded and mopped his brow Wade gave Murphy a significant wink. "Captain," he said, "if Mr. Oliver wants to go home now, I'll take him."

Murphy quickly smoothed off his look of surprise. "All right," he agreed, "that's good of you. What about keeping a man at the house for the rest of the night, Mr. Oliver?"

"Just as you say, certainly, captain. But I might just as well be alone." He smiled wanly. "You see, Captain Murphy, if I'd had my glasses on I'd not have missed. Pistol shooting is rather a hobby of mine."

Murphy walked to the door with him. Wiggins yanked at Wade's coat-tails and jerked him back.

"Hey," he whispered, "I see you give Murph the office. What's up?"

Wade lifted a cautioning finger. "I'll meet you at the office about noon, Wiggins," he said clearly. "I'm going home right after I deliver Mr. Oliver, and catch some sleep."

At the door, Murphy was asking Oliver if he had any idea why anyone should want to kill him. Oliver was emphatic in his answer that as far as he knew, he had no enemies. "I live a rather retired life," he explained with his apologetic smile, "and know few people intimately."

Murphy was about to ask more, but Wade nudged him. So Murphy contented himself with telling Oliver the he hoped they'd find the man, and Oliver explained hesitatingly that it might have been a housebreaker who had been forced to shoot because he thought he had been seen through the French windows. Murphy agreed affably as he closed the cab door and waved an optimistic good night.

Wade gave the driver Oliver's address and settled back. He offered Oliver a cigarette and lit one of his own. With a semi-gymnastic contortion, his foot slid the glass partition closed between the rear seat and the driver.

"Now, Oliver," he said, "who tried to shoot you?"

Oliver shook his head. "I wish I knew Mr. Wade." His voice was as vindictive as the voice of a harassed and nervous gentleman can be. "We'd go to see him."

Wade laughed. "Not we," he said. "I've got too much to live for."

Oliver did not answer. Wade spoke decisively.

"Oliver, I suppose you know my set-up on this case. What I know I print in the paper. Usually, that is. Not always."

"Yes, I understand. You're a reporter."

"Right, and tonight I'm a very busy one. I don't want to waste a lot of time beating around the bush with you."

Oliver gave him a surprised look and started to speak.

"Don't bother to interrupt," Wade said. He paused for a second, watching Oliver's weak eyes behind the heavy glasses. "Where did you get that ten thousand dollars, Oliver?" he asked. "And what did you do with it?"

Oliver gave a sigh, a deep sigh that sounded like an expression of relief.

"Young man," he said solemnly, "I'm glad you asked me that. I didn't know what to say about it. That money—was it ten thousand dollars?"

"Where did you get it?" asked Wade.

"I didn't know what to say about it," murmured Oliver. "I didn't feel—er—free to talk, and I didn't know what to do."

"Where did you get it?" asked Wade.

"During the ceremony," said Oliver. "The room was dark. It was dark, that is, except for an illumined devil's head in one corner. A large head. I designed it myself. I suppose this has been described to you."

"Yes. What about the money?"

"Not so fast, no so fast," Oliver urged smilingly. "I shall come to that. It was soon after the lights were turned off. The room was in almost complete blackness. I heard a voice say '147.' In a whisper, you understand."

"Your number is 147?"

"Yes. You must remember this was before the tellers had taken their places. Just at the beginning of the ceremony."

Wade nodded.

"When I heard this whisper, I was right alongside of the person who had whispered, and I turned around. I felt a touch on my arm. This person slipped something into my hand. A black leather wallet. The same voice whispered, 'Here's Parnell's money.' I took it."

"You knew it wasn't meant for you?"

"No—no indeed." Oliver edged forward and leaned closer to Wade, his thin forefinger marking his words. "You understand, Mr. Parnell had lost eleven thousand dollars to me in a private backgammon game one night last month, and had not paid off. I called him on it just last Saturday night. I thought this was that money."

He blinked behind his thick glasses. "I thought perhaps Parnell was a member of Dis and had taken this—well, er—spectacular method of paying off. I did not know how he knew my number, but I had no time to inquire, for the instant the wallet was passed to me the person passing it stepped back and in the dark could not be identified among the others. Then, after the ceremony—"

He stopped and mopped his forehead. "This, Mr. Wade, is what makes it extremely strange. Incomprehensible, in fact. The ceremony was about over, but the room was still dark. I felt two hands on my shoulders, and a voice said 'Come along and get the thrill of your life,' and the speaker pushed me playfully, but firmly, ahead of him."

"You are sure it was a man?"

"Well—I think so. The voice struck me as masculine, though it was a whisper. I went with him, unresisting. I thought it was all part of the game. He headed me for the cloakroom alongside of the ballroom entrance."

"Was it dark in the cloakroom?"

"No. The figure marched me to the wall, and said, still jokingly, 'Stand there and wait for the big moment.' I stood still—all in the spirit of fun, you know. In the spirit of fun, yes. The next thing that happened—" Oliver's voice rose, and his forehead was damp again—"was that I felt the tip of a gun under my ribs and heard a command to surrender the money. Of course—well, I was unarmed, so of course I gave up the wallet. I thought—yes, it is perhaps not sporting to say this of a dead man—I thought it was Parnell, getting his money back. I was angry, but quite helpless, you understand. Just as I handed over the money the voice told me to turn around with my face to the wall. I obeyed. I heard the door open and close and when I finally turned around again I was alone."

Wade considered a moment. "You did not recognize the voice at all?" he asked at length.

"O, no." Oliver shook his head ruefully. "Each mask has a muffled mouthpiece, you know, to disguise the voice. It's very effective," he added, clearing his throat—"you see, I designed it myself."

Wade smiled. "What about the number of the man in the cloakroom? Did you get a flash at that?"

"No. You see, he was behind me at first, then when he turned his back to go out I was facing the wall. When I got out and the lights were on in the ballroom, it was impossible to say which he was. About that time the photographer came up to take the picture, and the festivities continued until Captain Murphy came in and told us Parnell had been murdered."

END OF PART ONE

SHROVE TUESDAY

MARDI Gras.

The town was gold and shining. The streets rocked with music and quivered with laughter; banners floated from skyscraper towers and long silken festoons looped the windows, swirling the buildings in purple and green and gold, the crown colors of Rex, King of Carnival. Bands played on the corners and children danced in the street, while the sidewalks threw back echoes of half a million voices, for it was Mardi Gras, the golden holiday of New Orleans, when the town goes wild.

Roger Parnell's body lay in the morgue at police headquarters, but nobody had been found who mourned him. At noon Rex was going to ride through the shouting streets at the head of his parade, and at the steps of the City Hall the Mayor would give him the keys of the city, and Rex would lead his court on till his throne float stopped under the balcony where the Queen of Carnival and her maids waited for him, while the band played "If Ever I Cease to Love." The town was thrilled and waiting. Maskers asked one another about the murder, and some of them carried papers in their hands, but they spoke of it as of something that could wait till tomorrow for argument.

Downtown in the den of Dis the sun fell through the skylight on strange floats that would move through the French Quarter after the parade of Rex was over. They were no less magnificent than the floats of the merry Carnival parades, and they had required no less artistry in their design, but they were all strange and faintly sinister, making a pageant not of careless enjoyment but of something else—something weird, discomforting. The parade of Dis would be a spectacle that one would turn from with a sense of discord, an instinctive feeling that this, wildly beautiful as it was, was an intrusion alien to Mardi Gras. One would remember, watching the Dis parade, that a man had been murdered last night while these maskers danced, and one would remember that the name of their order was the syllable that began words of lost illusions.

But the Dis parade would not be on the street till afternoon. It was Mardi Gras morning, and the town thrilled to the coming of the king.

CHAPTER FIFTEEN

HE SAT negligently on the curbstone at the corner of Royal and Canal Streets, a circus clown whose white pantaloons were spotted with red rings as big as apples, and whose face had taken refuge behind a chalk-white mask split from ear to ear in a superhumanly jovial grin. He was not a very big clown, though the peaked dunce-cap that crowned his head added a deceptive tallness and the general broadness of his apparel suggested a robustness which his small person was obviously inadequate to support. He had occupied the curbstone for several minutes, oblivious of the crazily-garbed creatures who passed him or who stopped to gaze and trip a step to the rhythm of the banjo that he was strumming. A tiny Indian brave, aged about six, gave the clown a nudge with his toe.

"Sing a song, Mister Moddygraw?"

The clown turned his unbelievable grin. "Sure, Big Chief. I ain't here for nothing else. Listen." He thrummed brightly.

He had a high, clear voice, a voice that broke through the crowd like a shaft of light, and the clown's fingers crossed the banjo strings in a hurried final chord as his song stopped and he scrambled to his feet. The little Indian brave gaped at such rudeness, but the clown's cheerful "Sorry, see you later," was all he got, and he turned off toward Canal Street with a disappointed shrug. But the clown had forgotten the brave's existence, for he had scrambled up to meet a black-and-white Pierrette whose tilted head-dress failed to hide the flash of her red hair. He tucked his banjo under one arm and linked the other with hers, and they moved off down Royal Street.

"Been waiting long?" she asked.

"Just about ten minutes. I was having fun."

"Too bad you had to stop playing the banjo for that kid."

"Oh, I can't be playing a banjo all day anyway. I got too many things to do." He drew her close to the plate glass window of a shop. "What'd you want to see me about?"

She hesitated. Under her black domino he could see her bite her lip thoughtfully. "Don't let her know, Tony."

"I sure won't. How is she this morning?"

"Oh, she's not awake yet. It's only about eight-thirty. She doesn't know I'm out. I hope you didn't mind getting all dressed up like this, but I didn't want anybody to recognize us talking. She might be mad if she heard—she got pretty drunk after you left last night."

"Say, Lucy, I knew we oughtn't to left you by yourself. Was she hard to manage?"

She shook her head, and the early sunshine threw golden flakes on her hair. "No, and there were plenty of cops at the gate if she had been. Most of the time she's all right when she's drunk. But of course, last night—she told me Murphy had said awful things to her."

"Listen—" his voice was very low behind his grinning mask—"what's the chances that she—"

"Hus!" She glanced fearfully at the crowd shoving past them. "I—I just don't know, Tony. I woke up thinking about it. I don't know. I know she wasn't drunk before you came—you remember she wasn't a bit drunk when you took the picture—and she had been in a perfectly grand humor all evening." Lucy twisted the big black pompon at her belt. "The only time she seemed to be bothered at all was when she told me to look out for Mr. Ghent—number 47, you know, the one that turned out to be Mr. Parnell—and I did think she was sort of worried then."

"You know," he ventured, "I sort of think Ghent might be the baby we're after. He might have got out of his apartment after Parnell tied him up."

Lucy's slipper traced a line in the pavement. "But what would he do it for?"

"He mighta had a reason. Did he know Cynthia had been married to Parnell?"

"I don't know. But it's kind of a tough job to set out to kill all her husbands."

He chuckled. "Say, does she know you know about Parnell?"

"I don't think so. The day she burned all that stuff, I cleaned out the fireplace before she woke up, and she probably doesn't remember what she was talking about. She was awfully tight."

"Moddygraw doll-babies, lady? Nice Moddygraw doll babies—buy one for the lady, mister—Moddygraw babies, ten cents."

"Sure, I'll buy a doll-baby." Wiggins dipped into his pantaloons for a dime and made a selection from the proffered tray of tiny naughty dollies. "Look, Lucy—you pull the string and her skirt kites up in the back."

"That's not nice. You ought to be ashamed of yourself."

"Oh, but it's cute—don't you see? You pull the string—"

"Quit showing me that trash. You're a nuisance. Here I run the risk of getting fired to come out and talk to you about a murder—"

"Well, I got to have my lighter moments, ain't I? Take this nice baby and come over here to the wagon and I'll get you some cotton candy."

She yielded, protesting, but when Wiggins had led her to the pushcart at the corner and provided her with a great swirl of pink sugar fluff as large as her head, delectably mounted on the end of a stick, Lucy became insistent. "Look here, Tony, I've got to go. She'll be waking up and wanting ice water and tomato juice, and suppose I'm not there to give them to her?"

"Why don't you give me a break? She won't be up for another couple of hours."

"But I've got lots to do, and I am giving you a break." She drew him back against the side of the shop. "I brought you something I found," she whispered. "That's why I thought we'd better both mask."

"Yeah?" Wiggins galvanized with eagerness. "Gee, Lucy, you're smart. Evidence?"

She nodded. Her blue eyes peered anxiously through the slits in the domino, but the early revelers of Mardi Gras were noticing them not at all.

"Last night," she whispered, "after you had gone, I went around seeing that all the windows were shut. I walked along the side balcony, because Murphy had locked up the china-closet and I wouldn't have gone in there anyway. The balcony goes all the way around the house, you know, and I had taken a flashlight, because I was nervous. Outside the window of the china-closet—not right outside, but four or five feet away, on the balcony floor—I picked up this."

She reached inside her Pierrette costume and brought forth a little paper packet. Wiggins watched her breathlessly as she opened it, showing him a thin red silk cord, about eleven inches long. He peered at it curiously, then gave a smothered exclamation. The cord was the same dull scarlet as the Dis robes, but several inches of it had been stained almost black. He touched it, and the stained part was stiff.

"Lord," he whispered, "that's probably blood, Lucy." She started. "Don't let anybody hear you. I think it's blood too, because it's the same color as that spot on his robe. It just shows that for some reason whoever killed him threw it out there—or dropped it by accident, or something, because—well, I don't know why, but I thought I ought to give it to you."

Wiggins gazed at her with an admiration that was not wholly caused by her lithe little figure and her glistening hair. "You sure are a smart girl, Lucy. I'll take it to headquarters. They can put it under a microscope or something and prove it's blood, you know. Here—" he produced the stub of pencil that no newspaperman is ever without—"you write on the paper where you found it and when, and sign your name."

"I won't get in any trouble, will I?"

"Lord, no. I wouldn't let 'em hurt you, honey. They'll be so pleased they'll send you a bunch of flowers."

"Then I *would* be in a mess," she chuckled as she signed her name on the scrap of paper that concealed the red thread. "If I started getting flowers from police headquarters." She gave him the packet. "I've got to go now, honest. You'll be down taking pictures of the Dis parade?"

"Sure. There's a platform already built for photographers. I'll be on it."

"I'll look for you. So long."

Wiggins watched her twinkling ankles till she was lost in the crowd. He turned around briskly and made his way back to the office of the *Creole*.

He was tired. He had snatched but a brief interval of sleep between leaving the hospital and waking to answer Lucy's telephoned request to don a costume and meet her on the street; but Wiggins was too busy now to be bothered with remembering his weariness. He raced upstairs, took refuge in the lavatory to change his costume for his ordinary clothes, and hurried down to the city room to make sure there was no imperative assignment that would prevent his running over to police headquarters with the red yarn before it was time to photograph the Rex parade.

But as he entered the city room he encountered Wade, who was standing near the door talking hard and fast to another reporter. Wiggins sidled up to them.

"Hi, pops! Where's the fire?"

Wade wheeled and looked down upon him with relief. "So here you are, thank the Lord. Where've you been?"

"Out," said Mr. Wiggins with dignity. "I been busy, see?"

Wade sighed. "Well, we're all going to be busier than that. Where'd you go after you left the hospital?"

"Back here to that downy oak couch that some fools call a table. Did I play shut-eye!"

"So did I, damn it. Know what Chief Donahue did at four o'clock this morning?"

"Whew!" Wiggins fairly pranced with delight. "Don't tell me he pulled a murder down at headquarters."

"Worse than that," Wade retorted glumly. "He thought he'd pull a fast one while all the reporters were busy on the Dis murder—"

"And what did he do?"

"He raided the Red Cat. Got evidence enough to send twenty people to jail. Found papers proving Roger Parnell did own the joint—"

"Lord!" Wiggins vociferated with resentful fury. "That kind of break for the evening papers—and after all the morning papers have done for him—"

"Sure, but wait till I tell you what kind of break he gave them. The place has got the biggest assortment of controlled wheels ever seen in town. And dice that will hit and miss or do pretty nearly anything but give the customers an even chance."

"Whoops!" said Wiggins. "What was Donahue's idea?"

"I don't know. But you and I'd better get busy."

"Okay. We going out there? We'll miss the parades—that'll be—"

"No, we aren't going there. O'Malley's already gone, with Charlie to get the pictures. You and I are going up to police headquarters. The district attorney is back in town, and Ross Hildreth is waiting to be questioned now. You'll have to get a picture of him."

"Sure. Wait till I get some plates." Wiggins had started off, but Wade strode after him and stopped him at the door.

"Wait a minute," he added in a guarded tone. "This is graveyard. They cracked Parnell's strongbox and it was lousy with counterfeit money. That's why we're going down to the d. a.'s office. Hurry up."

CHAPTER SIXTEEN

DAN Farrell, district attorney of Orleans Parish, was in a state of exasperation. His desk was piled with police statements he had barely had time to glance at, and more were pouring in from the battery of stenographers who were typewriting angrily and badly in their indignation at being called to work on Mardi Gras morning. Weary policemen had talked and talked; avid reporters had stormed his sanctum since sunrise; witnesses had demandingly answered by telephone that they were not leaving town, and would tell him anything, if he'd only wait till the Dis parade was over; and the general sentiment of the town, which needed no explanation to Farrell, was that while a murder investigation was a necessary detail, the city administration would have reason to fear next election day if it tried to interfere with Mardi Gras. So Farrell had concluded that he might as well yield to spoken and unspoken tradition and let the Dis parade go on.

"For after all," he explained wearily to Murphy, "not one member of Dis has tried to get away. We've checked them all. And we haven't got far enough along to hold anybody."

"Only," said Murphy with stolid conviction, "Con Conroy."

Farrell sighed. "Conroy's going to be sprung in a few minutes. Valdon's got a writ."

Before Murphy could swear properly at whoever it was that had let Valdon know the whereabouts of his secretary there was a knock, and a clerk put in her head. "Mr. Wade and Mr. Wiggins of the *Creole*," she announced.

"Bring them in," Farrell said with involuntary enthusiasm, and as the door opened again to admit Wade's long languid figure and Wiggins hopping like a rabbit alongside of him, Farrell stood up with the first suggestion of pleasantness he had manifested that morning.

"Howdy, Farrell," Wiggins greeted him.

"Lord, boys, but I'm glad to see you," Farrell exclaimed. "Sit down and tell me what's been going on."

Wade slid his long self into a chair and faced Farrell across the desk. "I wish I knew. Murder. Knife and no fingerprints. A lot of poisonous personalities for suspects. What have you been doing?"

"Reading reports since seven o'clock." Farrell grimaced.

"Yeah?" Wiggins commented. "What about the Red Cat raid?"

"I'll come to that in a minute. I understand Donahue and his men did a riot act and they found among other things that the roulette wheels could be controlled."

"And that the late Mr. Parnell was the big squeeze," chirped Wiggins from his seat on a window-sill.

Farrell nodded.

"What about the queer money they found?" Wade inquired.

Farrell considered an instant. "They didn't find very much at the Red Cat. It looks as if the Red Cat had been gypped by somebody who put a little queer money into play. Parnell's box was full of it, though."

Wade thoughtfully scratched his chin. He looked at Wiggins and Farrell and Murphy in turn, saying nothing.

Murphy swore softly under his breath. Farrell touched a button on his desk and the clerk looked in.

"Bring in Hildreth," he ordered. "Tell the reporters they can come in and hear what he has to say but that they're to keep quiet while I talk to him. And bring your notebook."

The girl nodded. A moment later she ushered in Ross Hildreth, who was followed by reporters from the other papers. The newspapermen waved silent greetings to Murphy and Farrell and placed themselves around the wall, waiting; Hildreth stood uncertainly by the chair Wade had vacated, looking at his surroundings with the baffled air of a man who has waked up to find himself sleep-walking downtown in his pajamas. The district attorney was gravely polite.

"Mr. Hildreth? I'm Dan Farrell. Have a chair."

Hildreth sat down. He was tall and fair, and handsome in a foreign, sardonic sort of way; the first descriptive adjective that occurred to Wade on observing him was *intense*. His eyes were deep-set, and his hands, long and restless, were the hands of a man who has an insatiable desire for new experiences, and one felt that though he had been many places and known many sorts of people he was not and never would be satisfied, but must forever be seeking new towns and stripping new personalities, giving an extravagant response to every fresh stimulus. He was both fascinating and annoying, and as he sat down he regarded the district attorney with ill-concealed impatience.

"You're the district attorney? Good. I don't know a damn thing about this business of last night. I was in Baton Rouge."

He spoke rapidly, like a man hurrying to get done with a disagreeable job, and Farrell observed his somewhat uneasy glance at the clerk's fleet pencil.

"I've been told that you were in Baton Rouge, Mr. Hildreth. Just a minute." Farrell glanced up at a policeman who had come in with Hildreth and was waiting by the door. "This is Patrolman Dallison of Baton Rouge," he introduced. "Dallison drove down early this morning with Mr. Hildreth and came here with him. Tell us where you found Mr. Hildreth, Dallison."

Dallison took a step further into the room. "In the Heidelberg Hotel, Mr. Farrell. In his room."

"You went there in answer to a wire from New Orleans, I think?"

"Yes, sir. Me, I was at headquarters when we got the wire from here. It said a fellow named Hildreth was wanted in connection with a killing in New Orleans—"

"Really, this—" Hildreth interrupted, but Farrell politely silenced him.

"This is purely routine, Mr. Hildreth. Go, on, Dallison. What time did you get the wire?"

"About three o'clock, Mr. Farrell. So we called up the Heidelberg Hotel, and the night clerk said a fellow named Hildreth from New Orleans had been registered there since Sunday, and I told them it was police headquarters and had them ring up his room, but the phone didn't answer—"

"That was because—"

"We'll listen to you in a minute, Hildreth. Go on, Dallison."

"So I went on up to the hotel and went up to his room and the door was locked, but I knocked and knocked and finally this gentleman opened the door with a bathrobe on over his pajamas and wanted to know what the hell I was doing waking him up in the middle of the night, then I guess he noticed I had on a uniform and he looked sort of scared and asked me what I wanted, and I told him to get dressed and come on to New Orleans with me, on account of he was wanted down there. So he didn't seem like he wanted to come, but I said there had been a killing, and he started to get dressed and asked me a lot of questions which I couldn't answer, mostly on account of the wire from New Orleans hadn't given a lot of details, but he said his car was parked down on a side street by the hotel, and we used it to drive here in. He fussed a lot but he didn't use any violence."

"Thanks, Dallison." Farrell returned his attention to Hildreth. "Now, Mr. Hildreth, you can tell us what you were doing last night."

"Not a blamed thing," Hildreth retorted indignantly. "I don't know who killed Roger Parnell nor anything about it. I was in bed asleep."

Farrell patiently explained. "You understand, of course, Mr. Hildreth, that it's necessary to take statements from everyone who might know something about the motive for this crime. You are the only member of Dis, so far as we know, who claims not to have attended the party at Mrs. Fontenay's house last night."

"Then I'm the only one who couldn't have done the killing," Hildreth protested. "I tell you I was in Baton Rouge. I'd been there since Sunday."

"And you were in the hotel all Monday evening?"

"Yes. I had dinner in the hotel dining-room with a friend of mine. His name is Gilday. After dinner we went up to my room and he stayed about half an hour. It was about eight o'clock when he left. I read a magazine awhile and went to bed. It was early—about ten-thirty—because I planned to get up early and drive to New Orleans this morning."

"Were you in your room when the telephone rang?" asked Farrell.

"Yes. It woke me up. I didn't answer it because I thought it might be a call from one of my friends to join a party and I didn't want to be bothered. I went to sleep again before this officer came."

Farrell leaned back, studying Hildreth with thoughtful attention. "Dallison said your car was parked downstairs on the side street by the hotel. Is that where you usually leave it while you are in Baton Rouge?"

"I've never left it anywhere else, except on stormy nights when I've put it in a garage." Hildreth sighed with annoyance at the obtuseness of the law. "Baton Rouge is no big city, Farrell. Everybody leaves cars on the street all night."

"Yes, I know." Farrell took up his cigar from the ashtray on his desk and deliberately tapped off the ashes. "You were planning to drive to town this morning to take part in the Dis parade, I believe you said, but you didn't attend the party last night. Was it pressure of business that kept you away?"

"Well—no." Hildreth gave an uneasy glance at the reporters. "Is this for publication?"

"Not without my okay," Farrell answered with a quick glance at the newspapermen.

"Well—I suppose I ought to be frank. My wife and I haven't been living together for some time—I imagine she told you that when you saw her last night—and I thought it might embarrass her if she knew I was at the party. She had told me it was necessary for her to be there, as she's a member of the Council this year, so I stayed in Baton Rouge."

Farrell nodded. "You wouldn't have run the risk of meeting her in the parade?"

"Women don't ride in Carnival parades," Hildreth retorted shortly.

For an instant Farrell did not answer. He stroked his cigar along the edge of the ash-tray. Then, after a pause, he asked,

"Mr. Hildreth, have you any idea how Roger Parnell obtained your costume to wear to the party last night?"

"No."

"Was it at your apartment or your wife's?"

"Mine." Hildreth shrugged. "He might have stolen it."

"Wasn't your apartment locked?"

"Yes, but anybody could work one of those antique locks."

"Isn't that rather risky?"

"I suppose so, but I've got nothing of value there. It's only a temporary stopping-place. I moved in a month ago. Most of my things are out at my father's place on Bayou St. John."

Farrell nodded, looking keenly across into Hildreth's belligerent face. "Is it true, Mr. Hildreth, that you and Mrs. Hildreth are being divorced, and that you and Mrs. Fontenay intended to be married when the decree is issued?"

Hildreth flushed slightly. "That's true, but I don't see what it's got to do with this."

"Possibly nothing at all." Farrell glanced at his watch. "That will be all for the present, Mr. Hildreth. I think we have your address. You'll be good enough to remain in town, as we may need to talk to you again." He stood up.

"Oh, I won't run away." Hildreth stood up too. "Good morning."

He turned shortly and went out. Wiggins slid down from the window-sill and hopped after him, lugging his camera. The other reporters followed, in quest of a more elaborate statement, and Murphy plodded after them to make sure they heard nothing, he would not hear also.

Farrell gestured behind their backs to Wade, who turned and came back to the desk.

"What's on your mind, Dan?"

"These." Farrell opened a portfolio. "We combed out Parnell's apartment this morning."

"What'd you find?" Wade sat down eagerly.

"This isn't for the public."

"Damn. All right."

Farrell took several slips of paper from the portfolio. He smiled.

"Mr. Wade, the prosecution offers in evidence—"

CHAPTER SEVENTEEN

"Oh, hurry up!" pled Wade. "What have you got?"

"First," said Farrell deliberately, "four cancelled checks, all dated in January and February of this year, or in other words, within six weeks of Roger Parnell's death, drawn for sums of between two and four thousand dollars each and payable to Cynthia Fontenay."

"Whew!" Wade whistled.

Farrell was serious again. "What do you make of them, Wade?"

"She had an interest in the Red Cat, you know. Maybe this means Parnell paid her cut personally."

"That's reasonable. The Red Cat must have been a pretty profitable enterprise, then." Farrell turned over the papers. "Here are two more checks—five thousand each—payable to Fritz Valdon. Dated the third and tenth of January."

"Hm. Maybe a last effort to ward off the split they had later. What else?"

"A letter." Farrell took out a sheet of paper that looked as if it had been torn in half lengthwise. "Rather, I should say half a letter. Read it."

Wade took the sheet. The letter had been type-written, and the paper torn jaggedly down the middle, so that half of each line was left.

Parnell—
    This note will ser
the queen. Have whoever br
come yourself, present it
know everything is regular

> It is safely stowed away and
> need it. The whole thing so
> some vile plot to make a mu
> However, you have always had
> May your exit be full of h

Wade read the fragment and looked up with a scowl.

"This," he said, "is the sort of thing I'm no good at."

"Neither," Farrell admitted with a wry smile, "am I. Of course, it may not mean a thing—maybe it's just an old letter he meant to throw away."

"May—be," said Wade. "But I doubt it. The wording is rather odd. 'Present it . . . everything is regular . . . safely stowed away.' Sounds as if somebody was keeping something for Parnell that he was afraid to keep himself."

Farrell agreed. "The men found it folded up and put into an envelope by itself in a drawer of his desk. The desk was locked and they had to break it open. That makes it look as if Parnell was keeping it on purpose."

"Yes. And this about 'some vile plot to make a mu—'?"

"Here we are," said a well-known voice, and the door opened to admit Wiggins, chipper and cheerful, with Murphy at his back. "Picture of Cynthia Fontenay's next husband safe on the plate, Wade. Whatcha got?"

Wade glanced questioningly at Farrell, to receive a good-natured consent. "Show it to him. He's already given us one or two good leads. Murphy has seen it."

Wiggins puckered his monkeyish physiognomy at the note and listened to Wade's account of where it had been found. "Kinda cute, ain't it?" he commented. "Me, now, I think it's simple. 'This not will ser . . . the queen.' That means serve the queen. Cynthia's queen of the Dis business, ain't she? Click."

Farrell was listening with a certain amused interest. "What else, Wiggins?"

"Well, 'some vile plot to make a mu–' What about 'murder' as the rest of that word? Lissen. I'll read it. Say this is from Esther Morse. Now she's a nice girl. She can't help that bedroom stare, God gave it to her. But she's in some kinda jam with Parnell and she's been paying for same through the nose. Suppose he's got some letters. Lissen."

He held up the note, finishing each line as he read.

"Parnell—

This note will ser----ve the queen. Have whoever br----ings it or maybe come yourself, present it----and anyway, you can be damn sure everything is regular----about those lousy letters.

It is safely stowed away and----we will use violence if we need it. The whole thing so----bad it has got my goat and I know some vile plot to make a mu----rder.

However, you have always had----the nerve of a brass monkey. May your exit be full of h----ell or horror or something.

Now," he finished with a flourish, "how's that?"

"Very nice," said Wade, "except that it doesn't sound like Esther's kind of language. I don't think we are going to get very far this way. There's only one thing in that letter that I'm pretty sure about."

"What's that?" the other three asked, Murphy ending his question with a sigh of disgust at the whole business.

"'It is safely stowed away,'" Wade indicated the fifth line of the message. "That must mean the counterfeit money. If Parnell had not died you wouldn't have opened his box. The money was safe there."

"Hell," said Wiggins. "The trouble with you is you ain't had enough sleep. Why should somebody else have to write to Parnell to tell him money was in his own bank box?"

Wade laughed ruefully. "That's right. What about this 'come yourself, present it'?"

"You were right in the first place," said Farrell smiling. "We won't get anywhere this way—we all read something different in it. For my part I like the part about 'May your exit be full of—'" He put the note in an envelope.

"Wait a minute!" Wade pushed back his chair suddenly. "What about this? Somebody has something belonging to Parnell. He—or she—sends Parnell this note. Then he tears it in half. They each keep half, and Parnell can get back his property by presenting this half of the note and matching it with the other half, which is retained by the unknown. How's that?"

"Ve—ry good," Farrell approved slowly. "Maybe not right, but worth remembering all the same."

Murphy got up lumberingly. "You all can do all the fancy arguing you please, and it ain't no business of mine to stop you," he announced. "But meantime I'm going to check up typewriters. You get some photostatic copies of that letter made, Farrell, and I'll find out how many people who knew Parnell own typewriters. Then maybe we'll get somewhere."

Farrell laughed and agreed. "Perhaps you're wiser than we are, Murphy. Start on Dis members, will you?"

The telephone on his desk buzzed. He lifted the receiver.

"I know about it," he said after a moment's listening. "Writ of habeas corpus. Let him go." He turned back to Wade. "Conroy," he explained. "They found a judge to sign the writ." He took up the papers and began putting them back into his portfolio. "This murder," he went on, "is one with a lot of angles. The Federal men took up the counterfeit notes and are going over them. They won't discuss that part of it at all—of course, it's properly their province. But don't overlook it."

Wiggins grunted approvingly from his perch on the window-sill. "That stuff," he observed, "might be the junk they'd give you if you ever won out at the Red Cat."

"No," said Wade with a chuckle, "they didn't need that. Donahue proved that you couldn't win much or often."

"That may be another point," the district attorney suggested. "Somebody who lost big might have taken desperate steps to get revenge."

"Oliver," suggested Wiggins. "He got the dough last night. Maybe that tale he told Wade was a lot of apcray."

"Conroy," said Murphy vindictively.

Farrell shrugged. "Oh, get your mind on somebody besides Conroy, Murphy. I know he's been irritating, but he's not the only one." He sighed. "Listen, Wade. We'll have to chase down every possible lead and try to fit in the note, the counterfeit money and the gambling house. But right now I think we'd better stick to our first hunch of finding out everything that happened last night at the party. They tell me that black butler of Cynthia's is ready to talk. I don't want him here—too many reporters in the press room. I'll have him brought to the office of a friend of mine on St. Charles Street."

Wade took down the number.

"That letter," Farrell reminded him, "is strictly in the lodge till I release it. Also the fact that Parnell's strongbox contained counterfeit money." He looked at his watch. "You fellows go about your business now, and meet me in about an hour. We'll see the butler and then go over a report I'm getting on Oliver. Maybe we'll give the populace a real thrill at the Dis parade."

"Say," exclaimed Wiggins, jumping down from his perch, "I know something." With a grand gesture he reached for Farrell's telephone and called the coroner's office. "Hi, hots," he called into the mouthpiece. "What the coroner say? Yeah? Thanks. I'll come around and take a picture of the kids some day. Yeah, sure I will. Say, be careful of that thing, will you? Put it in a safe or something. We'll need it for evidence at somebody's trial."

He put down the phone and grinned at his astonished colleagues. "Now me," he said, "I'm nice. I tell the police what I know." Then, tersely and very grandly, he told them about the cord Lucy had found on the balcony.

"And," he added haughtily, "you apes can fool with butlers or crossword puzzles or old gents that make toys, if you wanta, but the chemist says the cord is stained with blood, see, and that's what I'm interested in." He picked up his hat and camera. "And what I'm saying," he added as he walked to the door, "is that where there's blood there's action, and I want some action. G'by."

The door slammed and Wiggins was gone.

CHAPTER EIGHTEEN

THE hands of the cathedral clock moved toward noon.

New Orleans looked like a fairy-tale town on a holiday. The crowds of maskers had thickened in the streets, and the crown flags of Rex streamed jauntily over the heads of a thousand peddlers selling every vendible kind of nonsense. The Mayor and the City Council occupied the reviewing-stand built on the steps of the City Hall, waiting to give the keys of the city to Rex. On the balcony of the Boston Club waited the Queen of Carnival and her maids. Every balcony and every window along the king's line of march was long since full of mummers, and those too abundantly merry to cling long to any single coign of vantage thronged the streets below.

Across the street from the City Hall was a platform, guarded by two policemen big enough to offer successful resistance to importunate maskers who pled to be admitted to the heights. But this platform, like that down by the Boston Club and another built at St. Peter Street and Jackson Square, was sacred, for it was here that photographers mounted to take the pictures of the floats of Carnival.

The policemen guarding the platform opposite the City Hall had grown a bit weary. They had said no so many thousand times that when a lanky figure, unmasked and dressed in the ordinary attire of business, emerged from the fantastic throng and put its foot on the lowest step of the scaffold both guardians stiffened their muscles and repeated crossly, "Can't go up. You ought to know that."

The objection was languidly good-natured.

"I'm Wade of the *Creole*. I want to speak to my photographer. He's up there."

The policemen acquiesced, and Wade bounded up the steps to where Wiggins, in company with photographers from the other papers, was making pictures of the maskers below them. Wiggins waved merrily, snapped the pictures he was busy with, and came over to the rail.

"Hi, pops. What's on your mind?"

Wade spoke in a low voice. "Keep your eyes open. I don't think anything's likely to happen here, but I might not see you again before the Dis parade. There might be some fireworks then."

"Sure." Wiggins nodded solemnly. "I getcha."

"You'll have a good chance to see what's going on from the platform. That's all I meant." Wade glanced around to see if he was being observed, but the other photographers were busy. "We're going down now to talk to Cynthia's butler," he added. "Farrell has had him brought to an office near here. Want to find out what scared him so last night."

"Okay," said Wiggins. "Tell him I said howdy."

"All right." Wade clambered down from the platform and began a laborious progress back to the law office that Farrell was using for Jasper's questioning; and as there was no way to make the journey except by pushing through the crowds, it caused him to make some weary reflections as to the general undesirability of people who committed murders on Mardi Gras. Farrell was waiting in the office.

"Got the butler?" Wade asked, sitting down and stretching his tired legs.

"He's here. I had him brought over from the Third. First, though, I wanted to tell you there's nothing much to be found out about Oliver."

"Mean he's the figure of mystery?"

"Either that or else he's the most innocent old fellow in town. He's lived here all his life. Family not rich, but left him pretty well off, and he's apparently made a lot of money out of his toy patents. He has spent a lot of time traveling around, and has learned all there is about what sort of things kids play with all over the world, and knows all about toy manufacturing. Keeps a workshop in his house. No friends to speak of. Has several old servants who have worked with him for years."

"Nil," said Wade tersely. "But he must know somebody, Farrell. How'd he get into Dis?"

"Oh, he knows a lot of people in a business way, and he seems to be on pretty good terms with two or three Dis members. He's had Hildreth out to dinner several times lately, and Cynthia once or twice, and occasionally he's met Conroy or Ghent downtown somewhere and has gone home with him for a drink. When I said no friends I meant no intimates that we could discover. We've got no evidence that any of those people know him well."

"Then that's a blank," said Wade disappointedly. He took out a cigarette and moved nearer to Farrell's desk to get a match. Farrell was frowning over the report in his hand.

He was evidently more concerned than he wanted to admit. Wade considered thoughtfully. Farrell, he knew, had a mind that was methodical rather than intuitive, and though he was expert at presenting evidence he had little talent for ingenious theorizing. "What about his gambling story?" Wade asked.

"Oh, he does gamble quite a lot, and they say that eleven thousand dollars at backgammon wouldn't be impossible for him. So his story there may be all right. He owns two racehorses, both of them very good, and they run regularly here at Jefferson Track and the Fairgrounds, and in Florida." Farrell referred to another sheet. "The doctor says there were no powder burns discoverable around that wound he got last night, but points out that because the wound was slight, and the bullet's course through the hair, powder burns would not be very likely to show. Oliver didn't lose much blood, so he might have been shamming weakness, but on the other hand a cantankerous old hermit might have been knocked to pieces by a thing like that. And what he said about his eyesight and his marksmanship are both true. They found bullets in the French window frame, and broken glass inside and outside of the room."

"Where's he now?"

"Down at the Dis den, getting set for the parade."

"His nerve seems all right," Wade decided, "but I guess he's off the cards till that's over. Let's have the butler in."

Farrell opened the door and gave the order. "I've put a man at Oliver's house," he added to Wade, "with orders to let me know as soon as he gets back. I think a little more conversation with him about what happened last night is going to be necessary."

"He's a nuisance to talk to," Wade warned. The door opened, and Murphy came in with Cynthia Fontenay's butler and a police stenographer.

"Here's Jasper," Murphy announced briefly.

Jasper stood just inside the door. His manner was as wilted as his one-time stiff shirt. He had no hat, and his hands fumbled with each other. Jasper was tall, and looked as if in his moments of dignity he might make an ideal butler, but for the present Jasper's moments of dignity were over. Farrell gave him an encouraging smile.

"Come over here, Jasper." As Jasper shuffled nearer the desk Farrell went on in his pleasantest manner.

"Now we don't want you to be scared. We're not going to hurt you. We just want you to tell us, as simply as you can, what happened last night at Mrs. Fontenay's."

"Yes, sir." Jasper's eyes wandered with relief from Murphy's uniformed figure to Farrell and his stenographer. "What's that young lady going to do, judge?"

Farrell smiled again. "She's just going to write down what you say so you won't have to be called back to say it again in case we forget anything."

"Yes sir. I ain't done nothin'. Before God I ain't."

"We aren't saying you have." Farrell glanced at the girl. "Ready, Miss Bond?"

Murphy took a belligerent shove at the interviewee's elbow. "Jasper," he demanded with preliminary emphasis, "have you been beaten or mistreated while in the hands of the police?"

"No, sir. Not at all. They treated me fine."

"Good," said Farrell. "And you're ready to tell us what happened last night?"

"Yes, sir, I am. I just didn't want to be in that jailhouse on Moddygraw, judge."

"All right, boy, tell us what you know about this business, and if we can we'll let you out right away."

"Yes, sir. I didn't mean to hurt nobody, sir. How come I got scared was I thought maybe they thought I'd hurt Mister Parnell. But when they tells me down at the jailhouse that Mister Parnell was stuck with a knife I just knew I wasn't your man."

Farrell smiled. "But why did you run away, Jasper?"

"Well, sir, I was just scared, judge. Just crazy scared. I said 'Jasper, get away,' and away I got."

"Were you in the china-closet when Parnell was killed?"

Jasper shook his black head vehemently. "No, sir. I was gone. Long gone, sir. Here's how come it happen, judge. When that boy come in about the picture-taking I told him to wait. Then, I go up on the gallery so as to stand by the door like Miss Cynthia tell me."

"When was that? I mean, what time was it?"

"Lemme see. That was just when the lights went out. Yes."

"All right, Jasper, you went up on the gallery. Then what happened?"

"I stood by that door and for a while everything was quiet. I had a crack in the blinds so I could see the carryin' on. We always has a time at those parties. Well—" Jasper grinned and then, remembering that this was serious business, sobered again—"well, I was lookin' through that crack and I see Miss Cynthia comin'. She come down the hall, by herself. Then she go in the china-closet."

Observing that everybody was listening with good-humored interest, Jasper proceeded with increased confidence in his own ability to get out of jail for Mardi Gras.

"Well, judge, I open the door so I can ask her if there's somethin' she want. But I hear her talkin' to somebody, so I don't go in. She sure was blessin' this man out."

Jasper sighed. "Well now, I ain't goin' let Miss Cynthia get in no trouble. She all the time treat me pretty nice, and she particular told me that if there was any rumpus at the party I was s'posed to look out for things. You see, sir, sometimes they gets a little bit lit, and sometimes Miss Cynthia she get a little bit lit too. So when I heard her blessin' out this man in the devil suit I figure maybe she wants protectin'. So I creep 'round to the back gallery where I can see through the pantry window. The window was shut, so I couldn't hear what she's sayin', but I open the blind a little ways so I can see in case he gets rough."

Farrell was interested. "And did he get rough, Jasper?"

"Sir," said Jasper with conviction, "he give her hell. He just bawl her out plenty. I stop to think if I ought to throw him out, and when I look in again that devil man is chokin' her. He's got his hands round her neck, judge—"

Jasper's voice rose and his gestures illustrated.

"—round her neck, and he's shakin' her—like so—" Jasper's eager hands closed on Wade's neck and Wade's startled croak was accompanied by a shake that nearly heaved him to the floor. "Just so," Jasper exclaimed eagerly. "Shake her like this—so—"

"Yes, Jasper, yes," panted Wade, extricating himself from the man's eager grasp as Farrell began to chuckle and Murphy angrily grabbed Jasper's shoulders with a "None o' that, you! Stand up straight."

"I'm all right, Murphy," Wade managed to say, feeling around his collar to make sure that he was. He put his feet on the floor again.

"Suppose you just tell us what happened, Jasper. I can understand." Farrell smothered his laughter and lifted a face of polite interest to the excited figure of Cynthia's butler.

"Yes, sir." Jasper, somewhat subdued, thought a minute to recapture the thread of his narrative.

"He was choking her," Farrell prompted. "What did you do?"

"Well, sah," said Jasper, "I just open that window as fast as I could and I heave myself through. I say, 'Jasper, you ain't goin' let no devil man choke any lady you work for.' So I heave myself through and I hit that devil man a knock in the jaw."

"Oh—you did, did you," said Farrell slowly. "Did he fall?"

Jasper grinned a broad ivory grin. "You bet he fall. He tumble down right where he is. And Miss Cynthia—"

"Yes? What did Miss Cynthia do?"

"Why, she run. She just put her hands up to her neck like to see if she got any breath left, and then she run. She get out of that pantry so fast I don't hardly see her at all. But that devil man—well sir, he bang the table with his head when he fall down and he just lie there. So I don't know what to do. I figure he been hit pretty hard, and I say, 'Jasper, somethin' goin' happen to you when you go hittin' gentlemen too hard.' So I just creep out of that window, and shut it again and creep around the gallery and wait till I see the light come on inside. Then I sneak in, and soon's I see Miss Cynthia she just say, quick-like, 'Jasper, go down and tell the photographer we're ready.' She don't act like nothin' happen at all. So I go down and tell the man he can come up to take the pictures."

"What time was that?"

"I ain't studyin' time. I just know I hit a man and if he's hurt there's goin' be trouble."

"I see. So you went down to get the photographer?"

"Yes, sir. I go down to get the picture man. Little fellow. He been talkin' to Miss Lucy. He and me go up and Miss Cynthia don't say nothin' to me. She don't look like there's any trouble at all. That sure is one smooth lady. After the picture man go she tell me to wait downstairs and she'll phone down if she need any more liquor. Well, I wait down there, and I'm keepin' out of the way of that man, judge. You know I couldn't let him choke Miss Cynthia. But I don't want him to see me."

"I understand," nodded Farrell. "What happened then?"

"Well, after while nothin' happen, and I wonder if that white man is come to. Seems like I just can't wait much longer. So I figure if I phone upstairs I'll ask Miss Lucy if they need any ice or anything and if there's been any trouble I'll hear about it. So I take down the receiver, and that phone is on the same line as the phone in a back room upstairs. And I take that receiver down and I hear Miss Lucy callin' the police."

Jasper heaved a mighty breath and his eyes rolled toward the ceiling.

"I was scared. Miss Lucy she say 'Police, come quick. There's a dead man here.' So I say, 'Jasper, get goin'.' So I go."

Farrell rested his chin on his hands and gave Jasper a long puzzled look.

"Miss Cynthia didn't mention the incident to you at all?" he asked after a pause.

"Judge, Miss Cynthia didn't mention nothin'. She let me stay in the jailhouse. I guess she was plumb scared too. But when I heard them say that man was knife-killed, I knew I didn't kill him. I had no knife. Somebody else kill him after I knock him over. So I figure I better talk with the court. So that's all I know about what happens, judge. Before God, it is."

Jasper stood beaming, his statement made. Through the window came faint strains of a band playing "If Ever I Cease to Love." Jasper's foot began to tap. He was eager. This was the song of Rex. If they let him go now, he could run around and see the parade.

Farrell had gone over to a cabinet in a corner of the room. He took out a thick package in a manila envelope. Opening it, he tilted the envelope and the pearl-handled knife that had killed Parnell slid to the table.

"Did you ever see that knife, Jasper?" Farrell asked.

But he might have spared the words. Jasper was staring down at the knife on the desk as if it epitomized all the awfulness in the world. His mouth was open and his eyes wide.

"Whose knife is that?" barked Murphy. "Yours?"

Jasper jerked back. "No sir, that knife ain't mine! I declare before God it ain't! That knife belong to Mister Fontenay. I seen it a million times."

"To Mr. Fontenay?" Wade repeated. "I thought he was in Europe."

"Yes, sir. But he left that knife when he quit Miss Cynthia. Miss Cynthia, she been usin' that knife to open letters. It been on the little desk in her sittin' room. I know that knife. Mr. Fontenay tell me long time ago, before he quit Miss Cynthia, that that's a fine knife. Not but two in the world like it. Mister Fontenay he have that for years and years. Mister Oliver give it to him. Mister Oliver is the only man got another one. And Miss Cynthia she been open' her letters with that knife ever since she up and quit with Mister Fontenay. Before God."

CHAPTER NINETEEN

WHEN Jasper was paroled according to promise, Wade and Murphy and Farrell squared their shoulders as though to brave a storm and stepped into the gay maelstrom of St. Charles Street. The crowds on the sidewalk surged back from the curb, jamming them against the wall. Twice, three times, Murphy tried to make a passage through the laughing multitude by use of his great voice and his gold badge, but it was no use. Rex was coming. It was his day to rule. Not only was it virtually impossible for the members of the throng to pack themselves more closely, but it did not occur to them to try to do it. Rex was coming. They paid no attention to more commonplace minions.

"If we can get to the curb," Wade suggested, "I think we can make it."

"Yeah?" grunted Murphy. He looked without appreciation at the shining confusion. "Well, hold in your elbows and duck."

They ducked. At least, they tried to. But those who have to attend to business on Mardi Gras are in a sorry plight. Every one of those jammed exhilarated maskers knew his rights. The idea was to get as close as possible to the steel cables that roped off the sidewalk, and to stay there; so long as there was no disorder, not a policeman on earth had the power to make them move.

Farrell got his foot out from under that of a hilarious Hindu and sighed. "We've got to get downtown," he said with determination. "If we let her get away now—take it slowly, and push."

Wade, shoved back and forward by the milling thousands, grinned. Already he could hear the music of the first band leading the Rex parade. Already, far up the street, he could hear the joyous cheers of the maskers greeting the king. The crowd around him was swaying to the rhythm of the Carnival song. A gayly bedizened pirate looked down at the Hula dancer beside him and began to sing—

"If ever I cease to love,
If ever I cease to love,
May I be stuffed with sausage meat,
If ever I cease to love."

The crowd around, dancing and throwing confetti, joined in the song.

"Damn!" said Murphy.

"Keep your elbows in," Wade advised. He chuckled. Murphy had folded his arms, and stood in the crowd like a rock in the midst of a heaving sea. Wade caught Farrell's eye, and they both laughed. The same thought had struck them both. They were ready to arrest a woman for murder. Ready, with all the forces of organized law and decency behind them, and were helpless; not by reason of those who thrived on lawlessness, but by the merry opposition of the holiday which is boasted as being the most orderly day of pleasure in the world. They were both close to sharing Murphy's impotent wrath.

Keeping as close together as they could, they had with infinite effort struggled ten feet. Wade paused for breath and looked around him. Mardi Gras. The banners and the confetti and the music. Countless thousands of sober men and women cheering a make-believe king. Insensibly, irresistibly, the thrill of Mardi Gras crept into him. The sky like thick blue velvet; the magic floats twinkling in the abundant sunshine; at the City Hall, a block or two away, the crown float of Rex halting while the Mayor and the City Council saluted Rex and passed him the keys to the city gates. Again the music sounded, the procession moved, the tinsel tops of the floats sparkled down the street. The crowds surged forward; the steel cables stretched and strained; the maskers riding the floats flung favors into the crowds—necklaces of glass beads, toys and trinkets of no value, which would be treasured by those who caught them till their grandchildren were old.

Mardi Gras. A Quaker girl, her lips a deep incongruous scarlet under her half-mask, drank a toast from a silver flask. An Indian chief stood beside her, his arm protectingly around her waist. The parade passed them; twenty floats drawn by mules, harnessed in gold and silver for this day of their glory. Between the floats marched the musicians, playing the gay silly anthem of the nonsense king. The Quaker girl began to sing the song, and suddenly Wade caught himself singing too—the merry song that was first sung in New Orleans by a little music-hall dancer named Lydia Thompson, and which, because Lydia Thompson so delighted the Russian Duke Alexis when he came to town to greet the first King of Carnival, has been kept ever since as the official anthem of Shrove Tuesday—

> "If ever I cease to love,
> If ever I cease to love,
> May dogs and cats quit chasing rats,
> If ever I cease to love!"

"Hey, you!" said Murphy. "Keep movin'."

Wade laughed and struggled obediently forward, through the crowd of maskers. Strange. They were going to arrest a murderer. He wondered if anybody else knew about Cynthia Fontenay. Perhaps somebody did. Somebody here. A glum-faced clown with a lugubrious smile painted across his white mask might be trying too to get down to Jackson Square, where Dis was to hold its revels, to warn her. Or perhaps the sober frocked friar pushing his patient bulk against the pack of humanity might be hiding his haste to get off in the other direction.

They forced their way on. Their progress was maddeningly slow. If they were held up now, with the Druids' parade following that of Rex, it would mean an hour's delay, and if in the meantime a warning whisper should have come to Cynthia, she could have slipped out of town by a back-street route, taking her secrets with her. Or possibly—and Wade went cold at the idea—possibly she had been warned already, and was triumphantly slipping past him now, in mocking anonymity. He looked at the maskers, trying to recognize her under one of the crazy costumes. A group of girls with purple pompons dancing on their white suits ran alongside him, singing Lydia's song.

"If ever I cease to love,
If ever I cease to love ...
May all the seas turn into ink,
May ravens all turn white,
May the Queen in Buckingham Palace die,
May we all get drunk tonight,
May cows lay eggs, may hens give milk,
May the elephant turn a dove,
May dogs refuse to eat fresh meat,
If ever I cease to love.
If ever I cease to love,
If ever I cease to love,
Potatoes will grow on a mulberry mow,
If ever I cease to love!"

With a grim fury they fought their way. Murphy pushed and shoved ahead of them. At length the last float had gone by. The crowds broke for a minute to shove into the street and run for a few steps in the wake of Rex and his pageant. In a minute, Wade knew, the Druids' parade would start, and it would be just as bad again. A sudden heave and a sweep of people caught him up. Murphy he could see just ahead of him; Farrell was lost to his sight. Propelled relentlessly, Wade moved out, blowing confetti from his lips and brushing ticklers from his ears. In another minute he had reached the steel cable, and he ducked under to stand in the street with the revelers. Murphy was there too, hastily gathering four policemen who had been patrolling the curb lines.

Farrell showed up in the middle of a bevy of sailor-girls who had formed a ring around him and were singing an invitation to come and play on Mardi Gras. Wade chuckled as the ring broke and Murphy and the four officers were shoved into the center. The girls laughed uproariously at the bellowing orders of the policemen. And then, with a storm of confetti and a blare of horns, they broke their circle and scampered off. Wade pushed his way to the officers.

"Get us through this crowd," Murphy was ordering. "We'll pick up a car over at the First Precinct and sweep down around the New Basin canal." He turned to explain to Farrell. "That gives us a chance to go down Esplanade Avenue to the river and then back to Jackson Square."

The police escort started, and pushing its way through the crowds that were already solidifying to cheer the Druids, cleared a passage to the far side of the street and through to the back streets by which they could make their way to the precinct station. Wade almost regretfully left the hilarious throng. Behind him he could hear the cries—"Here come the Druids!"

"I see the first float!"

"It hurts my eyes—it's so bright—it's lovely this year!"

In the distance the strains of Lydia's old song came faintly. He did not listen. His long legs keeping pace with the running steps of Murphy and Farrell and their panting escorts, Wade hurried off with them to arrest the murderer.

The back streets, where the parades did not pass, were nearly empty. They made their way to the nearest police station and hurriedly commandeered a car. With long sighs of relief they lay back on the seat and Murphy gave quick orders.

"It ain't time yet for the Dis parade," he explained as the car started. "I figure we'll run around through these back streets till we get as close to Jackson Square as we can, then well get out. There won't be any way to get to the square but to fight like we've been doing, but my idea is to get to the square, and then we'll be all right. Cynthia's due to sit on the balcony of the upper Pontalba building, facing the square, so the king of Dis can drink to her when he goes by, and she'll be there. We can slip inside the building and arrest her quiet-like, without anybody knowing what we're up to."

"And Oliver?" asked Wade. "He'll be riding a float, masked."

"We'll find out which float he's in. The parade won't start till the queen comes out on the balcony. They'll hold it up, thinking she's having an extra drink inside."

"And you'll nab him before anybody knows Cynthia's arrested?"

"That's the idea. Hey, Flanagan," Murphy called to the driver, "keep going! What's the matter?"

The driver, who had abruptly halted the car. turned a woebegone face to the back seat. But Farrell had already looked out and was sinking back with a groan.

"O my God, we forgot! It's the Zulu King!"

Wade, his elbows on his knees and his head between his hands, felt himself in danger of giving way to something very like hysteria. He wanted to laugh, foolishly, immoderately. The impossibility of doing anything on Mardi Gras was something he had frequently written about for the columns of his paper, but which he had never understood before.

Their progress was stopped. Before them was a moving sea of faces. Their ears were assailed by the slow dull thrump of jungle music and the soft swinging rhythm of laughter. Along the street, in marvelous savage panoply, rode the ruler of the Carnival, the Zulu King, grandly decked in a grass skirt and strings of beads and feathers and flowers, leading a line of floats on which rode singing revelers.

There was no help for it. They were halted. To try to force a car through that mob would be to cause a massacre and a riot.

"Wade," said Farrell solemnly, "if you don't quit giggling I'm going to throw you in the can."

"Sorry." Wade sighed and looked out. "This is the end of the parade, Farrell. They'll follow it around to Rampart Street, and as soon as they do we can have the road cleared. It won't be long."

"Please God," said Murphy devoutly.

They waited.

"We can get through now," said Farrell at length. He leaned and beckoned to the policeman on the corner. After a few words of instruction the way was clear. "Take any route you can," Farrell said to the driver. "Get us as close to Jackson Square as possible, then we'll get out."

The driver did his best. But three blocks from the square he stopped again. It was obvious that he could go no further. Even here, as far as they could see, the mass of human beings was solid.

"Lord!" said Murphy. "This is awful. I've never in my life seen so many people to watch a Dis parade."

But Wade, who had gotten out, understood. He heard the murmurs of conversation around him. These people in the street knew that somebody in Dis would probably be arrested for murder before night. As they pushed their way toward the square, Wade listened to what was being said around him, and smiled grimly.

There were some who were enthusiastic, who thought it was sporting to have the parade in spite of everything, to hold to the great tradition of Mardi Gras. There were others who said frankly that they thought it was indecent. There were some who devoutly prophesied that the wrath of heaven would descend on these people who had no reverence for death.

At last, after working with heroic determination that would have seen them through a war, they reached the square. They stopped. They looked at one another.

They had been defeated.

To get from the square across to the balcony where Cynthia was going to sit with her maids would have required an army tractor and a hundred more murders. The square and the surrounding streets were packed till it seemed that the walls must give in from the pressure of humanity against them. Balconies of the houses facing the square were loaded almost to the breaking point. The statue of General Jackson in the square was covered with maskers like a lump of sugar black with ants. Every tree was bending under its weight of occupants. The sheds of the French Market between the square and the river had been seized upon as vantage points. It was as impossible to move through those crowds as it would have been to walk through the tanglewood of a forest a million years old. This was an impasse.

Additional policemen, who had been detailed to guard the cables that kept the crowd off the route of the parade, were sweating with the enormity of their task. Murphy looked across to the balcony where Cynthia would sit. It was the only empty space in sight.

"We can't do it," said Farrell.

Murphy sighed and wedged himself against the iron railing of the square.

"No," he said, "we can't. But remember this. If we can't move, she can't either. She won't be able to leave that house. She's caught just as thoroughly as she'd be if we already had her in handcuffs."

Wade agreed. He glanced over to the guarded photographers' platform where he could see Wiggins, busily shoving plates in and out of his camera. Beside Wiggins sat a masked little figure in a Pierrette costume, who Wade instinctively knew was Lucy. The sun sparkled on her red hair with a brightness that reached him across the street.

There was a shuffle and a murmur in the crowd, a nudging of elbows and whispers that grew into a shout.

"There she is!"

There she was—Cynthia Fontenay, queen of Dis. She advanced upon the balcony, in the white robe and tiara of Dis, followed by ten figures in red devil costumes and masks. For a moment she stood quite still, holding out her jeweled scepter; Wade could see that she was smiling, quietly, triumphantly, as though she could hear the whispers and was proud that she stood serenely above them all.

"It was her house he was killed in. Some people say she did it. Did you ever see such nerve? Standing up there—"

"I think she's marvelous. That's what you call real courage."

"Indecency, I call it. Not caring—"

Cynthia smiled calmly down at the mob, as they strained and shoved for the sight of her. She was white and cool and shining, in her robe caught at the waist with a jeweled cestus, and the tiara of Dis on her bright golden hair.

"There she is," said Murphy stolidly. "She that murdered her husband last night."

Wade looked back at Cynthia. He looked at her cool effrontery, at her callous, triumphant smile. Involuntarily he shivered. He saw Wiggins briskly pointing his camera toward her and snapping.

Wiggins watched Cynthia as she held her scepter for the last time toward the crowd beneath, and turned to sit down. She chatted with her maids while they waited for the arrival of the king of Dis. He turned to look at Lucy.

"Lucy," he said in a low voice, "I never saw such a woman. She don't give a damn."

Lucy shook her head. "It took lots of liquor to brace up her nerve, Tony."

"I don't believe it. She don't look it."

"You'd believe it if you'd been with her all morning. But I don't see how she does it, anyway."

Wiggins was silent. Then he started. There was another cheer from the crowd.

"There they come!"

The music had sounded in the distance. The policemen pressed the mob back behind the cables. The space beneath Cynthia's balcony was clear. An attendant ran forward and set up a long step-ladder that reached up almost as high as the wrought-iron balcony rail. It was here that the king of Dis would climb up to present flowers to the queen, and to drink her health and shatter the glass on the pavement. Cynthia edged her chair a trifle forward, to look at the advance of the parade.

First came the musicians, playing, not the gay nonsense anthem of Carnival, but music that had been written for Dis. Queer, disturbing music, music that was not angry but that was not quite gay—music that had in it something of the suggestion of a rattle. Behind came the throne float of the king.

Wiggins focussed his camera and photographed the parade as it advanced. "Who's king this year?" he whispered to Lucy.

"Arnold Ghent. But don't say I told you."

Wiggins looked at the advancing floats. They were magnificent. They were artistic. But they were not beautiful. They were not like the floats of the other Carnival parade. These were in a vague disturbing sense, a defiance of the lovely tradition of Mardi Gras.

The title float, red and black, bore a wide arch proclaiming that the subject of the parade was "Things I Don't Want To Be."

Wiggins looked beyond. He saw a float that represented a rat in a trap—a gigantic red rat, kicking against the vast ugly trap that held its head. There was a lump of sugar as big as a house, swarming with man-size red cockroaches. There was a goldfish bowl, cunningly devised of steel wires covered with cellophane, in which hung a man covered with a gilt goldfish suit.

Wiggins shrugged with disgust. This was not Mardi Gras. This was— it was Dis.

He did not look at the floats that followed. He turned again to the king's float at the head of the parade. The king, his red devil suit half covered by a magnificent sable-bordered cape, rode under a canopy embroidered with red and black devils, and behind his throne leaped up red and yellow papier-mâché flames. Wiggins made a disgusted moue as he turned his camera full on the throne float and took the photograph.

The musicians ranged themselves in a semi-circle under the balcony. The ones leading the mules of the king's float brought it to a stop so that the king could reach the ladder. The music rose in a swift rebellious tempo.

Cynthia stood up. One hand rested lightly on the balcony rail, the other raised her scepter and held it toward the king. He stood and bowed low to her. The crowd shouted and then held its breath.

A page handed him a glass of champagne. He climbed the ladder. He drank to her, held the glass high, and flung it to the pavement. It crashed in a thousand bright splinters.

The page came halfway up the ladder and handed him an enormous bouquet of red roses. The king held them high, toward Cynthia.

She handed her scepter to one of her maids, and leaned forward, both hands out to receive them.

Then...

Every one of the thousands who saw the hellish pandemonium of the Dis parade had a different story of what happened then. Wiggins and Lucy, close on their platform, heard the shriek and the shattering noise and saw the ladder quiver and go under, hurtling Arnold Ghent back as Cynthia fell forward through the gap in the broken balcony rail, a white streak crumbling on the pavement below. They saw the mules rear in blind terror and dash madly ahead, and heard the wild panic in the square and the screams of those who were knocked down in the struggle for escape.

Afterwards, it was hard to say that they or anyone else had seen more than this. For Wiggins and Lucy had both leaped frantically down from the photographer's platform and had rushed forward to where they saw lying on the pavement under the balcony the broken white thing that had been Cynthia, and they knew, before Wade or Farrell or Murphy knew, that she was dead.

CHAPTER TWENTY

ON THE platform which fifteen minutes before had supported the cameramen, Farrell stood like a field marshal staging a retreat. Police reserves under Murphy and Chief of Police Donahue were gradually shaping the frantic crowd into order. Ambulances screamed their way through the side streets. One of them had already taken away Cynthia's body, and another had rushed Ghent to a hospital. Wiggins, who had bounded back up the steps of the platform, was making pictures as fast as his hands could work, and swearing at anyone who blocked his lens.

In a drug store that had been turned into a temporary infirmary Wade had found a telephone, and was pouring the story into the ear of a tense rewrite man. Looking out of the window he could see the police at work. Mounted men were carefully riding back the crowds, guiding them into streets where they could get away. A squad of traffic officers was roping off the space around the line of floats, most of which had been instantly deserted by their occupants, but one or two of which still held maskers who could not get off without help. The red rat was still in his trap, kicking violently and yelling for someone to lift the top that kept his head pinned in. The men who had led the mules were being aided by policemen in holding the mules back from the pushing mobs that were being gradually lessened by the press of bluecoats.

Murphy was everywhere. Wade could see him ruthlessly charging some straggler who had proved too agile for the police lines, and breaking off his string of threats to lift up a child and gently deposit her beyond the ropes out of harm's way.

From the window he could see the goldfish bowl, its imitation fish swinging from the wire by which it hung. "You might use the rat and the goldfish for a front-page box story," he added to the rewrite man. "I can't see from here whether there are any others who can't get out of the floats without help, but I'll let you know. Wait a minute—" as another of the reporters who had been hurried down to help cover the story came in with a statement. "Here's the police estimate of the injured.

"Twelve children and twenty grownups taken to Charity Hospital. Twenty or thirty arrests for interfering with police work—they're at the Third Precinct. Nobody killed—except Mrs. Fontenay—but it's a hellish thing to see and I wish you'd put in a line about the great work the cops are doing, and give Murphy special mention—he deserves it. Ghent was rushed off to Charity too. He may be badly hurt—you'll have to find out there. From what I could see, he fell backward when Cynthia's body struck the ladder, and landed on his float, breaking down the canopy that covered the throne. Farrell's here and doing a swell job. Wiggins sent in some plates—I suppose they'll have to do for the extra, but he's taking plenty more for the first night edition. I'll call again for the replate as soon as I get some more."

He hung up and went outside. The ambulances were still coming. A platoon of firemen had arrived with a hose-wagon and were hitching lines to a hydrant. The threat seemed enough for the crowd and they fell back. But only for a moment. There was a new rush at the far side of the square. More injuries, more arrests and a team of bolting mules; Wade dashed back to see what had happened and hurried over to the phone.

Wiggins was shooting pictures, using plates as fast as they could be delivered to him by copy boys hurrying to and from the office, ducking in and out of brawls and tangles, stepping out of the way of the mounted police, eluding the battling hoofs of scared mules, running here and there and stopping to shoot what he wanted. Wade smiled with a sense of admiring comradeship as he watched him. Wiggins, in his own fashion, was an artist.

At last it was over. At last the policemen had emptied the square, and formed a cordon before the house where Cynthia had been, to keep off curious sightseers. Wade joined Wiggins, and they walked over to the photographers' platform, where Farrell and Murphy were talking to Chief Donahue.

Wade climbed up to them. "Now that the extra's in," he said, "what are you saying about the death of Mrs. Fontenay?"

Murphy's big hands made a gesture of despair. "Wurra, wurra," he moaned, "I don't even want to think about it."

"Neither do I." Wade smiled with a sort of tense sympathy. "But we've got to."

Farrell, sitting precariously on the rail of the scaffold, sighed wearily. "Murphy thinks it was suicide," he told Wade.

"How about the coroner?" demanded Wiggins. "What does he think?"

"He's up there now." Murphy signalled to the balcony with a jerk of his thumb.

"As near as I can make it out," Farrell went on, "that old iron balcony rail broke when she leaned on it. She had to lean out to reach for the flowers." He sighed again, eloquently.

"Well, we better get up where the coroner is," Wiggins proposed briskly. "We can't get anywhere by just sitting here on the mourners' bench."

Chief Donahue shook his head disapprovingly. "Just another story, eh, son?"

"Think so?" Wiggins perked up indignantly. "Listen, chief. I didn't drive that dame to jump just by taking her picture, did I? If you ask me, this death can be chalked up against the building department. That balcony wasn't safe, was it? That rail is probably about a coupla hundred years old. She leans against it—bang! Then up pops the jamboree. Look what it cost me, willya?" Wiggins sadly displayed the ruin of his coat, torn to rags by his battling through the crowd for pictures.

"Hell," he went on grimly. "Murphy's conscience is all that's bothering him."

"Now what," demanded Murphy, "do you mean by that?"

"All right!" Wiggins shouted. "You say suicide, because you were after the dame for murder. I say accident, because she didn't know you were after her. How's that?" He turned briskly. "Come on, Wade, let's go up and see what the corner says. I'll bet any of you a new suit of clothes that he says accidental death."

They had reached the spot on the pavement where Cynthia's body had struck. Wiggins winced.

"It was—pretty terrible, wasn't it?" said Wade slowly.

"Shut up," snapped Wiggins. "What you doing—trying to make me cry? Listen. I could cry easy enough without you, but I ain't gonta. I'm here on business, see?"

Wade smiled, understandingly. He had appreciated his little partner's valiant efforts to cover up how he felt. Wade felt somewhat the same way himself. He wondered if Cynthia had jumped on purpose.

They went up the dark stairs that led from the corridor of the old building. On the second landing they turned into a doorway and went through a disordered living room, where masks and costumes had been thrown helter-skelter by Cynthia's companions in the frantic moments that had followed her death.

Four or five police officers and a half a dozen detectives stood around the door leading to the balcony. The coroner came forward as they entered.

"Just the men we want," he said to Murphy and Farrell. "Come over here. Matson's got the broken piece of grill-work. He picked it up and brought it in before some crazy souvenir-hunter could get to it."

Murphy nodded and asked one or two questions more, as Farrell and Wade leaned over the broken pieces laid carefully on the floor. "What does it show, Dr. Emerson?" Farrell asked anxiously. "Suicide? Or accident? Or can't you tell yet?"

The coroner shook his head. He looked at Farrell intently.

"Neither," he answered. "Murder."

CHAPTER TWENTY-ONE

"Murder?" Wade repeated.

"Murder?" he said again, incredulously, as the coroner nodded. "You mean one of those women on the balcony with her pushed her over?"

"They couldn't have," said Wiggins. He jumped forward to explain. "They didn't push her, doc. I was close. I saw. There wasn't one of 'em who coulda pushed her over."

Farrell gave him a silencing look. He was evidently more troubled than he wanted to own. "What do you mean, Emerson? Are you sure?"

"Sure," said Emerson succinctly. "I'll show you." He knelt down and gravely pointed to the two sections of wrought-iron railing that were lying on the floor. "This is bad business, Farrell, and I'm not denying you've got good reason to be upset. Whoever did this meant it to look like accident, and if it hadn't been for Matson's sharp eyes here we might have said accident at the inquest."

He beckoned them to sit on the floor by him, and indicated the broken railing again. "That rail was a solid piece. Of course it's old. But it has probably been reinforced at the supports many times since the building was first put up a hundred years ago. It's perfectly solid and safe. It didn't break of its own accord."

He indicated one broken end with a pencil. "Look," he said. "Here on the end you'll see two or three faint dents. That shows somebody used a hammer."

"My God," said Wade under his breath.

"Whoever did it," went on the coroner, "started with a file, and then, in order to make it look like a clean break, used a mallet or a hammer to finish it."

He pointed to the other end. "This is from the bottom. You can see it was filed completely through."

He peeled a bit of silvery lead-like substance from the end of the bar. "Solder was used to hold this side in place. The other side—" he turned the filed end toward them—"was filed almost through. The cracks were filled with what looks like gun-grease or shoe polish. I'm not peeling it off, as you'll need it for evidence at somebody's trial."

Farrell, who was crouching opposite him on the floor, examined the broken rail as though trying hopelessly to find evidence that the coroner was mistaken. There was an element of baffled despair in his movements. Wade, who knew what Farrell was feeling at this sudden proof that they must begin again to solve the mystery, did not try to make him speak. Instead he turned to Emerson.

"Then it's murder," he said flatly. "And the person who did it knew every detail of the Dis ceremony. He knew that the king's ladder would have its own support and not lean against the rail—that would have broken the rail inwards and would have caused a lot of inconvenience, but no death. He knew too that when Cynthia reached for the flowers she would have to lean over the rail."

Emerson shrugged, the final impatient shrug of the doctor who has spoken. "Murder," he said, "and mighty well planned."

Murphy grimly bit the end off a cigar. "And not a doubt," he added, "that a fall from that balcony would be fatal."

"Hardly any," Emerson agreed. "The balcony is about twenty feet from the sidewalk. Cynthia was leaning forward to receive the flowers, and I guess the murderer knew she would be. That would be almost certain to make her fall head foremost. The murderer was pretty clever."

"And damn desperate too," Murphy exclaimed with sudden anger. "My Lord, boys, do you get what he did? He was out to kill her, but he didn't care who else he killed in doing it—it was just by God's mercy that there weren't a hundred more deaths in that square. Do you get that?" He turned upon them with rising fury. "Boys, the man that did this thing is going to hang for it or there's no justice. If he don't I'll turn in my badge."

For a moment Wade was silent. Then, slowly, he got to his feet.

"I'm afraid you're right, Murphy. I thought Cynthia killed that man last night. I thought she came back in after the butler knocked him out, and stuck the knife in while he was unconscious. But she didn't. I wish to God we'd been here in time to arrest her for it, though—we'd have saved her life."

"Sure and we'd have saved a lot else, too," Murphy exploded. "There's thirty or forty people in Charity Hospital this minute because of this thing! And any of 'em might have been dead for all this murderer cared." He clamped on his hat. "Give us the report as soon as you can, doc. Come on, fellows: I want to get to work."

The others got to their feet. Farrell paused to speak again to the coroner.

"Look here, Dutreaux," Murphy called from the door, "I want Oliver."

"Oliver," Wade repeated. "That's not a bad hunch."

"Sure it ain't a bad hunch," Wiggins agreed. "Oliver had that ten grand, didn't he? He shot off a big fairy-tale about how he got it, didn't he? He mighta shot hisself in the back, couldn't he? Oliver ain't a bad hunch at all."

"But look here, you," Murphy added to Dutreaux and Wiggins jointly, "don't let anybody know how bad I want him. Just pick him up."

Dutreaux agreed. "Out to his house, I guess," he said. "He'll be coming in after the parade."

"I guess so. And have a couple of men out to get Conroy. That damn Conroy has got a lot of questions to answer."

"Okay, sir. I'll have them look for him."

"Now gentlemen," Murphy wound up, turning grimly to Farrell and Wade, "we'll waste about forty minutes in palaver if you like, and after that I'm going to put somebody on the books for murder."

"Fine." Farrell was smiling as though relieved to have something even faintly amusing to smile at. "We'll go to my office." He paused to speak to Dutreaux. "Get hold of the sister in charge of the emergency ward at Charity and find out how badly hurt Arnold Ghent is and how soon he'll be able to talk. He might know something about this."

"Get Hildreth too," Wiggins volunteered glumly. "Maybe he's the guy we're after."

They went down, through the police lines, and clambered into the waiting auto. Wiggins scrambled in beside the driver. Wade and Murphy and Farrell, in the back seat, were dourly silent as they drove toward the end of the square, which was still a-buzz with scattered groups talking about the near-riot that had interrupted the Dis parade. Wiggins had started an animated argument with the chauffeur about the relative value of mounted men and foot police in controlling a panicky mob, when suddenly there was a scream of brakes and the car swerved. The driver grew eloquently profane at a boy of about fifteen, who had come dashing out from behind another car. The boy laughed, and as the driver swore expertly at him, he pointed an automatic moviescope and caught the chauffeur's wrathful physiognomy before he ran off.

"Them damn kids," said the chauffeur under his breath as he started the car again.

"Look here, you," said Wiggins suddenly. "I gotta get out. You coppers can't drive and I don't wanta get killed. I'll come along."

The car pulled up to the curb. Wiggins grabbed his camera and jumped out.

"Where are you going, kid?" Wade called after him, "Well, I'm going by the *Creole* office a little while, and then I'll run up to your pow-wow. In the meantime, I got an idea."

"An idea?" Murphy frowned.

"Sure, an idea. Ever have one? They make you feel like you'd just swallowed a pineapple. See you later."

CHAPTER TWENTY-TWO

THE declining sun slanted through the bay windows behind Farrell's desk, throwing long bars of light across the smoke-swirled room. Murphy walked up and down the office, his hands clasped behind his broad back. Farrell and Wade sat at the desk, piles of Police Department memorandum sheets in front of them.

The faces of all three of them sagged with weariness, disappointment and defeat. They all felt as if they were facing a hopeless bafflement, fighting in the dark against a killer whose utter ruthlessness they had but just now realized, a killer so desperate that the lives of countless innocent men and women and children were negligible if they stood in the way of his purpose. They remembered those terrible minutes of panic in the square, and shuddered to think what might have happened but for good fortune and the efficiency of the police reserves. They had talked and talked, studying every report with acute attention and going over every detail their own memories could furnish, trying to find some flicker that would light their way to the man or woman they were seeking, and without result.

Now, for some moments, they had been silent. Farrell leaned back in his chair, one hand holding the fist made by the other, thinking; Wade leaned over, his chin resting on the back of his bony hand, smoking as steadily as though the murderer's name lay at the end of a chain of cigarettes; Murphy walked up and down, the thump of his feet making the only sound in the smoky room. Suddenly he stopped and wheeled toward the desk.

"This is the way I see it, boys," he announced. "Parnell was killed for one reason and Cynthia for another. But whatever prompted Cynthia's murder had something to do with her knowledge of Parnell's racket." Wade looked up, thoughtfully crushing out his cigarette. "But it strikes me, Murphy, that Cynthia told us about everything she knew when she admitted that she'd been married to Parnell and that she was collecting his tribute from Esther Morse."

Murphy stalked over to the desk and thumped his heavy forefinger on the sheaf of reports in front of Wade. "Look here, son. You've been studying these things for a long time, both of you. What makes you think Cynthia told you everything? She didn't tell a single thing that wasn't dragged out of her with pincers. She didn't own up about that marriage till Wiggins found it out. She didn't say a word about the money till we closed in on it—and I'm thinking the only reason she told about it then was because she realized that we could trace the bills finally."

Wade glanced at Farrell. Farrell nodded in affirmation.

"Then," Murphy was going on, "we find on top of her other sidestepping that she forgot to tell us about the row in the pantry with Parnell. Of course, she might not have known it was Parnell she had the row with, but we do know that if that fellow hadn't told us about the fight in the pantry we'd never have heard about it from Cynthia. Oh, she didn't have no trouble forgetting things, poor woman—maybe if she'd told us more she might have saved her life."

Farrell held up his hand for a pause. "Is this your idea, then—that each time you talked to Cynthia you got closer to the truth, and that whoever killed Parnell realized that she was gradually telling the whole story? And that he moved just in time to block our getting at the final facts?"

"That's it." Murphy banged the table decisively.

Farrell sat back again to think. Wade lit another cigarette, and as he blew out the match he slowly shook his head.

"Can't see it, Murphy. If you're right, the murderer had plenty of foresight."

Murphy scowled. "What do you mean."

"Well, it's like this, Murphy." Wade spoke deliberately, pausing between his phrases to set his ideas in order. "This thing today was no hurry-up job. It couldn't have been. Whoever killed Cynthia Fontenay had to cut through the balcony rail. That was done last night or maybe the night before or possibly before that. It couldn't have been done after daylight this morning. Hell, Murphy, the street under that balcony was full of people from sunrise."

"That's so," Murphy admitted reluctantly, but Wade was hurrying on.

"If he'd used a gun or a knife it would be easy to fit Cynthia's murder into an idea of panic. It would be easy to say then that one murder was planned and the other had to be done to cover up the first. But the way it was—I can't see it as an emergency killing."

Murphy kicked forward a chair and sat down. "What's your idea, Farrell?"

"Wade sounds right, but he may be wrong," Farrell said. "The balcony rail could have been cut very early this morning—just after your last talk with Cynthia."

"Assuming, of course, that the murderer knew what Cynthia told us," Wade put in. "But if Cynthia's murder wasn't planned at the same time as Parnell's, it was planned very shortly after. Remember, the murderer had just one chance of missing, and that was if the Dis parade had been called off."

"That's right," Murphy nodded. "The parade was necessary for the second murder scheme. But they didn't call it off. The murderer might have suggested that they have it anyway, or somebody else might have suggested it—or maybe they all did. Anyway, they all fell right into his plans."

"There's one thing we must remember," Farrell reminded them. "The murderer knew the Dis arrangements perfectly."

"I'll say he did," nodded Wade. "He knew—listen, there's one man I'd like to talk to. The fellow who set up the ladder. If the ladder Ghent climbed had been closer, and Cynthia hadn't had to reach so far out, she might not have leaned on the rail."

"A damn good hunch," Murphy approved. "We'll get him." He pressed the button on the desk and gave quick orders that the man who set up the ladder for the king of Dis be located and brought post-haste to headquarters. "What else are you thinking about?" he asked as he turned around.

"About that balcony," said Farrell, "draped in a lot of red and black hangings—the rail ready to collapse and the drapery hiding the break. Oh, it was beautifully planned. He's no fool."

Wade sat back and lit another cigarette, watching the smoke curl from the tip. He did not like the job that his friendship for the district attorney had thrust upon him. Years of newspaper work had rid him of a good deal of his native sensitiveness—or at least he usually thought it had, until he saw something like that still white thing on the pavement and that horror in the square. He remembered Cynthia as he had seen her last night—weak and bitter and jaded, but at the same time beautiful and very appealing, and perhaps bitter because she was fighting something the horror of which she had understood then better than he. He wished he had used more tact, and more sympathy. But after a moment his long training prodded at him—this was no time for being sorry. There were things to be done. He sat up.

"That's what we know," he said. "But there's something we don't know. We don't know who this murderer planned to kill besides Cynthia."

Murphy started. "What on earth are you talking about, boy? You mean we've got to sit back and wait for more murders?"

"I don't know," said Wade. "But look at this. Ghent was hurt. If he hadn't fallen on the canopy over his float he'd have landed on the pavement with her. Did the murderer want Ghent out of the way too? And why? We've got to answer that."

"That's true enough," Farrell admitted. "And assuming that the man who held the ladder was innocent, what about him? Suppose he hadn't stepped back in time? Wouldn't he have been killed too?"

The back of Murphy's hand rubbed his nose. "But why try to kill them?"

"My idea exactly, Murphy. Why?" Wade turned back to Farrell. "Ghent made it plain that he and Parnell weren't intimate friends. Parnell threatened him with death last night."

"That checked, didn't it?" Farrell looked at Murphy.

"Sure. Bedclothes burned, Ghent tied up and gagged. Of course he could have fixed all that himself if he wasn't level, but we checked the cab companies and found only one cab was called to that address. That cab picked up a masker and took him to Cynthia's. None of the cab companies took a masker from Cynthia's to Ghent's place. So it looks like Parnell was there, and did leave in a cab, just like Ghent said. Far as we can check his story, it's straight."

"All the same," said Wade, "I think a little talk with Mr. Ghent might be interesting. Maybe he's holding back on something he'd rather we didn't know. We'd better go at him pretty thoroughly, how is he?"

"Not so bad," Murphy answered. "They moved him uptown to a private hospital soon as the emergency people at Charity had looked him over. I think the doctors say he'll be okay in a little while."

"Then I suggest we grill him pretty soon," said Wade. He began to scratch on a wad of copy paper he had taken from his pocket. "This is the way it shapes up to me. Take Hildreth. There's always the chance he killed Parnell and doubled back to Baton Rouge, where he got into bed and waited for us to establish his alibi. Then as to Cynthia—what about that projected marriage of theirs? Cynthia couldn't marry Hildreth till Hildreth was divorced, and if we had any reason to believe she was in the meantime re-establishing an intimacy with Parnell, we'd have a pretty good case against Hildreth. We know Cynthia was doing Parnell a little favor about that blackmail. And don't forget that Hildreth and Ghent both have apartments in that building and either of them could have reached that balcony to file the rail without much trouble."

"Well, if you ask me," said Murphy heavily, "I don't see where a man's got such a damn lot of jealousy in him if he's getting married to a lady that's already had three husbands. But there's all sort of people."

Farrell chuckled. "Men have committed murder for women who've had fifty lovers, Murphy. No, I don't think we'd better overlook that motive in Hildreth's case. And speaking of jealousy, what about Mrs. Hildreth?"

"Right," Wade agreed. "She might have killed Parnell thinking he was Hildreth—the number-on-the-suit theory. She was at the Council meeting. She might have seen Cynthia and masker number 47 duck for the pantry, and she might have picked up the knife and gone after them. Suppose she sees Cynthia run out and then sees the man she thinks is her husband unconscious—or maybe only dizzy after being knocked down by the butler—anyway, he wouldn't be hard to stab."

"I thought," Murphy reminded him, "the fellow said the knife hadn't been around for awhile."

"Maybe Cynthia gave it to Hildreth and Mrs. Hildreth thought it would be an ironic instrument."

"And remember," Farrell added, "the balcony could have been prepared for Cynthia's death after we discovered the identity of the dead man. Mrs. Hildreth might have broken that rail before daylight this morning. Even though her plan to kill her husband had failed, after all, Cynthia was the one she'd be after most."

"I guess she figured she could get her husband later," Murphy surmised. He pushed back his chair and stood up. "Lord, boys," he said wearily, "I wish Cynthia had told us all she knew!"

"So do I," Wade agreed soberly. "But Cynthia can't, now."

"Do you think," asked Farrell, "that Cynthia didn't know who killed Parnell?"

"Well—either way. Suppose Cynthia knew Mrs. Hildreth had killed Parnell by mistake. From what Cynthia said last night, I gathered that she thought Parnell needed killing. And her knowledge would have given her a club over Mrs. Hildreth that would make Hildreth's divorce easy."

Murphy plumped himself back into his chair. "How about that note we found among Parnell's belongings? Where does that come in?"

"I don't know," said Wade. "What about you, Farrell?"

Farrell smiled hopelessly. "As far as I can see, we can get motives for these murders that will fit half a dozen people. What about Dick Barron? He lost that money at Parnell's gambling house, and lost along with it his good name and his father and the girl he was going to marry. If he learned later that the wheels at the Red Cat were crooked, there's plenty of motive, and a great many juries would say he was justified. If he knew Cynthia was helping Parnell blackmail Esther, there's another motive. Oh, he could have killed them both."

"But Cynthia's knife?" Murphy objected.

"That's not improbable," Farrell argued. "The butler said the knife had been missing—all he means is he hadn't seen it around. It might have been anywhere—in a bookcase, where she had left it after cutting the pages of a new book; in the guest bedroom; with the doodads on the whatnot. It's altogether possible that it was something the killer saw in a flash and picked up, in the same fashion that you might pick up a chair in a rough-and-tumble brawl."

"Say, listen," said Murphy ponderously. "Ain't you overlooking the chance that the knife wasn't the Fontenay knife at all?"

"You mean the one Jasper said Oliver had?"

"Sure." Murphy got up, his huge frame towering over the other two. "We know damn well Valdon and Parnell had one hell of a row about something. We know that Conroy had the money and said he got it from Oliver. Oliver we find on all our checking up is a fine upstanding first-class gentleman." Murphy's tone was ironic. "He's such a fine gentleman that he says never a word about the money at all until Wade pins him down. Then Oliver's yarn is that a good fairy gave him the money in the dark and a bad fairy took it away from him. Then he tells another fairy-tale about getting shot." Murphy struck the table. "Hell! Why couldn't Oliver be in on the Red Cat? He's a handy fellow with toys and knows all about springs and electricity. Maybe he fixed up them wheels. You recall that he said he had won the money from Parnell in a private backgammon game? Private!" Murphy snorted. "Maybe he was too smart to play in the regular sucker room."

Murphy banged the table. "Maybe Oliver had a row with Parnell and killed him, and Conroy got on to it and Oliver paid Conroy the ten grand to keep his mouth shut. Maybe Conroy told Valdon and when Oliver went home with Valdon for a drink Valdon wanted more money to keep quiet and they had a scuffle and Oliver got shot. So he runs home, empties his gun out of the window and tells that tale about being shot by a housebreaker."

Wade was listening closely. Murphy's story seemed to fit fairly well. If Oliver had killed Parnell with his own pearl-handled knife, the knife would certainly bring suspicion on Cynthia, or on someone in her house.

"And remember," Murphy was adding emphatically, "*Conroy told Wade about the money.* He was trying to make Oliver take the rap."

"Wait a minute," Farrell interrupted, "how do you fit the method of murder there? The knife under the robe?"

"Cripes," exclaimed Murphy. "You don't think a guy that invents toys would have such a lot of trouble figuring that out, do you?"

He leaned closer to Farrell for emphasis. "That guy Oliver would know all about how to file the balcony, rail, too. And he'd know all about Dis. He designed most of their claptrap, didn't he?" Murphy got up again. "I tell you, boys, Oliver's my candidate."

Farrell was suddenly hopeful. "What do you want me to do?"

"Hold that squint-eyed, coughing jumping-jack maker as a material witness without bond till I get finished with him. That's all. I'll do the rest."

The door of the office swung open. Farrell started indignantly, and then beheld Wiggins' head poked under a protesting officer's arms.

"Hey, Farrell!" Wiggins was yelling, "tell this monkey to let me in. It's important."

"Let him in," said Farrell with a grin, and as Wiggins struggled through and banged the door Murphy asked

"What have you got, kid?"

Wiggins was prancing. "Palenta, hots, pa-*len*-ta. And I got it all here." He marched up to Farrell's desk and gave Wade a big wink. "I brought ya everything I got. Everything. First, I brought this." He laid down the red cord with the dark stain. "And then I brought this." He reached into his inside breast pocket and pulled out an oblong object wrapped in a handkerchief.

"Now this," said Mr. Wiggins, "is a find."

"Hurry up, for heaven's sake!" Wade exclaimed. "What is it?"

"Now don't rush me, pal, don't rush me." With provoking slowness Wiggins unwrapped his parcel. "You see what it is, don't you?"

They gasped and started up. On the desk was a knife with a mother-of-pearl handle, in every detail the duplicate of the knife that had killed Roger Parnell.

Wade was on his feet. "Where in hell did you get that?" he demanded.

"Wait a minute, big boy, wait a minute." Wiggins airily waved his small brown hand. "That ain't all I brought you."

He marched proudly over to the door and flung it open. Crooking his index finger in a persuasive gesture he turned to his three impatient listeners.

"And I brought you this too," he announced. "Miss Lucy Lake, the smartest girl in town."

CHAPTER TWENTY-THREE

LUCY came in and stood an instant looking around at Farrell's austere sanctum and at the men who were waiting there, a trim little figure in a dark blue suit and a little hat that let bright ripples of her hair escape over her cheeks. Her big blue eyes were awed as she watched Murphy pull forward a leather chair and Wade turn over a fresh sheet of copy paper.

"Now don't you be scared, honey," Wiggins was admonishing with unnecessary warmth. "Just tell 'em where you found it and everything."

"Oh, you found the knife, then?" Farrell asked with interest.

"Yes, sir." Lucy sat down, very tiny in the big chair. "I found it just before I telephoned Mr. Wiggins."

"What time was that?"

"About twenty minutes ago."

"I see." Farrell gave her an encouraging smile. "You did quite right to notify us at once."

"I'm glad I did, Mr. Farrell. I'd like to do anything I could to help find out who—who did that to Miss Cynthia."

"We're glad you feel that way, and we want you to help us all you can," he assured her smiling. "Suppose you start by telling us where you found this knife, and how you happened to find it."

"Yes, sir, I will. Mr. Wiggins—" Lucy gave a bright blue glance to her champion—"Mr. Wiggins said the knife was important. I found it in a drawer at the bottom of Mrs. Fontenay's armoire. I went there to look for—" There was a break in her voice. Her slim little shoulders steadied themselves with determination, and her hand went up to her lips as if to stifle a sob. "I was looking—" the words came slowly—"for some things the undertaker—"

Her voice broke again. Wiggins slipped a consoling arm around her.

"That's all right, honey. We know how you feel. Just go ahead and cry if you want to."

Lucy looked up bravely. "There's no sense in my acting like a baby two months old," she said, and wiped her eyes. "The knife was under some lingerie in the bottom drawer of that lavender armoire in Mrs. Fonteney's room," she said, talking fast as though afraid she might break down again. "Tony had told me there was a lot of questioning about whose knife had killed Mr. Parnell, so the minute I found it I phoned him. I remembered it well, because it used to be on the desk in Mrs. Fontenay's sitting room."

"Do you remember when it was lost?" Wade asked her.

"O yes. Mrs. Fontenay had me look for it. She asked all the servants about it. It seems it was specially made and very valuable. That was about two weeks ago."

"Had you looked in the drawer where you found it, before today?" Wade asked.

Lucy puckered her forehead. "I didn't look for the knife there, Mr. Wade, but I must have gone into that drawer a dozen times."

"Then I wonder why you hadn't seen it before?"

"I don't know, except that it was at the very bottom of the drawer, under the tissue paper at the back. Just as if it had been hidden away."

"Anyway," said Farrell with a congratulating smile, "I'm glad you found it." He paused a minute. "Now while you're here, Miss Lake, there are one or two things we'd like to ask you. You knew Mrs. Fontenay very intimately, and we didn't, and you might be able to tell us something that will help us find out who wanted to kill her."

Lucy's slim fingers twisted together in her lap. "Mr. Farrell," she said slowly, "I'll tell you anything on earth I can. Last night—you weren't there, but I suppose Mr. Wade told you—last night I didn't want to say anything. She'd always been good to me, you see, and some of the things about her—well, they might not have sounded very well to people who didn't know her. But now she's dead, and I hope I can help you find whoever it was that killed her."

"Could you give us any lead at all on why anyone should want to kill her?"

"A lot of people didn't like her, I suppose. She used to say some people hated her, were jealous of her and all that. She said so often when she was drinking."

"She drank a good deal, didn't she?" said Wade. Lucy looked at him squarely. "Mr. Wade, she drank all the time, but I think she did it because she wasn't happy. I mean—she wasn't exactly unhappy, but do you know how people are when they don't care about anything very much, and have to drink before they can get any pep?"

He smiled. "Yes, I know what you mean. Tell me this. Was she in love?"

Lucy glanced questioningly toward Wiggins, who had perched on the arm of her chair. Wiggins patted her shoulder.

"Babe," he urged, "tell us about everything. The only one that can be hurt is the guy that pulled this job and he's got it coming to him."

"Well then—" Lucy looked back at Wade—"I guess she was. She was crazy about Mr. Hildreth. He was always around the house. He was there this morning."

"Oh, he was?" Farrell exclaimed. "Who else was there?"

Lucy took off her hat and brushed her hand across her red hair. "Mr. Conroy came before Mr. Hildreth. Mr. Conroy came about noon. That's the first time I ever saw him there, except last night. He said he wanted to see Miss Cynthia."

Lucy paused and glanced back at Wiggins, who pantomimed encouragement, grinning proudly over her head at Wade. She went on.

"Miss Cynthia had just gotten up, and was having her bath. I told her he was there, and she said take him some coffee and have him wait. Mr. Conroy looked terrible. I left him in the dining room, and when I came in he had found a whisky decanter and was having a drink."

"He looked terrible, did he?" Murphy put in with grim satisfaction.

"He certainly did. His clothes were all rumpled and his eyes were bloodshot. After I took him his coffee I went downstairs for a minute and Miss Cynthia rang for me. She had put on a negligee and she told me to tell Mr. Conroy to come in and to bring some whisky. She had already had her breakfast in bed. When I brought in Mr. Conroy and got the whisky Mrs. Fontenay told me to go down to the drug store and get some cold cream and a bromide. I think she wanted to get me out of the way so she could talk."

"Why do you think that?" Farrell asked.

"Because she always telephoned for things from the drug store. I had to wait a long time—there were a lot of people in the store as there always is on Mardi Gras—and when I got back Mr. Conroy and Miss Cynthia had gone out, and Mr. Ghent was there."

"What was he doing?"

"Nothing much. He was in the living room reading the papers. He asked me where Miss Cynthia was, and when I told him I didn't know he said he just wanted to know how she felt. I said she seemed all right, and he said 'Thank God for that,' and we talked a few minutes about last night."

"Do you remember what he said?" Farrell asked.

"He was very nice, but he didn't say anything special—just how dreadful it was, and that he couldn't understand it, and that he hoped Cynthia would be all right. He said tell her that he had been there, and would be home for an hour or so and for her to telephone him if there was anything he could do."

"Then he left?"

"Yes, sir. Just as he got up to go the bell rang, and I thought it might be Miss Cynthia. She goes—" Lucy stopped and swallowed—"she used to go out often without her keys. So I walked with him to the gate."

"Was it Mrs. Fontenay who rang?"

"No, it was Mr. Hildreth. He and Mr. Ghent shook hands, and Mr. Hildreth said he had been having a hell of a time with the police and that he had come by to see Cynthia as soon as he could get away. He said, 'We must spare her as much of this as we can, Arnold,' and Mr. Ghent said 'We certainly must. If you want me, phone my flat.' I let Mr. Ghent out, and Mr. Hildreth said he would come upstairs and wait for Miss Cynthia. He asked me where she was and I said I didn't know. He said 'Leave me alone for awhile. I want to think.' But before I went downstairs he asked me a lot of questions about last night and about how Miss Cynthia felt and what Mrs. Hildreth did. Then I went down. Miss Cynthia came back about five minutes later."

"Was Conroy with her?" Farrell asked.

"No. She was alone."

Farrell made a note on the paper in front of him, then looked up and signaled Lucy to go on.

"I told her that Mr. Ghent had been there and that Mr. Hildreth was upstairs waiting. She said, 'I hope you didn't say I was out with Con

Conroy.' I told her I hadn't mentioned him. She smiled and said 'Good girl. You should be in the diplomatic service.' Then she went up and a little while later she rang and told me to bring up some coffee. When I brought it she asked me where Jasper was and I said I didn't know. She got me to bring drinks for her and Mr. Hildreth, and as I left the room he said something to her that I didn't hear, and she called to me to tell anybody who came that she was out. After Mr. Hildreth left she rang for me again to help her get dressed for the parade."

"Did anyone else call," asked Farrell, "before she went out?"

"Mrs. Hildreth telephoned, and Miss Cynthia laughed and said she couldn't be bothered talking to her. She told me to say she was out."

"Was that all?"

Lucy thought a moment. "That's all I remember, except that she asked me what I thought of Mr. Conroy and I said he seemed nice but he was kind of hardboiled, and she laughed and said 'Honey, I love hardboiled men. They're such babies.'"

"She didn't seem worried then?"

"No. In fact—" Lucy conquered a suspicious quiver in her voice and then finished—"she was singing while she was getting dressed."

"Had she been drinking much?"

"She'd been drinking pretty steadily, but I don't think she was drunk."

"Then she went out?"

"Yes. She told me to go out and enjoy myself, and that I needn't be back till after the parade."

Farrell considered. Murphy took advantage of the pause. He walker over to where Lucy sat.

"Tell me, child, all Mrs. Fontenay's friends knew she was going to marry Hildreth?"

"O yes."

"Did Oliver know it?"

"Why, I suppose he did."

"You're sure he wasn't there today?"

"Absolutely."

"Did Mrs. Fontenay ever say anything to you about Mr. Oliver?"

Lucy pondered. "Ye—es, she did. Once she said something about his being an old woman."

"Anything else?"

"Another time she said 'Oliver is an old maid with all the public proprieties and all the private vices.' She told that to Mr. Ghent."

"Nothing else?"

"Not that I remember."

"All right." Murphy gave her a fatherly smile. "Thanks a lot, young lady." He glanced at Farrell. "That's all I wanted. Let her go now. Miss Lucy, don't you tell anybody what you've told us here. Don't talk about it at all."

Wiggins slid off the arm of the chair and tucked his hand under Lucy's elbow as she stood up. "Come along, honey. We'll run out and get a big dinner. You need it."

"Thanks a lot," Farrell said as Wiggins opened the door.

Lucy smiled over her shoulder. Wiggins made a lordly bow in Wade's direction, and they went out. Murphy took out one of his fat cigars and sat down on the edge of the district attorney's desk.

"Dan," he said decisively, "the knife that killed Parnell was Oliver's knife. I want Oliver held."

"I—wonder," said Wade thoughtfully. "There's something funny about that knife of Cynthia's. Down in the bottom of a drawer."

"Not a bit," protested Murphy. "That drunken Fontenay woman probably put it there and forgot all about it. Here's the point. Oliver may not have done this job, but he knows more about it than he's told. We can use the knife story to break down Oliver, and when he talks we'll get on to Valdon and Conroy and Hildreth and Ghent. Once we put the screws on—" he began to walk up and down again—"they'll all talk. It'll be the old story of seeing who can jump first to give state's evidence and get in the clear. An arrest works wonders to stimulate close-mouthed people."

Wade got up and leaned on the back of his chair, looking out of the window. He was not satisfied. A paper-knife had no business being at the bottom of a drawer under a pile of lingerie. "Just as if it was hidden," Lucy had said.

"Look here, Farrell," Murphy was saying. "I want to talk to Oliver first, and then to the others, and I want to do it without you." He was leaning over the desk, his big elbows spread wide apart. "This is going to be a real old-fashioned job. I'm going to get the truth if I've got to dig out all somebody's teeth."

Farrell started to object, but Murphy had not paused for breath. "O yes I will. Look, Farrell. Here's a murderer loose. He kills a man and a woman and he might have killed a dozen others." Murphy's face was red with wrath. "The man's a fiend, I tell you, and I'll have the truth out of him if it breaks me and kills him. By God I *will*, and nothing in the world will stop me!"

"You seem pretty sure you've got your man," Wade challenged softly.

"And why in hell shouldn't I be? That damn bunch of crooks. Tied in with a gambling joint that's got wheels and dice that ought to be in a circus. Oliver and Conroy and Valdon—particularly Oliver and Conroy. Practising illusions on us. Sticking a knife in a man and not through his clothes. Sawing a balcony rail so it looks right but falls to pieces. Doing some sleight-of-hand with the money Esther Morse forked over in the dark. That bunch needs smashing and I'm going to do it. What's that, Farrell?"

But Farrell was speaking not to Murphy, but into the mouthpiece of the telephone. "Yes, this is Farrell. Go ahead."

Wade was watching Murphy, who was pacing the little office like a caged animal eager to spring if the door could only be opened.

"All right," said Farrell into the telephone. "We'll come over. Right away, yes." He hung up.

"Ghent's doctor reports that we can talk to his patient now," Farrell explained as he walked around the desk and took his coat and hat off a tree in the corner. "I'll look up Valdon and have a talk with him while you and Wade go over to the hospital. We may want Conroy before the day is over. Anyway, I'm going to try to get Valdon to see it my way and tell us a few things about that fair-haired boy."

He grinned at Murphy. "Oliver," he added as he walked to the door, "will have to wait."

CHAPTER TWENTY-FOUR

ARNOLD Ghent was propped up in a bed strewn with the afternoon newspapers when Wade and Murphy were shown into his room. His sunburnt face, looking darker than ever against the white of his pillow, was enigmatic as he looked up. Wade wondered how much he knew.

"How are you feeling, Ghent?" he asked.

Ghent gave him a dour smile. "Oh, I'm in pretty good shape. No bones broken. I'm afraid I wrenched my back a bit, though."

Murphy drew up a chair and heaved himself into it. "Well, as long as you're all right, there's a couple of things we want to talk to you about. You had a damn narrow escape, young man."

"I seem to be going in for narrow escapes these days." Ghent looked away from them toward the window. "It was pretty ghastly," he said in a low voice. "One minute she was there above me, smiling, lovelier than I'd ever seen her before—and then the crash. I keep thinking I might have saved her—might have caught her as she fell."

"Now, boy," Murphy admonished soothingly. "You couldn't have helped it. You've got your guardian angel to thank that you weren't killed too."

Ghent turned to him with sudden vehemence. "No I haven't, Captain Murphy. It wasn't luck. It was because I'm a champion diver. As that ladder was struck out from under me I made a sort of turn in the air and sighted that canopy stretched over the throne on my float. If I hadn't been able to twist myself so as to dive straight for it I'd have shot to the pavement."

Wade was silent for a moment. "Do you remember what happened after that?" he asked.

"Not for the first few minutes. The first thing I remember is when they took me off to put me into the ambulance."

"Well, it's a devil of a business." Murphy's hands pushed back his mop of white hair. "I don't understand it, Ghent. That woman was so damned indifferent about the death of Parnell. He was a husband of hers—you knew that?"

"Not until I read it in the papers."

"Well, they'd been husband and wife, and this does seem like divine retribution. But it was no divine hand that sawed that balcony rail."

"No." Ghent shuddered. Wade, leaning on the foot-piece of the bed, was watching him thoughtfully. Wade had not forgotten that Ghent's account of what had happened in his flat the night before was not and could not be proved, and he searched with almost fearsome intensity for some suggestion that would demonstrate to him either Ghent's sincerity or its opposite.

"I don't know whether or not you realize it, Ghent," he began after a pause, "but you're probably going to be able to help us a great deal."

Ghent made a little deprecating gesture as though discounting a polite phrase. "I should like to, but I'm afraid I'm not logical enough to be a detective."

"That wasn't what I had in mind." Wade moved around the side of the bed nearer to him and spoke with emphasis. "It's evident, Ghent, that whoever killed Mrs. Fontenay was not at all loath to kill you with her." He paused to let this make an impression, glad to observe that Ghent was following him closely. "Now people don't murder without motive, Ghent, unless they're insane. Sometimes the motive that prompts a murder is one that to the outside world seems so trivial as not to be worth considering, and that's often the hardest part of investigating a murder—for the only person who could tell you about the motive is dead."

Ghent nodded slowly. "I think I understand you," he said. "You want me to tell you the name of someone who might have had a reason for wanting to kill me, because technically I'm the victim of a murder-scheme that didn't quite come off."

"That's it."

Ghent's heavy black eyebrows drew together in a meditative frown. He reached to the bedside table and felt for a cigarette. Wade struck a match for him and waited. For nearly a minute nobody spoke. Murphy, leaning forward with his elbows on his knees and the palm of one hand thoughtfully stroking the back of the other, was listening too, obviously hoping that here at last he would be given a pointer toward the dissolution of his bafflement.

"That's a very difficult question," Ghent said at length, with a faint smile. "Suppose I put it to you, Wade—who wants to kill you? Or you?"—to Murphy.

"Well, son, I've been shot at," Murphy admitted gruffly, "but I usually knew who it was. And I ain't been shot at this week."

Ghent chuckled, and then grew serious again. He looked back at Wade. "Sorry, Wade, but I'm afraid I can't answer you. In the first place, I don't know of anybody who'd benefit by my death, and in the second—"

"Valdon?" interrupted Murphy. "Conroy?"

"Certainly not," Ghent returned emphatically. "I've got only the most casual sort of acquaintance with them both."

"Hm," grunted Murphy. "That's what Mrs. Fontenay said about Roger Parnell."

"Did she?" Ghent smiled. "Only in this case it happens to be true."

"What about Hildreth?" Murphy prodded.

"Hildreth? Good Lord, no. Hildreth and I are good friends. Have been for years."

"Mrs. Hildreth?"

"Don't be absurd. What I was going to—"

"Say what you please, Ghent," Wade interposed, "but it's possible that somebody has tried to kill you twice and has failed each time."

He watched carefully for Ghent's reaction, but Ghent shook his head, and before he could answer Murphy spoke.

"What about that Barron boy? He was plenty sore at Parnell."

"But not at me. Listen, Captain Murphy. This sort of thing is foolish, because what I've been trying to tell you is that nobody has tried to kill me."

"You seem very certain," Wade countered.

Ghent looked up at him, leaning forward a trifle to emphasize what he said.

"I *am* certain, Wade. Your idea seems to be that this murderer, whoever he is, made up his mind to kill Cynthia, and figured that whether or not I was killed too didn't particularly matter. I think you're wrong. I believe the murderer had planned that everything should happen exactly as it did."

Wade was interested. He sat down on the edge of the bed. "Go on, Ghent. That's an intriguing theory, if you can support it."

"I think I can. Listen. The only thing we know about this murderer is that he's a man—or woman—capable of the most careful and detailed sort of planning. Roger Parnell's death took place under circumstances that made it impossible for suspicion to point directly at anybody. His going to a ball where nobody expected him to be, wearing Ross Hildreth's suit and passing himself off to Cynthia as me—that's too perfect for the murderer, Wade, to make it just a series of lucky accidents. The murderer must have contrived all that somehow for his own purposes—to delay your discovering Parnell's identity as long as possible, and to hide himself under a lot of confusion. Of course, it *might* have just happened so, but I doubt it."

Wade nodded. "That's reasonable. How does it lead up to your theory about what happened today?"

"Why, look at the way he contrived Cynthia's death," Ghent answered with a trace of impatience, as though annoyed at having to slow down his own volatile mind to match a slower and more meticulous pace. "The whole thing was perfectly devised. The man who arranged it isn't the type to leave anything to accident. If he'd wanted to kill me, he'd have schemed something whereby my death wouldn't have been left to chance. A man as careful as this man evidently is must have taken into account the fact that I'm a practiced high-diver. He'd also have remembered that there was a canopy over the throne float, and he must have known that I was skilful enough to dive toward it. He *knew* I wasn't going to get killed."

"Then you mean," Wade finished thoughtfully, "that his idea was to look as if he'd made a mistake—that he had intended to kill you, but that a lucky chance had saved your life?"

"That's exactly what I do mean," Ghent exclaimed. "You're overlooking the fact that there wasn't any way to be sure I'd be standing on the ladder when Cynthia fell. Her chair was in front of the others on the balcony, so that she must have been nearly touching the rail all the time. She might have stood up and leaned over to see the parade coming, or to wave to some friend of hers she saw in the square, and if she had, the rail would have given way—long before I was anywhere close to her."

"That's a pretty good notion, young man, a pretty good notion." Murphy edged his chair closer to the bed and put several questions about details of Ghent's explanation. Wade got up and walked slowly over to the window. He looked down at the street, thinking. Wade's reasoning processes were seldom swift, and he had few intuitive flashes. He liked an orderly presentation of ideas. But he was ready to admit that though Ghent's quick words and restless gestures annoyed him, what Ghent had suggested was probably correct. He turned back toward where Ghent and Murphy were talking and was about to put a question of his own when the door opened.

"Come right in," said a nurse's voice. "The doctor says don't stay very long, and don't let Mr. Ghent get excited."

"We won't. Thank you," Farrell's voice answered as the door swung inside, and the district attorney came in. With him were Valdon and Con Conroy.

Valdon sat down. Conroy leaned negligently against the bureau, one elbow resting on its glass top and one knee bent so that his foot supported him against the baseboard of the wall. He smiled at Murphy, Wade and Ghent with bland good nature while Farrell exchanged a few pleasantries with Ghent as a means of opening the interview.

"Valdon tells me he didn't take part in the Dis parade today," Farrell was saying. "Conroy admits he was there. Do you remember seeing him, Mr. Ghent?" Ghent glanced at Conroy and smiled. "Sorry," he answered, "but I don't. Of course, if Conroy had his mask on, I wouldn't have recognized him. I didn't see him at all this morning, that I'm sure of, except for a few minutes in the Dis den just before the parade."

"Did you two have anything to say to each other?" Ghent hesitated. Wade glanced at Valdon and Conroy. Valdon's face was stormy, but Conroy's as usual bore an expression of meaningless and exasperating innocence. "Not very much," said Ghent.

Farrell glanced at Conroy, whose smiling poise did not alter.

"The point, Mr. Farrell," said Conroy amiably, "is that Mr. Ghent and I had a bit of a row. Nothing serious, you understand, but he perhaps thinks that our friend the diligent captain here—" he bowed to Murphy— "might take it as grounds for throwing me into that rat-trap again. N'est-ce pas, Mr. Ghent?"

"Well, what happened?" insisted Murphy.

Ghent shrugged. "I'd hardly call it a row," he demurred. "I'd forgotten it till Mr. Farrell asked me when I'd last seen Conroy. After the floats had been driven out of the den I remembered something I had left in my locker, and went back into the den to get it. The building seemed to be empty, but when I got around to the lockers I saw Conroy. He looked as if he was trying to get into my locker. Of course I was pretty indignant for a minute, and asked him what the idea was, but as soon as he answered me it was obvious that he'd had a few drinks too many and had mistaken my locker for his. That was all."

"Oh," said Murphy meaningfully. "Trying to get into your locker, was he?" He grimly turned his chair so that it faced Conroy. "What do you say about this, young man?"

Conroy bowed. "Guilty as charged, I suppose." His smile was as guileless as a baby's. "I was confused and I did think it was my locker. That's my story, sir, and I am obliged to stick to it."

"M-*hm*," said Murphy. "M-*hm*." His grunt made it quite evident that he did not feel himself obliged to stick to it. "Now let me see. What's the number of your locker, Ghent?"

"Fourteen."

"And what's the number of yours, Conroy?"

"Thirty-two, sir."

"Quit being a chump, Murphy," Valdon exclaimed suddenly.

Murphy paid him no attention. "Are those two lockers on the same aisle, by any chance?"

"They are all in a row," Ghent told him. "The lockers are up against the back wall of the building." Valdon got up. "Look here, Farrell. It's time Murphy laid off this kid. He's been trying to frame him ever since last night. It's no crime to mistake a locker number in a half-dark building."

Farrell was not excited. "You're quite right, Fritz, it isn't. But minor incidents can't be overlooked in a case like this."

"Huh." Murphy settled himself back in his chair. "It's just one of those little things I'll be remembering." Conroy bowed again. "Don't crowd yourself Captain Murphy." He smiled at Valdon. "Take it easy, Fritz." Valdon gave a disgruntled turn on his heel. "All the same—"

"Hi, everybody! So we're all here!" chirruped an enthusiastic voice as the door opened and Mr. Wiggins, camera, tripod and all, bounced into the room. "How you be, Mr. Ghent? Good. Boss wants a picture of you in bed."

Farrell and Murphy had stepped aside to avoid being knocked down, for Wiggins was in even higher spirits than usual. He was setting up his camera. Ghent demurred faintly. "My picture—here in bed?"

"Oh, give the girls a break," Wiggins over-ruled. "You're too lucky to be left outa the paper, Mr. Ghent. Boy, I've seen you win plenty of cups, but I never saw such a pretty dive as the one you made off that ladder." He turned to the others, hands spread out. "Ain't it a fact? You know, that dive's gonta be—"

"Hurry and take your picture," interrupted Farrell with good-humored tolerance. "We're here on business."

"Sure, and ain't I here on business too? But I'll hurry. I just wanted to tell these gentlemen a piece of news they might like." He pranced happily toward the patient. "Didja know I got a permanent record of that dive? For pos-ter-i-ty." He brought the polysyllable out proudly. "Lissen, Murph. Remember when that half-witted chauffeur of yours nearly knocked down that boy in the street? The kid had a movie camera and I had an idea. Great stuff. He was up on the balcony next to the one Mrs. Fontenay was on, taking pictures of the whole thing, when she fell. I saw him there. So when I saw him again I figured what fun it would be if he had it all on the film, so I hopped out and grabbed him, and he swears he got it all. Of course I don't know, get me, on account it takes time to have it developed, but won't it be swell if it's there?"

He paused triumphantly, but the effect of his announcement had been astonishing. Conroy's bland smile had given way to an intent look strange to see on his cherubic face, as though his attention had been suddenly switched inward to the solution of a rare and dangerous problem. He glanced at Valdon, but Valdon was scowling darkly at Wiggins' elated face. Conroy's hands slowly tightened into fists, and were thrust into his coat pockets. Ghent had murmured "That's fine," but there was a momentary change in his expression, almost as though a shadow had fallen across his face for an instant and then had passed. Wade watched all three men, challenged as well as puzzled by their reactions, but Wiggins, blithely pointing his camera toward the bed, was chattering again.

"—so me personally, I think this messing up of Mardi Gras would be a crime even if there hadn't been any people killed. All set, Mr. Ghent? Okay—give us the old smile." He snapped the shutter. "Thanks."

"Now suppose you pack up," Farrell suggested smiling. "We've got a lot to talk about."

"Sure. Mug 'em and leave 'em, that's me." He whisked away his plates. "I got work to do myself. Well, so long, fellows. Here's hoping we—"

The telephone alongside the bed gave a long low buzz. Murphy picked it up.

"For you, Farrell."

Farrell took the receiver. "Yes? This is Farrell speaking . . . Oh—all right. You know what to do, don't you, until we get there? . . . Certainly, by all means keep him waiting. . , . Alright. Thank you."

He put the receiver back on its hook with a meticulous care which to Wade looked like artificial calmness masking excitement that he did not want to share. Farrell turned to Ghent.

"Sorry, but this makes me go back downtown. Hope you'll be all right and that we haven't bothered you too much."

"Not at all," Ghent answered. "I should be up sometime this afternoon or tomorrow."

"I hope you will. We won't take all your company with us—Valdon and Conroy can stay. I'll call you this evening, Fritz." He crossed to the door. "Come along, Murphy. You too, Wade—I'll drop you and Wiggins by the *Creole* on the way down."

Murphy, his mouth and eyes wide open with surprise, managed to contain himself through Farrell's genial leavetaking, but once outside in the corridor he fairly hissed, "What the hell, Dan?"

The district attorney glanced at Wade, who was leaning against the closed door in a negligent attitude that belied the closeness with which he was listening; and at Wiggins, who was goggle-eyed with expectation of something portentous. Farrell's face was grim.

"You wanted Oliver, didn't you?" he retorted tersely. "Well, we've got him for you. He's up at the Dis den. Deader than hell. Hildreth found the body."

CHAPTER TWENTY-FIVE

A POLICE searchlight made a glaring cone through the semi-darkness of the Dis den. Halfway down the cone of light stood the goldfish float that had been part of the Dis parade, the cellophane slope of the bowl reflecting bright patches that shone between the goldfish dangling inside and the excited group of men who were waiting impatiently for the coroner to scramble up on the float and complete the first step in the process of discovering how Mark Oliver had met his death. They felt angry, cheated and bewildered, for all they knew so far was that the crazy goldfish suit held Mark Oliver's body, dead from a bullet wound.

Wiggins, too full of energy to await the coroner's report, was hopping hither and yon like a grasshopper, flashing his lamps and snapping pictures among the floats that stood deserted in the shadows. The den was an enormous barn-like building admitting light only through a skylight and two small high windows in each of its hundred and fifty-foot walls, built according to the Carnival tradition which requires that floats for the parades be built in secrecy. The searchlight cut a piece out of the darkness, and Wiggins' lamps made momentary splotches of light; for the rest, the floats stood against the wall, their strange shapes just discernible.

Ross Hildreth stood with Wade, Farrell, Murphy and the group of policemen, looking oddly out of place with his light tan polo coat and his amber cigarette holder. "No, there was nobody here when I found the body," he was saying to Murphy with a trace of polite asperity.

The coroner climbed down from the goldfish platform. Following directions given them by Hildreth, the coroner's assistants had managed to remove one of the sections of the cellophane bowl, giving him access to the dangling body. Dr. Emerson walked over to where the others were standing. "We'll be moving the body in a minute," he said to Farrell, "just as soon as the police photographer gets through making the pictures for the Homicide office."

"What's the report to be?" Wade asked.

"Bullet through the right lung. I'll send over the post-mortem data right away."

Murphy made a gesture toward the bowl. "What do you make of it, Emerson?"

"What can I?" The coroner gave him a hopeless smile. "A man virtually in a glass case is shot in the side and the glass not even cracked. No weapon and no sign of one anywhere." He shrugged. "I'm glad my job is just to find out what happened and not how it happened, this time."

He clamped on his hat and picked up his black bag. "I'll be waiting on him at the morgue. Send him along when the wagon comes."

"Cheerful chap, isn't he?" Hildreth remarked to Wade as Dr. Emerson walked off.

"Very. But it's all in the day's work to him. No matter who's dead, for him it's just another autopsy."

Hildreth reached in the pocket of his polo coat and drew out a pigskin cigarette case. "It's odd," he said when he had fitted a cigarette into his amber holder and lighted it. "Odd, you know, about Oliver. I wonder what he had done to deserve this."

"It's even harder to understand than the others," Wade agreed. He was looking at Hildreth carefully. This was a strange reaction, he thought. Murphy had not heard Hildreth's remark, for Dutreaux had taken his chief and the district attorney off to one side and was making a many-gestured statement to them.

Hildreth glanced up at the bowl. "Rather like an exaggeration of a parlor trick," he observed.

He looked at the goldfish float with the air of a man studying some macabre work of art. Or perhaps, Wade thought, Hildreth suggested this simile because his spiked blonde moustache and the slight tilt of his derby, his careless elegance and his politely interested manner, all seemed so much more appropriate for a dilettante strolling through a museum than for the discoverer of a murder. Wade wondered if his attitude was a defense mechanism. In spite of his man-about-townish appearance,

Hildreth had an enviable record as an aviator during the war, and his ruthlessness overseas had contradicted his apparent casualness at home.

"It's like one of those riddles they hand out in intelligence tests," Wade remarked as he rapidly made a rough sketch of the bowl and the goldfish. "'A' is a man in a glass bowl. 'B' is a bullet in his lung. The bowl is not broken. How did 'B' get into 'A'? Two minutes to answer."

Hildreth smiled. "Some mechanically-minded chap might figure it out. I'm no good at mechanics."

"Except the sort that go with pursuit planes, eh?"

"And a dub even in that department."

Wiggins came scampering up. "Mr. Hildreth for a picture," he announced.

Hildreth grimaced, and Wade thought he was about to object, but after an instant he answered tolerantly,

"Shoot away. But make it as painless as possible."

Wade left them and walked closer to the float to examine it at close range. He noted that the arch curving above the bowl bore the ironic title, "Without a Secret."

The float was about twenty-two feet long and ten wide, and its edges were draped with red bunting that fell nearly to the ground on all four sides. In the center stood the bowl, about seven feet wide at its equator, made by stretching cellophane over four arched ribs that were fastened in the floor of the wagon. The ribs were nickeled, and at the top supported a nickeled ring about four feet across, over which fitted the glass top of the bowl. Across the ring was a metal X, the four arms of which hooked over the four ribs, and from the center of the X hung four strands of piano wire that fastened into the figure of the fish, two at the middle, one at the tail and another at the head. From a distance the arched ribs were hardly noticeable, and the piano wire was virtually invisible, so that the float presented the illusion of a goldfish in its bowl gazing back at a world that gazed at him.

The bottom of the bowl was decorated like a parlor aquarium with a brown papier-mâché castle and green cloth seaweed, and the floor, which was really the floor of the truck, was sprinkled with sand. In the sand were some splotches of blood.

"It's the devil's own device," Wade heard Murphy say behind him.

He turned around. "Tricky," he agreed soberly.

"It's like some damn fakir's trick," Murphy exploded. "We can't find a thing to show which way the bullet came in. The lid on the bowl is intact, the sides haven't a scratch on them, and there's no hole at the bottom of the truck. It's hell."

As an ambulance swerved past the patrolmen guarding the entrance and drove inside the den, Wade moved to one side. Two men carrying a stretcher got out of the ambulance, and a Bertillon officer followed them, unrolling a wide white sheet. "We may want to look for more prints," he called to Murphy. "We've got only one set so far."

"And they," Hildreth remarked grimly, "are probably mine."

Murphy shrugged. "We'll just move off and let these fellows do their work. There's some things we'd better get out of the way as soon as we can. Eh, Farrell?"

Farrell agreed. As they stepped out of the way of the ambulance Farrell turned to Hildreth.

"I'd like to check up on Dutreaux's report, Mr. Hildreth. You called headquarters as soon as you discovered the body?"

"I met Sergeant Dutreaux just outside and told him. He telephoned. I'd been here as long as five minutes, I suppose."

Murphy stroked his chin and glared. "I guess you pawed everything up pretty well?"

Hildreth gave him a polite frown. "I suppose so, if you want to call it that."

Murphy grunted.

"By the way, Mr. Hildreth," Farrell intervened, "had you asked anyone to come up here with you?"

"No. I was in something of a hurry." He smiled grimly. "Of course, if I'd had any idea of what I was to find, I'd certainly have brought along some unimpeachable witness."

Wade sat down on an empty goods-box and watched Hildreth as he stood leaning against one of the posts that supported the roof, carefully fitting a fresh cigarette into his holder. But Farrell seemed to be more interested in getting the broad outlines of the affair than in observing any minor reactions, illuminating though they might be. "What was the reason for your visit to the den this afternoon?" he asked in a business-like fashion.

"Why, I wanted to see Oliver. I called his house several times and got no answer. So I came here." Murphy bit off the end of a cigar. "Mighty brave of you to call us right up. You might have just ducked and left the body for someone else to find."

"O, no." Hildreth smiled. "It wasn't any demonstration of courage. I was afraid someone might have recognized me as I entered the building. I have a set of keys, you know, and I weighed the advantages. If I'd run away and had been seen my position would have been pretty bad. So I decided the wise move would be to call the police at once. Anyway, I met Sergeant Dutreaux as I was going out—after I had decided to telephone, but before I had had time to do it."

"Can you remember what you told Dutreaux?" Farrell asked. His voice was mild.

"The sergeant? I told him about how I came on Oliver's body. Is that what you want me to tell you?"

"Yes."

"When I couldn't locate Oliver by telephone I remembered that when I had last seen the float in the square, Oliver was still in the goldfish bowl. It occurred to me suddenly that he might have been forgotten in the shuffle. The police might have thought the goldfish was a dummy figure, and I knew if Oliver had been driven back to the den he couldn't have gotten out of the bowl by himself. So I rushed up here to let him out."

"What time was that?"

"Shortly after four. I had just come from the morgue."

His voice did not weaken as he spoke the last sentence. And yet, Wade reminded himself, Hildreth had been planning to marry Cynthia Fontenay. He wondered how any man could maintain an appearance of such complete detachment from personal tragedy.

Hildreth had not paused. "When I unlocked the main entrance doors of the den and came in, I saw the goldfish float parked over near the wall, about where it was when you came in. It was pretty dark in here, but I could see that the goldfish was still in the bowl. I was surprised that the figure was so still. It was simply dangling there. I struck a match, and saw blood on the sand at the bottom of the bowl."

"Did you open the bowl then?"

"I went out to my car for a flashlight, and when I came back in I took the top off the bowl and got inside of it. I had helped Oliver get into his things this morning, so I knew how to unhook the headpiece of the goldfish costume. I took it off. It was plain that he was dead. I started for a phone. As I reached the door, I saw a police car. Sergeant Dutreaux was in it. I told him what had happened."

"Where was the police car when you saw it?" asked Farrell.

"In the driveway."

"Had it stopped?"

"Yes, I believe it had."

Farrell did not speak for an instant, then asked, "You said you were going out to phone?"

Hildreth nodded.

"But there is a phone here." Farrell motioned toward the booth in a corner.

Hildreth smiled. "So there is." He reached into his pocket. "But you see—" his hand came out holding two fifty-cent pieces—"*that's* all the change I had. You can't put a half-dollar into a pay phone. So I had to go outside. There's a drug store about a block from here."

"I see." Farrell smiled. There was a drug store on the corner, and he knew it, but between the drug store and the Dis den was Hildreth's car. Whether Hildreth had been on his way to his car or to the store when he met Dutreaux was another of the annoying details that could not be proved.

"The policeman came in with me." Hildreth's suavity was still unruffled. "He confirmed my first judgment that Oliver was dead, and he, having a nickel in his pocket, phoned you from the booth in here."

"Say," Wiggins interrupted from a dark corner as Farrell was about to speak, "were you in the Dis parade today?"

Hildreth glanced across to where Wiggins, sitting on his camera, had been observing the proceedings. "No," he said briefly, and returned his attention to Farrell. "I was to have worn my regular Dis costume as a marshal. But you're holding it as Exhibit A, or something like that."

"You had planned to be in the parade, hadn't you?" Farrell asked.

"O, yes. On the king's float."

Murphy took it up. "You *were* in Jackson Square, though. Don't deny that, now."

"I have no intention of denying it," Hildreth returned crisply. "Certainly I was in Jackson Square."

"When Mrs. Fontenay was murdered," Murphy finished. "That's true, isn't it?"

"Yes." Hildreth looked coolly at Murphy. "You will find, Captain Murphy, that it was I who picked up her body and held it until the ambulance got through the crowds."

His answer was given with a certain quiet solemnity that puzzled Wade. It was as though he wished to remind them that in his own fashion he was mourning Cynthia's death.

"Where were you when the balcony rail collapsed?" Murphy demanded inexorably.

"Almost directly underneath it. I had placed the ladder for the king. I was—"

"Wait a minute!" Murphy barked it out. "You say you placed the ladder in position?"

"Yes," said Hildreth calmly. "I leaped aside just in time to keep myself from being struck. I was waiting to take it away after Ghent got down. It was pure luck I wasn't killed too."

"And you knew Ghent was the king, eh?"

Hildreth shrugged. "After your investigation last night, Captain Murphy, everybody knew everybody else in Dis. There was very little pretense at secrecy this morning. Of course I knew Ghent was the king."

Murphy's chest expanded. His cigar poked out at an arrogant angle as his teeth closed on it. "Well now, Hildreth, you know it's a theory of mine and of these gentlemen here that if that ladder had been placed closer to the balcony, Cynthia Fontenay might not have fallen."

Hildreth's eyes met Murphy's with frozen courtesy. "That's part of my theory too, captain."

"Oh, it is, eh?" Murphy nodded his head in ironic wonder.

Hildreth turned patiently to Farrell. "In fact, Mr. Farrell, that's why I came here this afternoon. I wanted to see Oliver about it. My thought was that if the ladder had been closer Ghent might have been able to hand the flowers over the railing to Cynthia, instead of her having to lean forward to reach them."

"And what, pray," inquired Murphy with plain incredulity, "did Oliver have to do with that?"

Hildreth looked at him. A little knot of muscle showed at each side of his jaw. His eyes narrowed. Wade, watching him, found now that it was not at all difficult to believe the stories he had heard of Hildreth as a fighter.

"Murphy," snapped Hildreth, "I'm damn sick and tired of your manner. I want to help you all I can, but I will not stand up here and let you smirk and suspect any longer. Either you'll treat me as a decent citizen until you're able to prove otherwise or I'll see you in hell before I tell you a few things I'm sure you don't know."

As Farrell started to speak Hildreth addressed him, more calmly but still with evident anger. "This man is preposterous, Farrell. I'm not so dull that I don't understand what he's thinking and of course I know it's part of his job to think it. But I will not be treated like an idiot any longer. Either Murphy changes his methods or I shut up."

Murphy had planted himself in front of him. "You're a pretty wise guy, Hildreth, but you might find it pretty hard to explain a lot of things." His face was close up to Hildreth's.

"Just a minute, Murphy," Farrell cut in. "Hildreth, you can either talk or not talk as you prefer. Murphy is entirely within his rights in asking you questions. You must remember that this is the third murder in less than twenty-four hours, and all of us are very eager—perhaps at times too eager—to find some definite clue to work on. If you prefer, you may address all your remarks to me instead of to Murphy and let me conduct the questioning, but several more questions there must be, whether you see fit to answer them or not."

"Sure," from Murphy. "Go ahead."

Hildreth was regaining his self-control. He shrugged. "Sorry. My nerves are bad. Dreadfully sorry." Murphy answered with a conciliatory wave of his hand.

"What I wanted to explain to you," Hildreth went on, speaking again with his characteristic easy detachment, "was that Oliver staged this spectacle. You know of course that every minute detail of a Carnival parade is worked out beforehand. Oliver had marked the pavement under the balcony last night. There were four crosses in red chalk, one marking the position of each foot of the ladder. As you know, it was a step-ladder and rather unwieldy. When I put it in place several policemen helped me. We simply followed the marks on the pavement. I handed the flowers up to Ghent, and stepped back to the curb. I wanted to see Oliver about the position of those crosses on the pavement, and that's why I'm here."

"How almighty inconvenient," Murphy whispered to Wade, "that Oliver should be dead."

Wade glanced apprehensively toward Hildreth, afraid that the whisper would make him angry enough to quit talking for good, but Hildreth, who was facing Farrell, gave no sign that he had heard it. Farrell was speaking.

"Can you substantiate the fact that Oliver marked the place for the ladder?"

"Why yes. There are others who knew it."

"I thought—" Farrell's words came slowly—"that the Dis arrangements were always secret."

Hildreth frowned thoughtfully. "They were, but I'm sure someone besides Cynthia knew Oliver was managing the parade. She told me."

Farrell nodded. After an instant's pause he asked, "You say you rigged up that fish float this morning? How did Oliver seem?"

"Truthfully," Hildreth answered after considering the query, "a bit nervous. He had the bandage on his head."

"What do you mean by nervous?"

"Well, he wanted to avoid people. Didn't seem to want anyone to know what float he was on."

"Anything else?"

"Not particularly. Just seemed to have his wind up a bit. I thought probably that attack last night had upset him, and I suggested"—Hildreth smiled wryly—"that he let me take his place. He wouldn't hear of it. Said something about being safer there than most places."

"Who else knew he was on that float?"

"That I can't say."

Farrell considered. "Is there anything more you can tell us, Hildreth?"

Several seconds passed before Hildreth answered. "Only this," he said finally. "I was going to marry Mrs. Fontenay. I am very eager to do what I can to help you. And that," he added smiling, "includes you, Captain Murphy. I'll answer any questions any time you care to ask them. Tell you anything I know, no matter how personal." His voice rose, and he ended almost fiercely, "All I want in return is the promise that I can see whoever killed Cynthia hang for it."

For a moment nobody spoke. Wiggins suddenly jumped up from where he had been sitting on his camera. "Well, I'm gonta tell you something," he exclaimed. "If you're right, I'm with you. If you're wrong, I ain't. I got a movie film of that parade. If it shows you standing where you said you were you're okay. If it don't—" Wiggins made a gesture with his thumb in the vague direction of the *Creole* office. "I'll get that picture pretty soon. After I look at it I'll call you up."

"And about the questions—" Murphy started, but Farrell interrupted him.

"We are very grateful for your pledge of co-opera-tion, Mr. Hildreth. Dutreaux, go to the door with Mr. Hildreth and tell the officers on guard there to let him out. If you have to leave town, Mr. Hildreth, please let us know before you go. We may want to see you later this evening."

"All right." Hildreth nodded curtly at them and walked away. Farrell watched him till he was out of earshot. Then he wheeled on Murphy.

"Order a squad of men here at once with plenty of lights," he said in an undertone. "Comb this place for a gun. And have somebody tail that fellow till you get further orders from me."

Wiggins, who had withdrawn back into the shadows, chuckled softly.

CHAPTER TWENTY-SIX

MURPHY had started on a run for the telephone booth.

Farrell, his hands deep in his pockets and his lips tight with grim determination, was walking stiffly up and down the great room. Dutreaux was consulting in low tones with the other men from headquarters. Wade was lighting a cigarette and casting a sidelong glance at Wiggins, whose mirth had not subsided. He walked over to him.

"What's so funny, half-pint?"

With the query Wiggins' soft chuckle broke into laughter that fairly doubled him up. Farrell turned on him with irritated swiftness and Dutreaux and his colleagues stared in amazement. Murphy, coming back from the telephone, glared at Wiggins with an animosity which said plainly that now at last they would get somewhere if half-witted shrimps would only behave themselves with decorum and not distract the progress of the law.

"What the hell is the matter with you, Wiggins?" Farrell exclaimed with annoyance. "I don't see anything so damn funny."

Wiggins choked and slapped his knee. "I'm sorry, but I all the time got to laugh when I see everybody go nertz at once."

As they stared in surprise he reached up and draped an arm over Wade's shoulder and laughed immoderately. "To see Murphy running for the phone and Farrell acting—"

He laughed derisively. Farrell's face was stormy. Murphy looked on open-mouthed, as though not certain whether this was something to be angry at or something that prefaced an exposure of a stupid act on his part. Dutreaux and the headquarters men were puzzled, some of them apparently inclined to share Wiggins' glee as a welcome break in a hard day and others evidently shocked by it. Wade chuckled in spite of himself.

"I know what you're thinking," said Wiggins, his risible faculties finally under control. "Hildreth admits he got inside the bowl to let Oliver loose. You doubt that's why he got in. He says he was going out to phone. You say, 'Horse feathers, he was gonta lam.' Then you look that dizzy bowl over and there ain't no bullet marks, and all you coppers chirp, 'Cripes! An inside job! He was killed by another goldfish.'"

Wiggins bowed grandly and proceeded. "So you put a tail on that guy Hildreth, figuring that he got caught short in his plans when Dutreaux showed up. Right?" The question was rhetorical, and Wiggins did not pause for an answer. "Murphy and the apes from the Bertillon office and Doc Emerson and Wade the Criminologist, all say, 'It's a pushover. If he had been shot from outside the bowl, there'd be a bullet hole. No bullet hole shows up. None in the bowl and none in the floor.'" Wiggins peered at them in scathing scorn. "That's what you say. Then you say, 'Hildreth admits he got in the bowl. He probably did the job and threw his roscoe away in here. We'll find it, and snap—Hildreth goes to the can for the murder of Oliver.'"

Wiggins bowed toward them again as he paused. They had listened with various reactions—Wade interested, Murphy with a puckered mouth that admitted grudging doubt, the headquarters men partly impatient and partly with enjoyment, and Farrell evidently a trifle disconcerted.

"Why isn't that a good working hypothesis?" Farrell demanded.

"A good working what?" Wiggins spread out his small brown hands to indicate magnanimously that he had no quarrel with working hypotheses. "Hell, it might be right. Sure. But first, you guys have missed the big point. I ain't saying Hildreth didn't knock that guy off. Maybe he did. But I know damn well," concluded Mr. Wiggins, "that he didn't do it that way."

"You do, eh?" This, in bellicose tone, from Murphy. "Well, would you mind letting us in on your secret? How do you know it?"

Wiggins thrust his hands into his pants pockets and strolled nearer the float. The Bertillon men had taken away the framework and sides of the bowl, leaving only the body of the truck. He looked it over and wheeled suddenly upon Murphy.

"Did you look under the truck? Oliver got his from below."

Dutreaux protested. "No, you're wrong there. We looked under the truck."

"Oh yeah?" Wiggins cocked a scornful eye. "What were you looking for, a machine-gun? Huh. Holes, eh? Perfect." He scanned the headquarters men. "Did any of you detectives ever ride on a truck? An old mule-truck like this? You all did, eh? Great."

He squatted down, his hands on his knees, and peered under the truck for a moment, then glanced over his shoulder. "Gimme a small crowbar outa that police car."

One of the men went for it.

"Now come over and see what I'm talking about," Wiggins ordered when the bar had been brought. He stuck his head under the truck and brought it out again as they gathered around him. "Now gimme your roscoe." One of the men on a gesture from Murphy handed over his gun. "Swell," said Wiggins.

He made his way around to the rear end of the truck and squatted lower, reaching the crowbar under. He grunted as though with a manful effort, and the others, watching, saw the two center boards in the floor of the truck spread apart. Wiggins made another prodigious effort, grunted and groaned, and the crack between the center boards widened. Then, as the crack spread to almost half an inch, the blue muzzle of Wiggins' revolver poked through and widened it still further.

"Sure!" Murphy banged the side of the float. "That's it!"

Farrell nodded slowly and Dutreaux's jaw dropped as Wiggins, wearing a broad smile of happy achievement, scrambled out from under the float. "It's just a gift." He winked at Wade. "And here I spend my life taking pictures of you guys."

He handed the gun back to the man who had lent it to him as Murphy patted him on the back. "Here," ordered Murphy, "brush that sand away."

Dutreaux brushed the bottom of the goldfish bowl clean. Murphy and Farrell bent over the middle boards, and Murphy nodded as Farrell pointed to two flat spaces about an inch long in the old wood, where a pressure had crushed the side of each board. A shiny and slightly concave indentation showed in the space on each plank.

"That's where the murderer rested his gun." Murphy meditatively stroked his jaw. "Well, I'll be damned."

"Wait a minute," Wade exclaimed suddenly. They climbed on top of the truck and he bent and looked at the spot where Wiggins' crowbar had come through. The crowbar had made similar marks on each side of the crack. "Look, Farrell," said Wade, pointing to the marks made by the crowbar. "Wiggins pushed the boards apart far enough to admit the muzzle of that gun he borrowed. There are marks from his crowbar, but no marks from his gun, because by the time he got the gun through, the crack spread out behind the crow-bar already wide enough to admit the muzzle of the gun without any hard pressure on the boards. But the murderer's gun made deep indentations at each side of the crack."

Farrell bent over. "Right. That means—"

As he paused to consider just what it did mean Wiggins was scrambling under the truck again. They could hear him rustling around underneath while they examined the marks made by the murderer's gun, vainly trying to decide what they meant. After about a minute Wiggins gave a yell.

"Hey, Wade! Come here! Look."

Wade jumped down from the truck. The drapery around the float made a box-shaped tent for Wiggins, from under which he was howling "Come under here and bring a light! Step on it!"

Grabbing a flashlight from one of the men, Wade pushed up the drapery and doubled up his gangling form to crawl under the truck. After an eloquent gesture toward the cause of his excitement Wiggins scrambled out and scampered toward his camera, giving Murphy a derisive wink as he passed. "Pull off those drapes," he shouted over his shoulder. "I think we're getting to first base."

Dutreaux and the headquarters men ripped the bunting aside, baring the rear right wheel of the truck. Wiggins crawled underneath with his camera and a flash lamp. Jerking his flash-gun out of his hip pocket he handed it to Wade. "Keep it away from your face," he advised breathlessly. "Sometimes they go bang,"

Maneuvering his camera into position, he lit a match and held it near the inside hub of the axle of the rear right wheel. Into the camera went a plate. Wiggins sighted two or three times, lit another match and burned his fingers.

"Let her go," he ordered.

Wade pressed the button and the flash lamp glowed.

"What the hell are you doing?" shouted Murphy from outside.

"Aw, keep your badge on, willya?" Wiggins called back impatiently. "We're doing your work."

Another flash lamp glowed. Wiggins snapped. The light showed a third time, and after this picture was made Wiggins scrambled out, with Wade after him. "Let's let him see it," said Wiggins, brushing the dust off his coat. "I gotta look after this suit," he explained to Farrell. "I done wrecked one in that riot."

Wade laughed. "I don't know what this means, Murphy, but it certainly seems to mean something." He stooped and indicated the wheel, the inside of which Wiggins had been photographing. "There's a lot of fishing-line wound around that wheel-hub. Must be about twenty yards of it. Good new fresh line."

"Fishing-line?" Murphy's face expressed unbelieving perplexity. "What the hell are you talking about?"

"Pick that bass drum of yours outa your lap and bend over and see," Wiggins suggested. "Fish line wound around the hub of the wheel. You know what fish line is, doncha?—they catch fish on it. Unless the fish are too smart."

Farrell was already on his knees by the side of the truck. "I see it," he said. "Murphy, order these men here to take off that wheel and bring it to my office. Be sure they cover it up and don't let it leak out. Don't print this, Wade, till we've tried to dope it out."

"Okay."

Murphy was giving his orders to Dutreaux. "Don't let anybody in here," he concluded. "Nobody, d'you hear? And have the Bertillon office make measurements of everything. Get ballistics on the bullet and photographs of this entire outfit. Get that?"

As Dutreaux indicated that he got it, Murphy turned to Farrell. "What next?"

"I think," Farrell returned smiling, "it might be profitable to go into a huddle at my office."

"Sure," assented Wiggins. He slung his camera over his shoulder. "Then we can play eeny-meeny-miny-mo with Valdon, Conroy, Ghent, Hildreth and all the other boys and girls—and arrest somebody. Ain't it fun? Now look at this."

He held out his hand, showing them a slab of steel about an inch and a quarter long and a quarter of an inch in width and thickness. In the center of the slab was a little hole.

"I found this tied on to the end of the line," Wiggins said—"just to make it harder."

CHAPTER TWENTY-SEVEN

FOR half an hour Dick Barron had been throwing short staccato replies across the district attorney's desk.

His answers crisply admitted everything the district attorney already knew and denied everything else. Yes, Dick had rapped at him, he had taken twelve thousand dollars from his employers last year. To pay his gambling debts. But why in hell keep discussing that? It wasn't any fun to remember, and everybody knew about it anyway. No, he did not know who had killed Roger Parnell. Nor Cynthia Fontenay. Nor Mark Oliver. The whole business was terrible, but why did they keep hammering at him?

His query was gotten out with an exasperation that had finally convinced Farrell that nothing of importance could be had from him tonight, so he bade him good-by, and as the door banged behind Dick, Farrell looked quizzically across at Murphy and Wade.

"That lad's a queer one," Murphy commented, frowning at the closed door as though he expected it to offer some explanation for Dick's oddness.

"Girl trouble, I think." Wade sprawled back in his leather chair and stretched his long legs in front of him. "I've noticed that Esther won't talk when we get on the subject of why she was paying blackmail to Parnell."

Farrell shuffled his reports. "However," he said wearily, "I don't think even Murphy believes that Esther Morse is concerned in these killings."

"But this Barron lad?" Murphy inquired vigorously. "He had plenty of motive, Farrell. Barron gets a bad clipping at the Red Cat and steals money to pay off; the theft is discovered and he's disgraced and his old man kills himself over it—or so the wise ones whisper. Then he finds that the Red Cat isn't straight and that Parnell owns it and that Cynthia gets a nice income from it."

"We've got no proof that Cynthia knew the wheels were controlled," Wade reminded him.

"Well, would Barron think about that? He'd say 'Here's the guy and the dame that's spending my money.' Bang—out they go."

Wade nodded reluctantly. "That's logical enough, Murphy. But why should Barron kill Oliver?"

"Who else do you know," Murphy demanded, "would be so smart about designing those contraptions out at the Red Cat?"

Farrell interrupted. "No. When I talked to Valdon this afternoon he said that so far as he knew Oliver had nothing to do with the Red Cat. He said that he pulled out himself when he found the joint wasn't level."

Murphy's mind leaped back to the gentleman who was engaging the major portion of his rancor. "What did Valdon say about Conroy?"

"He said Conroy represented a Chicago crowd that wanted Valdon to give them protection for a place they expected to open outside the city. Valdon also told me that Parnell was expecting to leave town pretty soon, and that if he got out Conroy's crowd were going to operate the Cat."

"Huh," said Murphy disgustedly. "Since when did Valdon get so eager to tell the police things he thought they ought to know? Valdon says Oliver never was in the Red Cat, but he didn't explain how Oliver happened to have the ten grand that Conroy took away from him at Cynthia's does he?"

"Maybe," ventured Wade, "Valdon doesn't know."

"It's been my experience," Murphy assured him, "that when a crime's committed in his neighborhood there ain't much he don't know. Why couldn't Valdon do this job himself? We know Parnell and Cynthia had a row in the pantry. Suppose Valdon came in after the butler had knocked Parnell down and the row started again. Parnell and Cynthia would be trying to get Valdon to keep on protecting the Red Cat. There's a row and Parnell gets killed. Cynthia knows Valdon did the killing—so out with Cynthia."

"Nice," commented Wade. "But what about Oliver?"

"Well—Oliver—" Murphy paused, thinking.

Farrell read a report for a moment, then looked up. "The man I'm interested in," he told them, "is Ghent."

"Ghent?" Murphy grinned. "Me too, Farrell. He's slick. Too almighty slick. I've been laying out a couple of pipe-lines to find out about Ghent."

"Yes?" Farrell prompted with interest. "What did you find?"

"Just that he spent a lot of money and had a lot of lady friends and one of them was Cynthia, and that he never did very much work. Just played golf and tennis and went swimming and won all those diving championships."

"I've been thinking," said Farrell slowly. "We've got only Ghent's story of how Parnell came to his rooms last night and tied him up. Suppose Ghent knew for some reason Parnell was to be at the party. Suppose Ghent came there and killed him, then went back home and fixed up his apartment to support that story ho told."

"But why should he kill Parnell?" Wade objected.

Murphy sprang up. "Look—how about this?" He leaned over the desk and talked fast. "Here's something we didn't think of. Suppose Ghent was in love with Cynthia himself and was jealous because she preferred Hildreth. Suppose Ghent went to the party. He sees a guy with Hildreth's suit on—we'll have to take it for granted that he knew the number of Hildreth's suit. He's got it in for Hildreth on account of Hildreth has beat him in getting Cynthia's affections. He hears a racket in the pantry and cracks the door open and sees this guy he thinks is Hildreth trying to beat up Cynthia. The butler leaps in and knocks the guy down, and Ghent is plenty mad and as the guy starts to get up Ghent leaps in and kills him. But Cynthia hadn't run so far that she didn't see him do it. She threatens to tell, so Ghent sneaks out on the balcony before dawn and files through the rail. He knows he can dive, so he ain't afraid of hurting himself."

"Fine," said Wade. "But what about Oliver?"

"Damn Oliver," said Murphy.

Wade got up. "But you can't ignore him, Murphy. Whoever killed Parnell and Cynthia had some reason for killing Oliver." He turned and faced Murphy and Farrell. "I'm thinking if we're smart we'll look for the person who had a reason to kill Oliver. That's our missing link. Oliver wasn't in love with Cynthia. He wasn't mixed up with the Red Cat." Wade jerked his chair forward and sat down again, his elbows on the desk, talking with slow, punching syllables. "The only way Oliver seems to be involved with this bunch at all is that he had that ten grand last night. And I've got a notion that what he said about it might possibly be the truth."

"That fairy tale?" countered Murphy. "Boloney."

"Well, consider this." Wade began checking off his statements on his fingers. "First, we know Esther was paying blackmail to Parnell. Cynthia said Esther gave her the money last night, telling her it was the last payment. Parnell was planning to leave town. Cynthia says she gave the money to Parnell. Got that?"

They nodded.

"Oliver's story to me in the taxi last night was that somebody nudged him in the dark, whispering '147.' He turned around and the mysterious nudger handed him a wallet, saying 'Here's Parnell's money.' He thought it was a gambling debt, and took it. Then somebody got the money away from him at the point of a gun."

"I'm listening," said Farrell dubiously.

"All right. Cynthia said she had told Parnell she would deliver the money at the ball to an agent. 'When Parnell said he didn't know anybody who was a member of Dis, she told him that Arnold Ghent was a member. Parnell came to the ball himself, and told Cynthia he was Arnold Ghent. He had on a suit with the number 47 on it. So here's my hypothesis. The room wasn't absolutely black during the ceremony—there were some lighted devil's heads and such crap—suppose in the dark Cynthia sees a suit with the number 47 on it, and hands the wearer of the suit the money. But the suit is really 147—the figure one is hidden in a fold of the cloth, maybe. She whispers '47,' and Oliver, who hears her, thinks she's saying '147.' She gives him the money, thinking she's giving it to Ghent, and he takes it. Right so far?"

"Mhm," said Farrell with a slow nod. "Reasonable."

"But Conroy sees this. He hears the whisper, 'Here's Parnell's money.' He decides to get his hands on it, and does so in the fashion described by Oliver. We know Conroy had the money when he was searched."

"Well, well, well," said Murphy ponderously. "So that's why Parnell tried to beat Cynthia up—he said she hadn't forked over the money, and she said she had." He sat down. "So you think Conroy's our best bet, Wade?"

"I don't know. Conroy doesn't look like a man who'd kill three people for ten thousand dollars. If it was a tremendous sum, I'd say yes."

Murphy heaved a sigh. "I ain't trusting that Conroy," he reminded them. "Him with his moon-face and curly hair."

"I'm not trusting anybody who was there last night," Wade retorted grimly. "All I'm saying is that as I see it Oliver is the crux of our—"

The telephone buzzed. Murphy picked it up.

"Good!" he chortled. "Fine. Bring it in as fast as you can." He grinned broadly as he turned around. "Dutreaux reporting. He's got the other half of that note we found in Parnell's flat. It was written on Oliver's typewriter. So that's something about Oliver, and it might give us a lead to run down."

Wade was not optimistic. "A note written to a dead man on a typewriter owned by another dead man—" he shook his head.

"But because it was written on Oliver's typewriter," Farrell reminded him hopefully, "doesn't necessarily mean that Oliver wrote it. It may get us somewhere."

"How that Conroy—" Murphy began insistently—"you listen to me and quit grinning. I know a slick guy when I see one. And that Conroy, he's slick. He's too smart. Sure," he insisted, "decent people don't know how to handle the police. That takes experience. And Conroy," he finished ruefully, "acts like he's had experience."

Farrell chuckled. "He does. We'll accept your testimony on that, Murphy."

Wade was preoccupied. "I'm still favoring Ghent."

"He's easy enough, if you can get around Conroy," Murphy exclaimed. "That business of being tied up is old stuff. I'd say Ghent's a lively prospect. He's too Johnny-on-the-spot to suit me. I've got a habit of being suspicious of a fellow that's hanging around when there's a murder going on."

"Don't forget Hildreth," Farrell interpolated.

"Oh, Hildreth—I can't see him in it." Wade shook his head. "Nobody has suggested that Hildreth and Cynthia weren't very fond of each other, so there's no motive there, and for the life of me I can't see why he'd want to kill Oliver or Parnell. Nothing seems to tie him in except the fact that Parnell was wearing his suit, and Parnell might simply have taken that without asking."

Murphy stroked his chin. "Maybe you're right," he admitted grudgingly. "But that don't let Mrs. Hildreth out. Jealousy, as we said before, killing Parnell because she thought he was Hildreth, and Cynthia because Cynthia had vamped her husband."

"Very good," Wade rejoined with a sigh, "but WHAT ABOUT OLIVER?"

"O Lord." Murphy sank back, discouraged.

Wade shook his head. He was as depressed as Murphy, but he could not avoid the conviction that the death of Oliver confronted them with a riddle to which none of them had as yet managed to suggest a solution. Valdon, Ghent, Hildreth, Conroy, Mrs. Hildreth, Dick Barron, even Esther—all of them had been involved in personal relationships with Parnell and Cynthia, but what about Oliver? Oliver was an unprepossessing but apparently harmless old codger—and yet he had been murdered in the street before thousands of people, by a diabolical piece of ingenuity that proved that his murder was the result of long and hateful scheming. What, in heaven's name, Wade wondered, had Mark Oliver done?

There was a knock, and Dutreaux came in, his lean face creased with the jovial grin of the man who has achieved something of merit. They greeted him eagerly, and he gave Farrell a big manila envelope.

"Here it is, chief," he announced triumphantly.

"Where'd you find it?"

"Well, sir, it was quite a job." Dutreaux settled himself to a smoke with the air of a man who richly deserved it. "We found the typewriter and checked it with the photostatic copy of the note. Then we started to ransack the house—not all of it, because we didn't have to go through but three rooms. The note we found on the bureau in the old guy's bedroom, stuck under an ash-tray."

"Another herring." Wade gave a low disappointed laugh. "Just stuck there for anybody to see, Dutreaux?"

"Yes sir."

As Murphy opened the manila envelope Wade shrugged, but bent eagerly over the torn half-sheet of paper. Farrell hastily took the photostatic copy of the half they had found in Parnell's flat and laid the two pieces together. The note was easy to read:

"Parnell—

This note will ser----ve as does a courier's ring from the queen. Have whoever br----ings it in case you do not come yourself, present it----to me and if it fits I'll know everything is regular----and will give up the money. It is safely stowed away and----available at any time you need it. The whole thing so----unds charming to me. Like some vile plot to make a mu----sical comedy dramatic. However, you have always had a flair for the unusual. May your exit be full of h----igh spots and thrills."

"Unsigned." Wade said it, with another fatalistic shrug in which Farrell joined him.

"And unsolved," Farrell added.

Dutreaux sighed. Dutreaux plainly had no great opinion of the appreciative powers of his superiors. For the love of mud, his sigh said forcefully, it wasn't his fault the bloomin' thing had no signature, was it? He'd been sent to find the other half of that letter, and he'd found it, just like he'd been told to do, and here they were acting just like it was proof that he hadn't done his duty in not finding a signature too. Dutreaux's mouth puckered into something as close to a pout as so wide a mouth could achieve.

Wade gave him a sidelong grin. "A policeman's lot," he agreed sadly, "is not a happy one."

Dutreaux had no mind for whimsical quotations. "Well sir," he suggested hopefully, "it says money, don't it? Maybe it means the counterfeit money."

"Hell," said Murphy gloomily. "Parnell was planning a getaway, wasn't he? He'd need good money to take with him. That counterfeit money is another one of those little things we've got to worry about."

"Then I guess we can say," Dutreaux volunteered, "that whoever wrote this here letter has got all the dope we want, or else he's dead."

"It answers the 'what about Oliver?' question," Wade said suddenly. "The murderer was keeping some money for Parnell and Oliver knew about it, because this note was written on Oliver's typewriter. Or possibly Oliver was keeping the money and Parnell sent a friend of his to get it, and the friend decided to keep the money and kill Oliver and Parnell."

Farrell nodded. "That's our most reasonable theory so far," he agreed. "I'm mighty glad you found this, Dutreaux."

Dutreaux gave a magnanimous shrug. "Oh, that wasn't nothing. Nothing at all, sir."

"Wait a minute," exclaimed Wade. "Put it this way. No matter who had that money of Parnell's, the murderer got his hands on it and wanted to keep it. He put Parnell's half of the letter back in the desk, so Parnell wouldn't miss it and get suspicious. After he had killed Parnell he went to Oliver's house to get Oliver's half of the note, so that Oliver would have no proof that anybody had been keeping anything for Parnell. That's when Oliver got shot. The murderer intended slipping up to Parnell's flat and taking that half too, after Parnell was dead, but headquarters men were ransacking the place and they found it. He knew we'd check it up and find it was written on Oliver's typewriter, so he sneaked in and laid the other half on Oliver's bureau where he knew we couldn't help finding it."

"D'you think Mr. Oliver suspected all this?" Dutreaux inquired.

"I don't know. But the fact that Oliver knew about the transaction makes it sure that he would get suspicious sooner or later."

Murphy poked his finger disconsolately into his ruddy cheek as though to gain comfort by feeling its healthy elasticity. "Then I guess," he offered sourly, "there ain't nothing to do but get a court order to look in everybody's safety-deposit box to see who has a lot of cash stowed away, and if you'd been on the force as long as I have you'd rather try to swim the river ninety times before breakfast than try to get in the safety-deposit boxes of people who ain't got nothing proved on them."

For a moment Wade stared scowling at the thickening darkness beyond the windows. Then he wheeled around.

"Listen—I've just realized something. This means we've struck bottom somewhere. The murderer sneaked out and put that note where he knew we'd find it. It means that somewhere in our bungling along we've come damn close to him, and he's scared. I feel better. Much better. Because when criminals get scared, they get stupid."

CHAPTER TWENTY-EIGHT

WITH his right leg stretched out in front of him and his left up on his desk, bent around his typewriter, Wade sat musingly reading the page that projected halfway above the platen. It was two hours since he had left Farrell's office and rushed in to make a new lead on his story. It had not been easy, for he did not want the murderer to guess that the police really thought he was getting scared enough to be stupid. But re-reading his final draft of the new lead, Wade decided that it would do. He grinned up at Wiggins, who sat hunched up on the desk, his chin on his knees, and rolled the sheet out of the typewriter.

"Take this to Mr. Koppel," he called to a copy boy, and showed Wiggins the carbon.

Wiggins puckered up his small face.

"Good story," he decided. "But the way I see it is that before long this dodo's really gonta get upset and knock off somebody else."

"Well—he might."

"Sure, why shouldn't he? What the hell's one murder more or less to a guy like that? Anything can get to be a habit." Wiggins felt in his pocket and found the rear end of a chocolate bar, which he bit with conviction. "All these apes that have been talking better pull down their shutters, or the first thing that'll happen, we'll be out taking pictures of another good guy gone to heaven."

Wade was ruminative.

"How do you think Oliver was killed, shrimp?" he asked.

"I dunno. I guess the guy rigged up a rod and tied the fish line to it. It don't seem possible that the murderer crawled under the truck and went bam just when the band struck up." He rolled up the tinfoil wrapper of the chocolate bar and threw the little ball of it under the desk. 'Who's Murphy voting for?"

"Anybody and everybody. I think he'd like to hang Conroy and Hildreth and Ghent and Valdon all at the same time, with Mrs. Hildreth thrown in for lagniappe."

Wiggins spied Wade's cigarettes alongside the type-writer and helped himself. "All I'm waiting for is for that film to come back. Where you keep your matches?"

"Here's one. When will you get the film?"

"Tonight. I sent it out of town to be developed so no smart guy could give us a lickin' on it. Koppel sent some cub with it. I hope he keeps his face closed."

"Got any idea what you'll find on it?"

"I dunno." Wiggins contemplated the spiral of smoke.

Wade got up and reached for his hat. "I'm going over to the Greek's to get a little indigestion. I'll be back in a little while. If that film shows anything phone me."

"Okay. And say, if you should happen—"

The copy boy came running up to interrupt. "City desk wants you, Wiggins."

Wiggins slid down from the desk-top. "I hope they heard from that cub." He walked toward the door of the city room with Wade. "What I was gonta say is, if you should happen to see a good-lookin' hunk o' ham on the counter bring me a sandwich, willya?"

Wade promised and went out. He walked slowly along toward the lunchroom. Street cleaners were already busy whisking away the debris of the last Carnival parade, and newsboys shouted the first editions of the morning papers. Wade kicked a litter of confetti out of his way and walked on with his head sunk between his shoulders, thinking.

The chilly night air was an annoying stimulus, strong enough to make him conscious that there was something at the back of his mind but not strong enough to bring the tantalizing hint into his consciousness. There was something he should have mentioned. Something that was probably important.

He turned into the Greek restaurant where reporters for the *Creole* got hurried lunches between stories. The night man greeted him.

"Evening, Mr. Wade. You got something on your mind?"

"No," said Wade gloomily. "I wish I had."

He went over to a table by the wall.

"Now this thing you were asking about—" Murphy unwrapped the length of bloodstained yarn—"it may be very valuable as a clue but we've had little luck with it so far. Dutreaux says every store in the city that might handle it has been checked and at only one place do they find an exact duplicate."

"Where? What store?" Lucy bent forward eagerly.

"A little hole in the wall over on Rampart Street. Fellow named Binton runs the place. He says that he bought a job lot of it about a year ago and sold quite a lot of the skeins this year. But his trade is about ninety-nine per cent negro."

Lucy's brow puckered. "Did he make any sale to a negro man recently?"

"Dutreaux says he asked him that, and that Binton says he's quite sure that he didn't. He says he sold a lot of it to negro women. They use it for mending sweaters, or socks. But there's no doubt that the stuff he handles matches this absolutely." He smiled at Lucy affably. "Oh, I know what you're thinking, young lady—you've got Jasper in mind."

Lucy smiled back at him but did not commit herself.

Farrell walked up and down the library of his home, his head lowered on his chest. Farrell was essentially practical; he knew that in a few days the police department would begin receiving severe scorings from the newspapers, and that in a few days more it would be the district attorney's turn to face public outcry for solution to the Mardi Gras murders. But he felt as hopeless as though he had suddenly been ordered to read a page written in a lost language. The details of the case threw themselves again and again, mocking and baffling, into his mind.

The two pearl-handled knives. The red cord with the bloodstain. The counterfeit money found at the Red Cat and in Roger Parnell's strongbox. The letter torn in half. The mysterious blackmail payments made by Esther Morse to Parnell. The gun fastened under the goldfish float, to be fired when the fishline grew taut and pulled the trigger.

Farrell paced his library. He could hear the clock in the hall ticking out the remaining minutes of Mardi Gras.

Suddenly he stopped. He picked up the phone and called a number.

"Murphy?" he said after a half-minute. "Hurry over to my house. Business is going to pick up right away."

Sergeant Dutreaux waited under a banana tree in Jackson Square with the immobile patience that is characteristic of cats, Chinamen and policemen when their minds are on their work. He managed to keep well hidden in the shadows that lay like soft velvet over the grass. It was getting colder, and Dutreaux shivered, but his eyes did not waver from their contemplation of the entrance of the house diagonally across from him.

He stiffened with attention. A man came out and turned back to close the door. He walked to the curb and got into the coupe that was standing there. Dutreaux had edged toward a police car parked near the gate of the square. He got into it and waited. As the coupe turned the corner, Dutreaux slammed his foot on the starter.

Wade had come back to the table. "Wiggins on the phone, Steve," he told the night waiter. "Bring me an artichoke with lots of French dressing. And fix a sandwich for him."

Steve smiled. "Very splendid special one, eh? Lots of pickles?"

"Yes. He likes pickles," Wade answered absently. That wispy hint kept dancing around on the edges of his mind.

"Why don't you eat something?" Steve demanded. "Thinking is very hard work. You have to take care of yourself."

Wade abstractedly plucked the first leaf off the artichoke.

Fritz Valdon went into police headquarters and took the elevator up to Farrell's office. Esther Morse was waiting in the anteroom with Mrs. Hildreth. They were talking to a police sergeant.

"Does this sort of thing go on forever?" Sophie Hildreth asked with a chastened petulance. "Captain Murphy called me up a little while ago and said I was to come here. Something important, it seems."

"He called me too." Valdon shrugged. "I couldn't resist coming. Curiosity. Conroy refused. Told Murphy to come and get him." Valdon chuckled. "If they're not ready," he added after a moment, "I'm going to take a walk. Will you ladies join me?"

Sophie and Esther said no.

Lucy told the cab driver to wait.

She walked to the weatherbeaten frame house that squatted back in the corner lot. Folks sitting on their doorsteps threw her a passing curious glance and went back to their gossip of Carnival day festivities.

The taxi driver sat back and smoked. Lucy was talking to a middle-aged negro woman on the porch of the corner house.

The woman went inside. Lucy waited. After a few minutes the woman came back with a little package, which Lucy put into her purse.

"You sure I don't have trouble for this, Miss Lucy?" the woman asked anxiously.

"Not a bit. I promise. Provided you don't tell anybody. Here, buy yourself something pretty."

"Thanks, Miss Lucy."

Lucy smiled good-by and got back into the cab. "To police headquarters," she said.

Arnold Ghent drove out toward Oliver's house. When he got there the streets were packed with a curious crowd pressing as close to the house as the police guards would let them. Automobiles were parked on both sides of the street. Ghent found a space a block away and left his car.

He tested the lid of the rumble-seat, apparently to make sure it was locked, and walked toward the house. He seemed quite unconscious that he was being followed.

After a few moments he came back to his car. He looked at his watch. Eleven-thirty. He had been requested to be at the district attorney's office at twelve.

He started back toward town, driving speedily, but not so speedily that another car had not time to edge in just behind him; and the driver of the second car, wearing a cheerful smile, beat Ghent to his destination.

"We're going to hang you for this. We got you right. *Dead* right."

Murphy looked with stern assurance into the face of the man who sat beside him. Farrell was in the front seat with the chauffeur. The district attorney's face, reflected in the mirror over the wheel, was lined and grim in the light from the dashboard. He turned around toward Murphy's prisoner.

"You can make it easier on yourself, if you talk," he suggested.

But there was no answer.

The car paused for a light, then edged ahead. Murphy eyed his prisoner harshly.

"You'll talk later, Barron—don't worry."

Dutreaux's car hung close to the tail-light of the car ahead. The traffic was heavy along upper St. Charles Avenue, and Dutreaux knew better than to take any chance on losing his man now.

It had been a good exciting ride. The man in the car ahead had driven up toward the Dis den and had stopped his car a block away. Then he had parked the car and walked. As he neared the entrance Dutreaux had seen the two patrolmen on guard, chatting and smoking. Evidently the man he was trailing had seen them too, for he had kept on walking. Dutreaux, deciding that the walk would probably only take him around the block, had run back to his own car and waited. He had been right. The driver of the other car had reappeared after a few minutes, and the chase had started again.

A red light held them up just above Canal Street. Dutreaux pulled alongside the curb and got out of his car. He walked to the car he had been following and opened the door.

"Hello, Hildreth. I'm Sergeant Dutreaux. Remember me?"

Hildreth nodded without any apparent surprise.

"Well, they want you at headquarters." Dutreaux got into the car and slammed the door. "Let's go."

The light changed to amber and then to green. The car moved forward.

Conroy padded happily along a back street, smiling his fatuous smile at the newsboys shouting the newest details of the Mardi Gras murders. Nobody observing his pleasant progress would have guessed that he carried a freshly loaded automatic under his armpit.

He turned into a street so narrow that it was almost an alley, and walked around newspaper trucks and their loaders. Nobody noticed him. Inside was the roar of presses, and just beyond the door the shouts of newsboys as they got their allotment of morning papers.

Without hurry, or any appearance of stealth, Conroy entered one of the many back doors and walked into the *Creole* building.

ASH WEDNESDAY

CHAPTER TWENTY-NINE

THE cathedral clock struck midnight.

Carnival was over. It was the day of penance and prayer. It was the day when all New Orleans goes to church, to plead understanding for its exuberance and forgiveness for its sins. But today there were many among the devout who when they crossed themselves as the first minute of Ash Wednesday ticked across the clock prayed also for deliverance from the strange new terror that for the first time in New Orleans had made Mardi Gras horrible.

Farrell and Murphy, Wade and Wiggins and Lucy, all made their way feverishly through the tangle, praying in their own way that they might be getting close to the end.

Wiggins heard the twelve strokes that signaled midnight as he bent over the tins that held the fluid known in photographers' rooms as "soup." The small red light at the side made his face insouciantly diabolic as he poked in a practised finger and stirred up the solution.

He whistled brightly while he watched the dim gray outlines on the enlarged negative take form. Crushing down the impulse to haste that rose in his soul he slowly swished the solution across and across the film in the narrow pan. At last he held the negative up to the light and studied it. He squinted his eyes and moved the film back and forth between himself and the red glow.

"Lord!" said Wiggins.

He could feel his heart thump. But he must not hurry. If you hurry with a negative you might as well go back and take the picture over. And this picture was one that could not be taken over.

Triumphantly Wiggins pranced to the door. On a cutting table in the next room were long loops of narrow motion-picture film from the boy's camera. Wiggins brushed them aside and pressed his enlarged negative dry. Then, switching on the full lights of his developer he bent over to sight the glow on the frame.

A figure walked softly and slowly through the door-way from the darkened room at Wiggins' back. The sharp glare of the arclight shed only a dull scattered glow in the shadows by the door. Wiggins still bent over, carefully studying the negative in his development frame. Then, without turning around, he reached up and switched off the arclight, and a concentrated spot shone from the machine that was hung from the ceiling.

He heard it coming before he felt it, and tried to duck. For an instant, through the blinding earthquake in his head he heard thumps and noises. Then it got dark.

"Miss Morse," said Lucy fervently, "I think that's the lowest, ungodliest, lousiest—I beg your pardon, but that's how I feel about it."

Esther half smiled. "I've been feeling that way for a year. But what could I do?"

For a moment Lucy said nothing. She sat very still, her chin cupped in her hand, looking at Esther. They were alone in a little cubbyhole of an office that opened off the anteroom leading to Farrell's sanctum. They had been alone there for half an hour, talking.

"Miss Morse," inquired Lucy, "is that sable?"

"Yes." Esther suddenly reached out and put her hand over Lucy's. "I wish you'd call me Esther," she said.

Lucy got up. She looked down and then looked up again. "Honey," she responded, "anybody that wears sables is Miss to me. I was just thinking what a shame it is that you shouldn't have any fun."

"I—I hope you didn't mind listening," said Esther. "Sometimes you get desperate. You simply have to talk."

"Mind? For the love of Mike, didn't I drag you in here and *make* you talk?" Lucy frowned. "I'm just thinking."

"You're a darling," said Esther.

"Please omit flowers," said Lucy. "I've got something on my mind." She put both hands on Esther's shoulders. "Listen. You stay here till I get back. Don't move."

"Where are you going?"

"Outside. Don't go away. Wait for me."

Lucy shut the door softly behind her. Esther stood up, and walked restlessly over to the little window and back, and then back again, wondering if any girl in the world had ever before carried such black despair as hers.

Dick Barron was repeating over and over again the same story that he had told Murphy and Farrell when they picked him up. Murphy was bending over him with his blunt wagging finger within an inch of Dick's nose.

"We got you cold, didn't we?" he roared. "What were you doing in Oliver's garage? Trying to find things, weren't you? There's no use, my boy, we trailed you from the time you left your house. We'll tell you just where you drove and what way you got there. You might as well come clean now. You're hooked."

Dick looked at him with desperate steadiness. "I told you I went there because I got a phone call telling me to meet someone. That's the truth. I tell you it's the truth."

Murphy picked up a photostatic copy of the torn letter that lay on Farrell's desk. "Now look, my lad, what about this note? Didn't you write to Parnell telling him that you had the money Esther Morse was going to give him for the last payment on that blackmail? Didn't you say that you had it and that if he sent the other half of the note that you'd send it to him? And didn't he come for it himself? And when he came didn't you say it was at Cynthia Fontenay's house and for him to try and get it?" Murphy stopped for breath.

"Now, boy, I don't want to be hard on you. We know that you were just made a fool of by that crowd that was fighting Parnell for his gambling joint. You tell us the whole story, and we may be able to save you a lot of trouble."

Dick looked at Farrell pleadingly. Farrell seemed impervious to pleas. But he said, not unkindly, "Tell Murphy what you know, Barron. He'll get it out of you sooner or later."

Dick's body sagged hopelessly. "Have you all gone crazy?" he exclaimed. "I *didn't* kill Parnell! I didn't kill Cynthia! I didn't kill Oliver!" He started up from his chair but Murphy pushed him back and held him there with his hand on Dick's chest.

"The hell you didn't. You killed them all or you helped kill them." He leaned over and shoved his red face closer to Dick's. "You know somebody played you for a chump. Now get even. They're trying to make a sucker out of you. Come on. Talk." Murphy's hand slipped over and closed fiercely on Dick's fist. "Talk! Talk or by God I'll break every damn one of your fingers. *Talk!*"

A long ring on the buzzer checked his wrath. He straightened up. Dick sat up in his chair, his hand numbly feeling the beads of sweat on his forehead. Farrell pressed a button on his desk.

Wade burst into the room. He saw Dick and stopped.

"You're just in time, Wade," Murphy said enthusiastically, as Wade started to speak. "We've got one of the guys in the Mardi Gras murders."

Wade stared at Dick. "How long have you had him!"

"About an hour. What's the matter?"

Wade shrugged. "Nothing much. Except that you've got the wrong man." He smiled at their startled faces. "Get that kid out of here for awhile. I've got the guy you want, down in the back corridor."

Accompanied by a police orderly, Dick Barron came into the anteroom and looked around with the bewildered air of a man who steps from the dark into the glare of a bright light. Lucy, who had been sitting by one of the vacant desks, got up and came toward him.

"Please," she said to the orderly, "can I speak to this gentleman without you listening?"

Dick glanced wonderingly down at her determined little figure. "What do you want to tell me?"

"Nothing. I want to ask you things. Is he under arrest?" she inquired of the orderly.

"Well, sort of." The orderly grinned.

"I'm working with Mr. Wade and Mr. Wiggins of the *Creole*," said Lucy. "And I've got to ask Mr. Barron something important. Special orders."

"Up here?"

"Right here."

"If you let him get away you'll be under arrest yourself."

"I'll be responsible," said Lucy. "You get that, Mr. Barron? If you try to get away I'm under arrest. Now come over here in this corner and talk to me." Dick laughed, partly in relief at being separated from Murphy and partly in amusement at Lucy's cool determination. "What do you want, Lucy?"

"Plenty. Sit down."

He obeyed. Lucy stood over him, sternly.

"Did your father commit suicide?" Lucy asked pitilessly.

Dick started. His mouth shut in a thin line. Then he answered.

"I think so. It was digitalis. For God's sake, Lucy, what do you—"

"Where were you the night he died?" she demanded. "On the way to Pass Christian."

"Can you prove it?"

"Certainly. Why?"

"Why were you going to the Pass?"

"I wanted to see Esther. She was at a hotel over there. I went back home as soon as I got the wire, and I never did see her."

"Have you ever talked to her? I mean alone?"

"Not since the jam over the money. Why, Lucy?"

"Then," said Lucy in a low voice, "I guess you didn't know that for a whole year she's been paying blackmail to Roger Parnell because he told her that he had absolute proof that you killed your father because you had to have his money to pay your way out of all the trouble you were in."

"My God!" Dick sprang up. "Lucy, if you're lying to me—"

She wondered how it was possible for a man to live with his heart thumping so loud that she could hear it. "Lucy," he said in a voice so strange that she had to watch his lips move to be sure it was Dick and not somebody else nearby speaking, "how do you know this?"

"She told me. She was nearly crazy and she had to tell somebody. She thought maybe you had killed these other people too. I'm a girl and she's a girl and we've got feelings in common so when I saw she couldn't live much longer without talking I got her off by herself and made her tell me."

Dick did not answer. He stood still, so white she thought it strange that he did not faint, his hands opening and closing.

"Can you prove that alibi?" she asked. "Is there anybody that knows your father was all right when you left for Pass Christian?"

"Of course. An old friend of his who lives in Chicago was with me."

She grabbed his arm. "Come on. She's in here." She threw open the door of the little office and saw Esther start up. "Here he is, Miss Morse. He didn't do it. He can prove he didn't."

Unmindful of the little choking cry that burst from Esther's throat, Lucy started to close the door. Then she remembered something else and put in her head.

"Please don't forget I'm responsible for you, Mr. Barron. If you try to run away we'll both be under arrest."

She ran downstairs and jumped into a cab. "To the *Creole* office," she said.

Wiggins opened his eyes to find that though his head ached and pounded it rested on Lucy's lap, and her lap was so soft and warm and delightful that he didn't care if his head kept aching forever. He wriggled his neck and looked up into Lucy's anxious blue eyes. She smiled, and he smiled back, but his head hurt and his eyes stung so that he closed them again, and felt Lucy's hand stroking his forehead.

"How'd you get here?" he asked her.

"I just this minute came in. I went down to police headquarters to see you, but you weren't there, so I hung around awhile and came on over here. I've got something I'll show you later. Will he be all right, doctor?"

"O, yes," said another voice. "But he got a bad bump. He'll need some rest."

Wiggins opened his eyes again to look up at the doctor, and winked. Koppel, the city editor, kneeling on the floor by him, gave his shoulder a gentle thump. "I'll leave you with your nurse," he said. "You're in good hands and you deserve to be. You caught yourself a murderer tonight."

Wiggins sat up. "Yeah? Where is he?"

"Wade and a couple of cops took him to headquarters." Wiggins felt his bandaged head and grinned over his shoulder at Lucy. "That's good. Who is he?"

"Conroy," said Koppel.

Wiggins jumped up, laughing.

"Oh, boy!" he shouted. "Let's go, Lucy."

CHAPTER THIRTY

As the door closed behind Dick and the orderly Murphy leaned ferociously toward Wade.

"Who have you got?"

"Con Conroy."

"Conroy? If you're making a monkey out of me—"

"I'm not," Wade retorted shortly. "He tried to knock off Wiggins."

"Wiggins!" exclaimed Farrell. "Wiggins! What the—"

"That's how I feel about it too."

"Wiggins!" Murphy sat down with a thump. "Sure and I don't blame you. When people kill their own friends that's police business. But when they get after a kid like Wiggins—"

"You ought to see the guys down at the *Creole* office. It was all we could do to get him out without a lynching." Wade grinned.

"Did you see the rest of them outside?" Farrell asked. "Murphy told me to get them all here tonight."

"No, we came in by a side door. We've got him cold, Farrell. I'll file the bill of information myself. Here's how it happened."

Wade sat down on the desk. "I'd been talking to Wiggins about eleven o'clock. He was waiting for that movie film to come in, and when I went out to eat he told me to bring him back a sandwich. After I got out on the street something started to bother me, but I couldn't remember what it was till Wiggins phoned me that the film had come and for me to hurry with that sandwich. On my way back to the office I remembered that Wiggins had warned me against a fourth Mardi Gras murder—he said he figured that the murderer wouldn't mind another killing if somebody got too close on his trail. I recalled that Wiggins had talked pretty generally about his film and what he expected it to show, so I ran to the office and beat it up to the third floor, where the photographers' rooms are."

"Cripes," Murphy blurted, "is that where you got Conroy?"

"Yes. I ran right back to Wiggins' headquarters—the photographers' shop is quite a way back from the front elevator—and as I rounded a corner back in the building I heard a hell of a racket. The rooms were dark. The only light was the developing light above the table. I got a glimpse of Wiggins rolling under a table with his head busted, and somebody slipping out, so I went for the guy and yelled bloody murder for somebody to come help me. It was Conroy. When we got his gun and persuaded him that we meant business we called the city desk and they got a couple of cops off the street to bring him in."

"Holy saints," said Murphy fervently. "And how is the boy? Badly hurt?"

"I don't think so. But if he is, you'll never hang Conroy." Wade smiled grimly. "We'll take care of him."

Farrell shook his head. "This is pretty awful. That kid Wiggins. Let me have a look at Conroy." He got up. "Who's outside?" Wade asked.

"All of them, I guess," answered Murphy, getting up and going to the door. "Do you want them in?"

"Sure. Make it fast. We'll stage it in the other office. Just announce that you're booking Conroy. They've got a right to know it's over."

Farrell and Murphy agreed and went out. Wade hurried through the side door into the corridor, where Conroy was standing with several policemen and reporters, answering their questions with his familiar smiling insolence.

"I don't know whether to thank you for saving me from your ferocious colleagues," he observed as Wade approached, "or to kick you downstairs."

Wade's face was grim. "Don't talk about kicking, Conroy. You might put bad ideas in these boys' heads."

Conroy looked them over appraisingly. "Quite a crew, aren't they? All loyal to the Alma Mater, eh? Three big cheers and a tiger for the *Creole*. Die for dear old Wiggins." He laughed softly. "You fellows must think I'm a real hard guy."

Another of the *Creole* reporters took a threatening step toward him. "We don't think you're hard. A bird that has to slug a shrimp like Wiggins with a jack can't be so tough."

"And you had a gun, too," observed Kennedy of the *Telegram*. "It's a wonder you didn't bring a mob with you."

The others added their derision. "Where do you want this mug?" they asked Wade.

He told them. Kennedy shoved Conroy along. The others helped with the shoving. Conroy looked up at Wade and winked.

"I'd hate to cross you fellows up," he remarked blandly. "But you've climbed the wrong tree."

"Stow it and keep moving," said Wade shortly. He left them outside and went into Farrell's office.

They were all there: Dutreaux and Hildreth, Valdon and Ghent and Mrs. Hildreth, and Esther and Dick sitting together. Wade looked them over carefully as Farrell spoke.

"You're just in time, Mr. Wade," Farrell said rising.

The door burst open and Wiggins and Lucy, arm in arm, appeared on the threshold. Wiggins winked at Wade and rubbed his bandage head. Lucy smiled proudly. Murphy beamed upon them and found them chairs.

"Yes?" said Wade significantly in answer to Farrell. He paused a moment. "Mr. Farrell, *The Morning Creole* wants to file information demanding an arrest for the murder of Cynthia Fontenay, the murder of

Roger Parnell and the murder of Mark Oliver, as well as the attempted murder of Anthony Wiggins."

Everybody in the room turned to stare at Wiggins. He smiled back at them.

"The *Creole*," said Wade, "also wants to deliver to the state the man against whom this information is filed—Con Conroy."

There was a quick nervous buzz from everybody. Valdon sprang to his feet. "I don't understand this, Farrell."

Wade had opened the door. He motioned Conroy and the other reporters in. The murmur quieted down, and they stared at Conroy. Conroy stood only just inside the door, smiling.

Wiggins got up. He felt his head, grinned and walked over to Farrell's desk.

"Say, Mr. Farrell, I do hate to spoil my pal's show, but Conroy ain't the guy." He wheeled around. "Here's the one you want."

He dived past Dutreaux and Murphy with a shout.

"Come and get him! Quick! He's got a gun!"

CHAPTER THIRTY-ONE

WIGGINS dashed into the press-room of police headquarters and made a leap for the telephone connecting with *The Morning Creole* office. "Gimme Koppel," he shouted.

With one finger of the hand that held the receiver he edged up his turban of bandages so as to uncover his ear.

"Koppel? It's all over. Ghent confessed. Yeah. Wade's cleaning up the story and Charlie's making the pictures. The plates are coming in with O'Malley."

He winked up at Lucy, who had followed him in and was perched on the edge of the table.

"And say, Koppel. Get this in the lead, huh? The murderer confessed when confronted with evidence supplied to the state by Lucy Lake— Miss Lucy Lake. Aw, in your hat, Koppel—you know how to spell it. L for lovely, U for European, C for psychology, Y for yum-yum. Last name Lake—like Lake Pontchartrain. No! cut the kiddin'. L-A-K-E. Here's Wade now. All right."

Wiggins jumped up and handed the telephone to Wade. "Koppel says tell it to a rewrite man and make it fast. Give him the works."

He scrambled up on the table by Lucy as Wade took the phone. Wade edged the chair closer to the desk. He held his wad of notes in a hand shaky from weariness, but as he leaned forward toward the mouthpiece his grin was jubilant.

"This is Wade. I'll dictate a lead for the re-plate edition. All set? Lead paragraph:

"'The dawn of Ash Wednesday saw the end of the Mardi Gras murders.' (Indent new paragraph.)

"'Arnold Ramsey de Clifford Ghent confessed at 5:15 this morning to the murders of Roger Parnell, Mrs. Cynthia Fontenay and Mark Oliver. The confession came at the end of a three-hour grilling by Captain Dennis Murphy of the Homicide Squad.' (Got that? New paragraph.)

"'Ghent's confession came when he was confronted with proofs of his guilt secured by Cornelius Augustine Conroy (middle name like St. Augustine, Florida), an investigator for the United States Treasury Department; Miss Lucy Lake, who was personal maid to Mrs. Fontenay; and Anthony Wiggins, staff photographer of *The Morning Creole*. (Sure, that's straight about Conroy. Wait a minute.)"

Wade looked up and winked at Murphy, who had just come into the room cheerfully smoking a fat cigar. With him came a troop of reporters heading for their own typewriters and phones.

"—And don't forget," Murphy was exulting, "we never laid a hand on him. When he broke he broke all over. He just sat up and spilled it out."

Wade had turned back to his phone. "All clear with that lead? All right, I'll give you the notes for the rest of it. Koppel wants to replate right along, doesn't he? Fine. Here it is."

Again his long shaky fingers arranged the scrawled notes in front of him. "Take Wiggins first. The developed roll of film from the boy's camera showed plainly—get this—that Ghent started his dive off the ladder *before* Cynthia leaned over." He listened a moment. "Right. He knew it was coming. Wiggins made a series of stills that shows it clearly. Enlargements of the movie film, yes. Ghent sprang back just a split second before Cynthia touched the rail, but it's enough to show that Ghent knew the rail was going to break. That's right. If Wiggins hadn't blabbed, he'd not have gotten that sock on the head.

"Now here's what Lucy did." Wade shuffled his notes.

"Lucy thought the piece of bloodstained yarn she had found must mean something. Remember, that's the stuff the police located the store on, but couldn't go any further. They seemed to be up against a blind wall. So Lucy went out and visited the servants of all the suspects. The woman who cleans up for Ghent and Hildreth identified the yarn as being like some she had seen in Ghent's room. Yes, she cleans up both their apartments—they're in the same building. Ghent had had the stuff for some time; she bought it a couple of months ago to fix a lounge cover. She even had a piece of it in her house that she'd brought home to mend a sweater. The rest she had left at Ghent's. That's probably the piece he used. O well, there's a little sap in the best of them. What? Don't rush me—I'll tell you in a minute what he used it for.

"Now Conroy—Cornelius Augustine, if you don't mind. He put in the knockout slug. Ghent had stubbornly insisted that the police could not take a lot of circumstantial evidence and hang the murders on him. After he had seen the Wiggins and Lucy evidence he admitted it looked bad, but he defied Murphy to show a motive. Murphy brought in Conroy. I think the old Turk thought Ghent and Conroy might have been in on the jobs together. Confederates, yes. Well, Conroy handed both Murphy and Ghent the surprise of their lives.

"He formally charged Ghent as a counterfeiter, displaying the credentials of his own authority from the Treasury Department. And to clinch it—he told Ghent that he had found his counterfeiting plates. Six of them. For ten, twenties and fifties. He found them in Ghent's car, under the rumble-seat."

Wade paused. "I'm coming to that.

"Here's the way the plates fit in. First: Conroy told Ghent that the government had a perfect case against him. Second: He named Ghent's partner, Mark Oliver, deceased. Third: He told Ghent that the plates suggested a very nice motive for at least two of the murders.

"That seemed to be enough.

"Ghent asked for a cigarette and a cup of coffee. Murphy got him all fixed up from the restaurant across the street. Then, very calmly, without urging or apology, Ghent told the complete story of his plot and purpose in killing the three who are dead and in attempting to kill Wiggins, who is very much alive and qui vive this minute." Wade grinned at Lucy, who straightened up and shook Wiggins' impudent arm from around her shoulders.

"Ghent's motive," Wade went on, "was money. Real money. Parnell had known Ghent for a long time, and when he split with Valdon he began to be afraid Valdon would knock him off for the Red Cat bankroll. So he got his capital turned into cash for his run-out and cached the money with Ghent, who promised to hold it ready for Parnell's blowoff.

"That was like a little gift from heaven to Ghent.

"You see, his job was to do the contact work for the counterfeiting outfit. He handed out the phony bills to the agents and collected for them. So when Parnell came into his parlor, Ghent agreed to hold the money for him, and as soon as Parnell left he ordered out a bale of green goods from Oliver and changed bad money for the good.

"Yes, Ghent has it, but he won't say where. Sure, some lawyer will get it."

Wade lighted a cigarette and waited.

"All right. The next step. Parnell was greedy or he might still be alive. He had been blackmailing Esther Morse.

"That's it—the same one. Very nice. How the hell should I know? Come on, take this stuff. Parnell wanted to make one more haul from Esther. He figured this would be his last chance to score, so he made it a good one. He told Ghent about it and offered half the money to Ghent if he'd go and get it. That was Monday afternoon.

"At first Ghent agreed to take Esther's money. Then Parnell opened up and told him that Cynthia Fontenay was going to make the collection for him at the Dis ball. All Ghent had to do, Parnell instructed, was to receive the money from Cynthia. This gave Ghent the idea on how to commit the murder."

Wade waited, then with a confirming "That's it," went on with the story.

"Monday night, the night of the ball, Ghent called Parnell. He asked him to hurry over to his flat. "When Parnell arrived, Ghent told him that it was all off. He insisted that he wanted to get clear of the whole thing. Parnell was disappointed, but he agreed. Ghent then demanded payment for his part up to date. Parnell demurred, and Ghent suggested that he could well afford to pay him out of the money Cynthia was to get from Esther. Then Parnell told him that he couldn't collect it; that he had to leave that night because Valdon had turned the heat on and the Red Cat was going to be raided. Sure, use Valdon's name. What the hell—this mess has knocked him out for good.

"Ghent sympathized with Parnell and offered a play whereby Parnell could collect. He agreed to help Parnell get into the Dis ball if Parnell would give him part of the money that Esther paid over. Get it? Sure, it was perfect.

"Ghent told Parnell that although it would be impossible for Parnell to get into Dis by himself, that he (Ghent) could arrange it for Parnell to go and pretend he was Ghent. You must remember that Parnell had already arranged with Cynthia to deliver Esther's money to Ghent.

"Parnell agreed to all proposals and asked for the money Ghent had been keeping for him. Ghent turned over the green junk he had substituted. Parnell left to deposit it in the Day and Night Trust Company, where he had his safety deposit box. What? Oh, Ghent had kept it in an antique chest in his flat.

"Then Ghent got busy. He knew Hildreth, who lived upstairs, was going to be out of town all night. He knew that Parnell had no idea about the Dis regalia. That made it easy for him to work out the method of the first murder which the police found so puzzling."

Wade waited a moment. "All right. I'll stand by." He lit a cigarette and turned gratefully to take a cup of coffee Lucy was holding out to him. After a moment he received the signal from the other end of the wire and went on.

"Ghent had a knife that belonged to Cynthia. Oh, he says she gave it to him, but I think that's the hooey. Anyway he had it. Now, when Parnell came back from putting that bale of hay in the safety deposit box, and put on the costume Ghent had ready, Ghent told him that a knife worn over the heart was a necessary part of the outfit. He explained it by telling Parnell that this was the ultimate sign of authentic membership; that if there was any question one of the monitors felt for the knife. If it was there, 'Pass, brother.' If not, 'Scram.' You get the idea.

"Parnell swallows this, so Ghent, who had worked this pleasant little angle out while Parnell was banking, loops the red yarn inside the lining of the robe and hangs the knife on it by the hilt. That leaves the knife hanging inside the robe with just a knot of the yarn on the outside.

"Now to kill Parnell, all he has to do is gather up the loose cloth of the blouse part of the robe around the handle of the knife, and plunge the blade in. That's what he did. Then he pulled out the red yarn by the outside knot and the police had the fun of guessing how come Parnell's cloak had no hole in it. But for Wiggins they would have taken the slant that the murderer had dressed his victim after the crime. Right."

Wade turned over two more sheets of his notes and slowly sipped his coffee, throwing Lucy an appreciative grin as he swung back to the phone.

"Cynthia Fontenay is the next one up. The police, believe it or not, were right about one thing. The balcony rail had been filed. Ghent changed the marks for placing the ladder and he held the flowers just out of Mrs. Fontenay's reach. Teased her to death, that's it. He admits all this.

"Now here's the motive for that murder: After Ghent told his cock-and-bull story to Murphy about being tied up in bed and threatened with death by Parnell and not being at the ball, Cynthia got him off in a comer privately and told him that he had been at the ball and she knew it.

"Listen, sap. Of course he was there. How do you think he killed Parnell? After Parnell left for the Dis ball in a taxi, Ghent drove his own car over near Cynthia's house. He went through the gate without any trouble and went up to the ballroom. He knew Parnell was there in Hildreth's costume; so it was an easy matter for him to keep his eye on his man. Just before the meeting of the Dis Council, when Parnell left to go to the back of the house, where he was going to tell Cynthia to deliver the money to him, Ghent left the ballroom and went into the courtyard. He stood behind some banana palms and waited for a chance to get a whack at Parnell. He mentioned that he saw Wiggins come in and talk to Lucy, and he also saw the butler Jasper on the balcony. He saw Jasper leap in the china-closet window. Wiggins couldn't have seen that from where he was, even if he'd been looking up there instead of at Lucy.

"Recall that Cynthia was having a row with Parnell because she had given Oliver the money by mistake. Jasper, if you remember his angle, put an end to the struggle by conking Parnell with his ham-like fist. Right. Well, when he saw Jasper beat it, Ghent went up to take a look.

"Through the window he could see Parnell knocked out cold. You can get the picture: Ghent climbing in the window, checking by the suit number that the man on the floor is Parnell, grabbing the handle of the hidden knife, and then while music played in the front of the house, sinking the dagger up to the hilt in Parnell's manly bosom. Curtains for Parnell and Arnold Ramsey de Clifford Ghent has become a murderer.

"It was an easy job for him to slip out again. He waited behind the bananas till Wiggins had gone, then watching the movements of the servants carefully, he went out through the gates. He said that he slipped off his robes just before he opened the gates, and stuck the robes under his coat. Then he went home and trussed himself up in bed for the police to find. He knew they'd come sooner or later, because he knew Parnell had pretended to Cynthia to be Ghent, and when they found he wasn't, that would raise the hue and cry.

"Everything went perfectly, he said, until Cynthia said that she knew he was at the ball. For Ghent, smart as he might be, forgot that Cynthia and Hildreth were pretty fond of each other and that Hildreth would naturally have told Cynthia he wouldn't be able to make the ball. Cynthia evidently doped it out from the number of people on hand that Ghent must have been there."

Wade waited for a comment. "But don't be feeling sorry for Cynthia. According to Ghent's confession, she agreed to keep quiet if he paid her off. She only wanted all the money that Esther Morse had given her for Parnell and a cut-in on the Red Cat money.

"Sure. Ghent said she figured the play right away.

"He agreed to everything, he said. Then he made plans to kill her. Yes, isn't he?—awfully nice chap.

"After he left Cynthia's house he went out to Oliver's place. He wanted to get Oliver's duplicate of the knife that had killed Parnell, so he could plant it on Cynthia's premises. What? No, stupid. He wanted the police to think that Oliver knew something about the killing and he figured that they'd find Oliver's knife eventually. Oliver already had been implicated in the handling of the ten thousand dollars that the police found on Conroy. Ghent swears that he didn't know this, but that he sensed Oliver was hiding something. Sure, he knew him well. They were partners in that queer money racket. Ghent said he knew Oliver would be looking for a payoff on that counterfeit money he had passed on Parnell, and that he had to stall. The more trouble Oliver had, the better for Ghent. Oliver, you see, had an excellent reputation. Ghent figured that if he could keep Oliver involved in Parnell's murder, he could kill Oliver and make it look like suicide. That's the reason he wanted Oliver's knife. Exactly—so it would be missing.

"Incidentally, Oliver's story of the shooting out at his house was true. Ghent said that when he fired at Oliver, he meant to kill him and to dress it up so it would look like suicide. Oliver surprised him by getting to his feet and blazing away, so Ghent lammed out.

"It was after this that he fixed up the trap for Cynthia. The balcony rails were covered with bunting, so it wasn't hard to conceal himself from the street and file through the ironwork. The apartment behind was vacant.

When he got through with this, he went home and doped out a way to kill Oliver. It was then that he thought up the big Fishbowl Murder. He had an old derringer. It was a .48 caliber, single barrel, rim-fire. Police, by the way, ask that whoever picked it up return it to headquarters.

"I'm coming to how it got lost. Ghent turned the derringer into a death machine by tying back the trigger. It's an old trick that old-time Western gunmen used so they could fan the hammer of a revolver. The trigger is pressed back. In regular firing position, that's it. That means the hammer is ready to fall any time you let it loose. Ghent blocked the hammer with a piece of steel about an inch long. He put it between the hammer and the bullet. That's it—a prop. The steel kept the hammer up, but just as soon as the block was jerked out, the hammer fell and the cartridge exploded. The rest is easy.

"The fishing line on the wheel had been tied to the block of steel and fastened to the wheel-hub. Ghent said he threaded it through the loose planks on the wagon and left the slack on top under the white sand in the bottom of the float. Every revolution of the wheel took up more of the slack and wound it around the hub.

"Ghent rigged all this up in the Dis den just before dawn. He seemed mighty proud of this notion. He separated the planks with a little crowbar, and put the derringer in place, and the pressure held it. When the gun fired, he knew, the noise would be muffled by the bowl and the brass band and the cheering multitude; and since the kick from a .48 derringer is terrific, the gun dislodged and fell to the street."

Wade listened. "That's it. The motive for this one was money. Ghent wanted the counterfeiting plates for himself.

"I guess Ghent planted the knife in Cynthia's armoire while he was alone in her house Tuesday morning, with the servants all downstairs. Conroy took her out to try to make her tell something about the counterfeiting racket. But apparently, he says, she wasn't in on that.

"And that," said Wade with a long sigh, "is the three murders."

He turned from the phone and grinned across at his sleepy-eyed confreres, who were at their own phones calling hurried details to their own rewrite men. Wiggins rubbed the back of his bandaged head and gave Murphy a placid smile.

"Gonta hang this guy, Murph?"

"Huh," said Murphy. "If we don't we'd better burn the rope."

Kennedy of the *Telegram* hung up the receiver of his phone and came over. "Statement from Farrell," he said. "Going to use every means to get a quick trial."

Wiggins automatically grabbed for the *Creole* phone. "D.A. to ask for quick trial," he reported when he got through to Koppel. "Murphy confident of conviction."

Kennedy chuckled. "Everybody else in the clear, Murphy? What about Dick Barron?"

"Sure, he's all right—" Murphy grinned at Lucy—"but I guess that's Miss Lucy's story. They do tell me she's been playing Cupid."

The reporters looked inquiringly at Lucy, but she only smiled.

"Then that's about all, I guess," said Kennedy. "You're a lucky guy to crack this one so fast."

Murphy scratched his ear. "I guess I am. It's a bad business, boys." He walked over to the window. There were pink streaks across the sky. "A bad business," he repeated.

"We'd better get hold of Conroy for a feature," said Kennedy. "And now," he demanded of Murphy, "what about you? The Mardi Gras murders are over. You've done a good job." He grinned. "You're an old copper, Murphy, and we all like to see you come through. You've been chasing cut-throats and killers for twenty years and more." Kennedy paused and looked at the others significantly. "There's a rumor around, Murphy, and we fellows would like to get the dope on it from you. They're saying that this is your last murder case, that you're going to retire on pension and raise chickens. Is that true?"

Murphy smiled and puffed on his cigar.

"Come on, Murphy," Kennedy urged, "give us the story. You're on the crest now. What are you going to do?"

Murphy picked up his hat. "I'm going to mass, that's what. This is Ash Wednesday morning. You'd do well to come with me and forget the damn lies you hear around this building." He strode out.

The reporters grinned as the door of the press room slammed behind him.

THE END